PRIZE SURPRISE SWEEPSTAKES!

This month's prize:

A FABULOUS SHARP VIEWCAM!

This month, as a special surprise, we're giving away a Sharp ViewCam**, the big-screen camcorder that has revolutionized home videos!

This is the camcorder everyone's talking about! Sharp's new ViewCam has a big 3" full-color viewing screen with 180° swivel action that lets you control everything you record—and watch it at the same time! Features include a remote control (so you can get into the picture yourself), 8 power zoom, full-range auto focus, battery pack, recharger and more!

The next page contains two Entry Coupons (as does every book you received this shipment). Complete and return *all* the entry coupons; **the more times you enter, the better your chances of winning!**

Then keep your fingers crossed, because you'll find out by November 15, 1995 if you're the winner!

Remember: The more times you enter, the better your chances of winning!*

PVC KAL

PRIZE SURPRISE
SWEEPSTAKES

OFFICIAL ENTRY COUPON

This entry must be received by: OCTOBER 30, 1995
This month's winner will be notified by: NOVEMBER 15, 1995

YES, I want to win the Sharp ViewCam! Please enter me in the drawing and let me know if I've won!

Name_____

Address _____ Apt. _____

| City | State/Prov. | Zip/Postal Code |

Account #_____

Return entry with invoice in reply envelope.

© 1995 HARLEQUIN ENTERPRISES LTD.   CVC KAL

PRIZE SURPRISE
SWEEPSTAKES

OFFICIAL ENTRY COUPON

This entry must be received by: OCTOBER 30, 1995
This month's winner will be notified by: NOVEMBER 15, 1995

YES, I want to win the Sharp ViewCam! Please enter me in the drawing and let me know if I've won!

Name_____

Address _____ Apt. _____

| City | State/Prov. | Zip/Postal Code |

Account #_____

Return entry with invoice in reply envelope.

© 1995 HARLEQUIN ENTERPRISES LTD.   CVC KAL

"You might as well call me Mike. We're going to be seeing a lot of each other."

"We are?" she asked. The prospect was unsettling. Nina was disturbingly aware of his overwhelming maleness. Detective Lieutenant Mike Novalis was one very handsome man. Which, Nina told herself sternly, could only complicate the mess she was in.

The last thing she needed right now was to be attracted to this man. Any man. She was going to have her hands full just finding out what kind of person she was.

He turned a little and looked directly at her, and then he smiled. Nina was shaken by the wave of heat that flickered through her. She froze, determined not to react to him. *I cannot let myself trust this man. He thinks I'm lying.*

Then another thought came, one she had been fighting to hold at bay. *What if I really did do something wrong?*

Dear Reader,

This is another spectacular month here at Silhouette Intimate Moments. You'll realize that the moment you pick up our Intimate Moments Extra title. *Her Secret, His Child,* by Paula Detmer Riggs, is exactly the sort of tour de force you've come to expect from this award-winning writer. It's far more than the story of a child whose father has never known of her existence. It's the story of a night long ago that changed the courses of three lives, leading to hard lessons about responsibility and blame, and—ultimately—to the sort of love that knows no bounds, no limitations, and will last a lifetime.

Three miniseries are on tap this month, as well. Alicia Scott's *Hiding Jessica* is the latest entrant in "The Guiness Gang," as well as a Romantic Traditions title featuring the popular story line in which the hero and heroine have to go into hiding together—where of course they find love! Merline Lovelace continues "Code Name: Danger" with *Undercover Man,* a sizzling tale proving that appearances can indeed be deceiving. Beverly Barton begins "The Protectors" with *Defending His Own,* in which the deeds of the past come back to haunt the present in unpredictable—and irresistibly romantic—ways.

In addition, Sally Tyler Hayes returns with *Our Child?* Next year look for this book's exciting sequel. Finally, welcome our Premiere author, Suzanne Sanders, with *One Forgotten Night.*

Sincerely,

Leslie Wainger
Senior Editor and Editorial Coordinator

Please address questions and book requests to:
Silhouette Reader Service
U.S.: 3010 Walden Ave., P.O. Box 1325, Buffalo, NY 14269
Canadian: P.O. Box 609, Fort Erie, Ont. L2A 5X3

ONE
FORGOTTEN
NIGHT

SUZANNE
SANDERS

Silhouette

INTIMATE™ MOMENTS®

Published by Silhouette Books

America's Publisher of Contemporary Romance

For Zachary

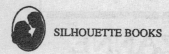

SILHOUETTE BOOKS

ISBN 0-373-07672-X

ONE FORGOTTEN NIGHT

SUZANNE SANDERS

has published biographies and books on historical subjects, but *One Forgotten Night* is her first romance novel. She found that writing a romance novel was "a lot more fun than writing nonfiction, and also much more demanding." She enjoys the challenge of imagining a fantasy situation and then creating a logical framework in which it could occur.

Suzanne lives in Oregon, which she considers the perfect state for someone who can't decide whether she prefers the mountains or the sea. Her favorite pastimes include hiking, reading (history, mystery and, of course, romance) and exploring the Pacific Northwest.

Dear Reader,

I love romance. As a teenager, I read Daphne du Maurier's incomparable *Rebecca* and fell hopelessly under the spell of its brooding, haunted hero and its imperiled heroine. Since that time I've read and loved hundreds of romances, from the lush historicals of M. M. Kaye and Katharine Gordon to the exciting contemporary fiction of writers like Linda Howard and Nora Roberts. And now I feel tremendously honored to have my own first romance novel published.

Writing this book was exhilarating—in the way that the hardest, most demanding work can be exhilarating when it's directed at a cherished goal. One of the biggest thrills I experienced was the way the characters came alive as I worked, revealing aspects of themselves I hadn't foreseen and sometimes taking the story off in new directions. I hope that Mike and Nina and the others will come alive for you, too, and that you'll enjoy reading *One Forgotten Night* as much as I enjoyed writing it.

In a world so full of books waiting to be read, the greatest gift an author can receive is the gift of a reader's time. Thank you very much for yours.

Suzanne Sanders

Chapter 1

Even before she opened her eyes she knew that something was wrong. Her head ached dully, and she was lying on a surface that was much too hard to be a bed. She lifted heavy eyelids and blinked at the dazzle of a bright light overhead. Beyond the light was darkness, a windy void that she knew was the night sky. Cool air blew across her face. Suddenly she realized that she was lying outdoors, on concrete. What was going on?

Someone knelt next to her. She wanted to sit up, but her body felt heavy and very, very tired. It would be so much easier just to lie there.... She struggled to turn her head, to look around, but her muscles refused to obey. Panic welled up. Then a hand rested firmly but gently against the side of her face, and strong, sure fingers moved along the line of her jaw to the fluttering pulse in her neck. A man's voice said, "Hang on, sweetheart, you're going to be fine." The voice was deep and reassuring. Her panic ebbed. The unknown speaker continued to talk to her in a soft, comforting voice. She was cold, an aching cold that seemed to reach outward from her very bones, but the place where his hand touched her throat was warm. She let her trembling eyelids fall shut: she was not alone.

Then she felt, rather than heard, a bustle of new arrivals. Someone wrapped a blanket around her; she was being lifted. "You're all right, it's okay," a new voice, a woman's, said in a tone that was at once soothing and professionally impersonal. "There's been an accident. We're taking you to the hospital."

An accident. Going to the hospital. She was dimly aware that there was something...something you were supposed to do if you had an accident, something you were supposed to remember. Dizzily she groped through the fog that threatened to swallow up her senses. Aha! That was it; she remembered now. Gathering her fading strength she whispered hoarsely, "I hope I'm wearing my good underwear."

Just before she passed out she heard a short, surprised laugh somewhere behind her.

Mike Novalis watched the flashing red ambulance lights recede down the street. A couple of blue-and-whites had pulled up, and uniformed officers were taking names and witness statements from the small crowd that had gathered. Novalis grimaced: even at one o'clock in the morning, even in a deserted and decaying part of town, there was always a crowd. Flashing lights, sirens, the hint of violence or danger—it brought them out of the woodwork, hungry for a cheap thrill. And you're right here with them, Novalis told himself. Is there really that much difference? It was a question he'd asked himself before. Lately it was getting harder to answer.

He shivered. It was cold, and he had left home in a hurry, throwing on his jacket over a T-shirt. Now he wished he'd grabbed a sweater. There was a damp rawness in the night air and a halo of mist around the streetlight at the end of the block. Turning up his jacket collar, he headed for his car, beckoning to one of the uniforms.

The cop hurried over. He was a young black man, with short-cropped hair and an air of barely suppressed excitement. Novalis sighed. The kid had to be a rookie. He hadn't been on the force long enough to discover that shootings were routine. "What do you need, Lieutenant?" the younger officer asked eagerly.

Novalis checked the cop's name tag and then cocked his head at the little crowd, which was beginning to disperse. "Anything good, Simms?"

"Not so far," Simms said. "Mostly people who showed up when the ambulance came. But we've got the guy who called 911. My partner's getting his statement now."

Novalis hesitated for a moment, leaning against his car. Nothing here required his attention. He could go home, crawl back into bed—turn off his police radio this time, damn it—and try to get some sleep. But something bothered him. He thought of the woman in the ambulance. He'd found her lying in the street like a broken doll, one of those old-fashioned dolls with delicate porcelain skin.... He shook his head impatiently to dislodge that oddly touching image. He'd seen too much in his years on the force to start getting sentimental. Still, she hadn't looked like a hooker, or like an uptown yuppie cruising for drugs or excitement. What had she been doing on this street? His instincts told him that something in the picture didn't quite fit.

Instincts? jeered a voice inside his head. *Remember what happened the last time you trusted your "instincts"?* Novalis quelled the mocking voice, pushing his self-doubt deep down where he couldn't hear it. He realized that his jaw was clenched and that his hands had balled into fists; he forced himself to take a deep breath, wondering if Simms had noticed. Simms probably knew about Novalis's private nightmare. They all knew. Nobody talked about it, though—at least not when he was around. He glanced at Simms, saw only bright-eyed attentiveness.

"I'm going on to the hospital," he decided. "Call me there with the statements and whatever you get from forensics." He clapped Simms on the shoulder and climbed wearily into his car. Only when he started to drive away did he notice the dark stain of her blood on his fingers.

The next time she woke it was in a hospital room. The antiseptic odor, the echo of long hallways and the white acoustic ceiling tiles told her at once where she was, but she wasn't alarmed. Her body felt warm and light, and she floated in a pleasant, unconcerned haze. A woman in a nurse's uniform was snugging a blanket over her. She noticed idly that the nurse wore an engagement ring. A nice little stone, she thought drowsily. Just under a carat, the cut's nothing special but the color is good. . . .

"Ah, you're awake," she heard a man's voice say, and a white-coated doctor stepped up to the side of the bed. "How are you feeling?" The bed moved, jogging her up into a sitting position. Suddenly her senses prickled. Like an animal that senses someone's near, she felt eyes were watching her. Craning her neck, she saw that there was a fourth person in the room.

He sat unobtrusively in a corner by the head of the bed. He wore a beat-up brown leather aviator's jacket over a wrinkled blue T-shirt and jeans, and his shaggy black hair was overlong; he certainly didn't look like a doctor. His thick dark brows were drawn sharply down into a V, and he looked impatient. As he intently watched her the dreamy lassitude that had enveloped her began to melt away. Heat invaded her body as, with a tingle of heightened awareness, she reacted to the intensity of his gaze. He was waiting for something. For her. Deep inside she trembled at the thought.

"How are you feeling?" the doctor asked her again, and she dragged her gaze back to him.

"Fine, I guess. What happened?" Her voice sounded strange and weak. Like a dark cloud on the horizon, moving swiftly nearer, her feeling that something was terribly wrong was growing stronger by the second. She just couldn't pin down what it was.

"You had a minor injury—" The doctor paused and glanced toward the dark-haired man. "That is to say, you suffered a slight head wound. But don't worry, you're going to be fine."

"A head wound? How?"

The dark-haired man rose from his chair in a single lithe motion and stood beside the bed. He was several inches taller than the doctor and more athletically built, with broad shoulders and a muscular, long-limbed frame. He looked down at her for a moment, and in his eyes was a flicker of some expression that she could not quite read. "Someone shot at you," he said.

"Shot!" Her voice cracked on the exclamation. "How—? What—?" Her confusion was so vast that she couldn't finish either question. He was still looking at her, and despite the bizarre unreality of the circumstances she couldn't help noticing that his eyes were a fathomless blue, several shades darker than the faded T-shirt that was stretched tight over his chest. His gaze was watchful but guarded, as though he wished to give nothing away. "Who *are* you?" she asked.

In a gesture eerily familiar from movies and television, he pulled a leather folder from inside his jacket and flipped it open to show her a gleaming badge. "Detective Lieutenant Mike Novalis," he said crisply, and she felt a pang of loss. It was totally irrational, she knew, but for some reason she'd been sure that this man was someone she knew, someone close to her.

"I'd like to ask you a few questions," he said. "Did you see the person who shot you?"

There was that horrible word again. *Shot.* This couldn't be happening. Every instant she grew more certain that something was badly wrong. If only her head would stop hurting for a minute she could figure out what it was. She put her hand to her forehead and felt something stiff and smooth. A bandage.

"It's all right," the doctor said comfortingly, with an irritated sidelong glance at the policeman. "The bullet just grazed your temple. You have a tiny crease—it probably won't even leave a scar."

The policeman stood waiting. Novalis, that was his name. His *name!* Suddenly she knew what was wrong, and the knowledge was as shocking as a blow. She felt sick and dizzy, as though she were standing on the brink of a deep, dark cavern that could swallow her up if she made one false step.

She looked at Novalis, the doctor and the nurse, and then, in a voice that shook despite her desperate effort at control, she said, "Who am I?"

There was a moment of startled silence. Detective Lieutenant Novalis broke it. "You're saying you don't remember anything about the shooting?" His voice was carefully neutral, but she thought his gaze sharpened.

"That's exactly right. I don't. I don't remember *anything!*" She heard the rising shrillness in her voice and fell silent, afraid to give in to the sick terror she felt. She pressed her lips together to stop their trembling and, to keep panic at bay, forced herself to focus on the silvery stethoscope around the doctor's neck. She felt as if she were trapped in a dream. A bad one.

"If you don't mind, Detective?" The doctor took her hand and felt for her pulse.

"Sure, Doc," Novalis said. "You take over. I'll just sit here until you get this sorted out."

Novalis retreated to his chair. But she was conscious of his brooding gaze as she sat stiffly upright, trying to still the clamor of her thoughts while the doctor looked into each of her eyes in turn. Then the doctor handed her a black leather shoulder bag. "Your name is Nina Dennison," he told her gently. "This bag is yours. It has your identification in it. Does that name sound familiar?"

She clutched the bag to her; its soft leather felt cold to her touch. She mouthed the syllables of the name—her name—several times. "No. It doesn't. What's wrong with me?"

"Well, Nina, as I told you, you have a minor head injury. You're perfectly all right physically—we've taken X rays already and there's no damage. But sometimes these injuries can cause memory loss."

"Amnesia," Nina said. She felt stunned. The word seemed so—so dramatic. Not the sort of thing you ever expected to happen to you. But then you never expected to get shot, either.

"Exactly. You appear to be suffering some form of amnesia. There's no need to panic, but let's find out how serious this is. What's the first thing you can remember?"

"Waking up just now—no, wait, I remember waking up once before. I was lying on the ground. They were taking me to the hospital, I think," she said slowly. "Yes, and someone laughed."

Novalis cleared his throat. "That was me, I'm afraid." He leaned forward. "I was first on the scene when the shooting was called in."

"And you *laughed* at me?" she said indignantly.

"No, not at you." He seemed uncomfortable. "It was—well, you said something funny."

"What?" Then she remembered. Joking about her underwear, of all things. She must have been in shock. "Oh, never mind," she said hastily. Novalis grinned as he leaned back against the wall, and she all but gaped in surprise. His grin was a minor miracle; it transfigured his face, making his stern features look almost boyish. One thick, dark brow angled playfully, and light sparkled in the blue depths of his eyes. She found herself smiling back at him as though they'd just shared a secret.

At that moment Nina remembered something else from her first awakening. An impression of strength and security: a hand touching her face and a voice comforting her. An unexpectedly intimate voice. A voice, she now recognized, that belonged to Detective Lieutenant Novalis. She looked searchingly at him, but he was no longer smiling. Once again he was aloof and unfathomable.

The doctor said, "So you remember being brought here. Do you remember, oh, what you had for dinner last night?"

Nina shook her head.

"Going to work yesterday?"

She could only shake her head again, filled with blank dismay. Work? She didn't even know what she did for a living.

"How old am I?" she asked.

"According to your driver's license, you're twenty-seven years old. Let's see...how about your family? Any names, or images that come to mind?"

"No." Her voice was almost a whisper. She felt utterly alone. But she must have a family of some sort; perhaps the bag would give her a clue. She glanced at her ringless left hand. Apparently she wasn't married. The hand seemed alien to her, like a piece of statuary, and she studied it for a moment, taking in the long fingers with short oval nails, the clear polish. When she flexed her fingers, she felt taut thighs under the blanket. She gazed curiously at the outline of her legs. All at once she was overwhelmed by a frightening sense of facelessness. She didn't even know what she looked like. Panicked, she surged up from the bed—too quickly. Her head spun and she staggered.

A strong arm slipped around her shoulders, supporting her, and she was pressed against a solid masculine chest. "Take it easy," Novalis murmured in her ear. She looked up, startled. He must have crossed the room in a flash to reach her before the doctor or nurse could react.

"Thanks," she gasped.

"Don't try to move too fast," he advised her. "You've had a bad shock on top of some painkillers. Take a moment to get your bearings." He was still holding her tightly with one hard-muscled arm. His jacket was open, and she felt the steady beat of his heart, the heat of his body through the thin cotton of his shirt. His warmth, his strength, touched the cold knot of fear inside her. She relaxed against him, wanting to feel his other arm around her, too, pulling her even closer to his heat....

Suddenly Nina was embarrassingly aware of what she was thinking. She stiffened and pulled away from him. I must still be in shock, she told herself. No matter that she'd thought she sensed some kind of bond between them earlier—this man was a stranger, just doing his job. Then Nina became belatedly aware of a current of cool air on her backside. She realized that she was wearing only a loose hospital gown and, glancing over her shoulder, she saw to her horror that it was gaping wide open at the back.

She clutched the gown shut behind her. Novalis took a robe from a wall hook and draped it over her shoulders. He met her accusing stare blandly, but his left eyelid flickered as though he had repressed a wink. Undoubtedly, she thought, he had had himself a good long look. She felt herself blushing.

"Is there a mirror?" she said with as much dignity as she could muster.

Novalis ushered Nina into the bathroom. "You okay?" he inquired, and when she nodded he flipped up the light

One Forgotten Night

switch and closed the door. Alone in the tiny cubicle, Nina turned to the mirror. In the unflattering glare of fluorescent light she solemnly surveyed herself.

The face in the mirror was pale and strained, with dark shadows under the greenish hazel eyes. Wonderingly, she touched her cheek. Her skin was smooth. She smiled experimentally. A few fine lines formed at the corners of her eyes, but her teeth were even and white. Her features, while not classically beautiful, were interesting: broad high cheekbones, a firm chin and a wide mouth. Not bad, she decided.

A bandage slanted rakishly across her forehead like a pirate's head scarf. Long, tumbled red-brown bangs fell over the bandage; thick, tousled hair grazed her shoulders. *So I'm a redhead.... Hmm, hope it's natural.* She wore small, plain silver hoops in pierced ears. She was tall and seemed well built.

Nina looked at the mirror for a moment and then slipped out of the baggy robe and drew the gown over her head. She appraised her body like that of a stranger: the full, firm breasts with dark nipples puckered tight against the sudden chill, the gentle curves of belly and hips, the faded scar on one knee. How had she gotten that scar? Falling off a child's bike, maybe, or tripping in her first pair of too-high heels? She searched for an answering memory. Nothing. She touched the scar gently and wondered how many other secrets this body held. *My* body, she reminded herself.

Do I have a lover? She thought of Detective Lieutenant Novalis waiting outside, and of how eagerly she had responded to the nearness of him, and her breath caught in her throat. "Be careful," she whispered to the image in the mirror. She put the gown and robe back on. She noticed that her toenails were painted a deep, lustrous burgundy—a splash of color in the sterile little room. Those red toenails cheered her a little. The doctor and the detective were talking when she stepped out of the bathroom. They looked up hopefully. "Anything?" the doctor asked. "Sometimes the mirror jolts the memory...."

"Nothing. Sorry."

"Amnesiacs often suffer loss of short-term memory, or they lose knowledge about their own lives," the doctor said. "Many times it's only temporary. Let's see how well oriented you are otherwise. Do you know what year it is?"

Nina named the year, the month, the day. She knew without thinking about it that the city outside the window was Philadelphia. She allowed herself to feel just a little encouraged. The doctor asked, "Can you name the president?"

Nina did so unhesitatingly. Then she added glumly, "But I can't remember whether I voted for him or not."

Several hours passed. Dr. Perrone called in a neurologist and a psychologist. They established that Nina seemed to have lost all memory of her personal life and the events leading up to the shooting. Yet her intelligence and her ability to make decisions were unimpaired. There was no medical reason why she shouldn't leave the hospital. On the other hand, she carried an insurance card and could stay in the hospital for a few days if she wanted to do so.

"Let me get this straight," she asked Dr. Anderson, the neurologist. "If I stay here, do I have a better chance of getting my memory back? Is there anything you can do for me?"

Dr. Anderson shook her head regretfully. "There's no treatment for amnesia—only the passage of time. I can't make any promises, but we do know that most cases of amnesia clear up eventually. Sometimes the memory comes back suddenly, often within a very few days. Sometimes it comes back slowly, in bits and pieces, over a long period of time. But sometimes, Nina, it doesn't come back—at least not all of it. I have no way of telling what will happen in your case. If you feel comfortable going home, you can certainly do so. It might even jog your memory.''

The psychologist, Dr. Tooley, chimed in. ''This must be very frightening for you. It might be better for you to spend a few days here until you're over the shock.''

''No,'' Nina said decisively. ''I'm going home. Right now there's only one thing I want—I want to find out who I am. I can't do that sitting here.''

She glanced at Detective Lieutenant Novalis and thought she saw a fleeting look of approval on his face. He had been in and out of the room during the doctors' examinations, and for the past half hour or so he had been sitting quietly, fidgeting a bit but making a visible effort to control his impatience. Nina wondered why he was still there. She had amnesia, after all; she couldn't tell him anything about the shooting he was supposed to be investigating.

Nina raised a hand to her bandage and shuddered. She had escaped death by an inch. It was disturbing to think that her life, only a few hours long as measured by her memory, began with an act of violence.

''Do I really need this thing?'' she asked, pointing to the bandage.

Dr. Perrone smiled. ''I guess it is a little conspicuous. I'll replace it with a smaller one, all right?''

''Please. I have enough problems without looking like the Mummy.''

When the doctors withdrew for a conference, Nina took her clothes and bag into the bathroom to get dressed. It would feel good to get out of the hospital robe; her clothes were unfamiliar, but at least they were *hers*.

At the time of the accident she had been wearing a plain but expensive black brassiere, nearly new, and matching lacy panties. Nina almost laughed. So she *had* been wearing good underwear, after all. She had also been wearing a black turtleneck sweater, a pair of jeans with a narrow leather belt and dark gray walking boots. Everything was stylish and of good quality without being flashy. So far, so good, Nina said to herself as she laced her boots.

But as she straightened up, she met the shadowed eyes of the stranger in the mirror, and her composure cracked. When talking to the doctors she had felt strong and capable, ready to tackle the problem of her lost memories, certain that they would return. Now that certainty was gone. Nina felt only emptiness and a desolate sense of loss. Suppose her memory never came back? What was she going to do? She huddled on the toilet seat and cried for five minutes. The tears dried to sniffles, and she blew her nose forlornly on a strip of toilet paper.

The doctors' questions had seemed endless. They proved that she could remember things like the dates of World War I—but not her own birthday. Enough questions. Now it was time for some answers.

She grabbed her bag and burrowed in it for a wallet. Her Pennsylvania driver's license said she was born on February 17. *That makes me an Aquarius. Wait a minute—how do I know that? Do I believe in astrology?* The wallet also held nearly eighty dollars in cash, and several credit cards. *So I'm not going to starve. Not immediately, at any rate.*

The shoulder bag contained a zippered red nylon pouch. *That's got to be makeup.* Nina's spirits rose a little. She washed her tear-streaked face, rinsed out her mouth and put on some blush and lipstick. Ruffling her hair with her fingers, she took stock of herself in the mirror. Superficial though the changes may have been, they made her feel better. Now she was a person instead of a patient. And if she fluffed her bangs just right, she couldn't even see the little Band-Aid at her temple that covered the place where she'd been shot.

Mike Novalis smothered a yawn as he waited for Nina Dennison to come out of the bathroom. He wasn't sure why he had stayed. She wasn't going to give him a state-

ment about the shooting, that much was clear. He just
hated loose ends.

Earlier he had phoned Simms at the district offices and
told him to run checks on the ID in the Dennison woman's purse and coat. Now he was waiting for Simms to call
him back. Maybe Nina Dennison was nothing more than
the unlucky recipient of a stray bullet. As for what she had
been doing when that bullet caught her—well, it looked as
if he'd never know. *Forget it,* he told himself. *If she says
she doesn't remember anything, there's nothing you can
do.* He'd take Simms's call, close the file and go home.
And then he'd catch up on some sleep.

But he felt an insistent tug of curiosity. Everything about
this woman was a puzzle. She'd looked so fragile and
helpless lying there in the street—and then, less than half-
conscious, she'd made a joke. In the past few hours she'd
proved that she was no delicate china doll. She had intelligence, strength, flashes of temper. He liked that.

He also liked the way she looked, Mike admitted to
himself: her green-gold eyes, her full lower lip and that
tantalizing glimpse he'd had through her hospital gown of
long slim legs and the creamy curve of a hip. She had felt
good leaning against him. At six foot one, he felt out of
sync with petite women, but Nina's head had nestled into
exactly the right spot on his shoulder. *Oh, yeah, it would
be all too easy to get turned on by this one.* When she had
gasped, her warm breath against the base of his throat had
started his pulse pounding there. It had taken all his will-
power not to wrap his arms around her and pull her closer.

Mike rubbed his hand wearily across his face. He knew
he shouldn't be letting his thoughts wander like this. But
it wasn't often that he came across a woman like Nina
Dennison. Too bad that when he did, it was in the line of
duty. No one knew better than Mike that that put her off-
limits. *And someone tried to kill her,* he reminded him-

self. *For all you know, she's mixed up in a drug deal gone bad—or something worse.*

The beeper in his pocket signaled him to call Simms. He went down the hall to a bank of pay phones.

"That you, Lieutenant?"

"Yeah, Simms, what've you got?"

"The Dennison woman lives alone, as far as her land-lord knows, so it probably wasn't a husband who shot her. And she looks clean, doesn't have a rap sheet."

"That doesn't mean she's clean, Simms," Mike said. "It just means she's never been caught."

"Uh, right, Lieutenant. Sorry."

"Just something to keep in mind. But you're right, there's no evidence of anything hinky." *Just a hunch, and no one's gonna trust my hunches.* He sighed. "There's no reason to think she's anything but a random target, some-one who was in the wrong place at the wrong time."

"Except for one thing, Lieutenant. Check this out. I talked to the doorman at that address you gave me, the office building. Dennison works there, all right. She works for Zakroff and Duchesne. You know," Simms prompted when Mike didn't respond. "The gem dealers."

Then Mike got it. "Son of a—"

"Lieutenant," Simms interrupted excitedly. "The chief wants to talk to you right away."

The gravelly voice of Morris Hecht, chief of detectives, came over the line. "Simms says your victim's got *amnesia*," he said, his voice heavy with irony.

"That's what the doctors tell me."

"Do you believe in coincidence, Novalis? I don't," Hecht continued without giving Mike time to reply. "When we've got an undercover investigation by the Justice Department, the Treasury Department, Interpol and probably the goddamned Boy Scouts of America for all I know, and then there's a shooting, and the victim just happens to work for the company that's being investigated, well, then I don't believe in coincidence at all. The feds're probably gonna take this over.''

Novalis grunted. He shared his chief's ire toward federal agents who were overeager to muscle in on anything remotely connected with their investigations. To make matters worse, the feds often seemed to relish keeping the local law enforcement out of the picture and in the dark.

''One good thing,'' Hecht continued, ''is the feds are stretched pretty thin on this right now. I'll turn in a report, but it'll probably be two, maybe three, days before they do anything. So until then you stay on this woman's case, Novalis. Find out if she's connected. But don't get in the way of the boys from the Bureau.''

''I got it. I'll keep in touch.''

''And, Novalis—'' Hecht's voice was grim. ''Don't screw up on this one. You can't afford it. Anything goes wrong, and you go down.''

Mike was silent. He knew Hecht was right. What was there to say?

''Amnesia.'' Hecht snorted dismissively. ''That only happens in the goddamned movies.'' He hung up.

Novalis saw the neurologist hurrying down the corridor and stepped into her path. ''Dr. Anderson, I need to talk to you. Can you confirm that the Dennison woman really has amnesia?''

''You want to know if she's faking it?'' The doctor's voice was impartial, but her eyes glinted with faint disdain behind her glasses. Novalis didn't let it bother him. He was used to asking questions that made people uncomfortable.

''Yeah, that's what I want to know.''

''Well, I suppose you have to consider the possibility. In my professional opinion, Nina Dennison's amnesia is genuine. Her reactions have been normal for this type of trauma, and cases like hers are not really uncommon. But

there's no way to prove it, if that's what you're after. A
clever person can fake amnesia."

"Thanks, Doctor. You've been a big help."

Mike Novalis was thoughtful as he walked back to
Nina's room. His cold eyes and the set of his jaw startled
an impressionable young nurse's aide, who scuttled out of
his way. Mike didn't even see her. And by the time he
reached Nina's room, his expression was one of polite
neutrality. *You don't know anything yet,* he cautioned
himself. *Wait and see.*

When Nina came out of the bathroom, she found Mike
Novalis alone in the room. If he had heard her crying he
gave no sign. Instead he looked her over appraisingly.
"Very nice," he remarked.

Nina felt oddly self-conscious. She plucked at the sleeve
of her sweater and said, "At least I like my clothes."

"Yeah, they're nice, too."

Before Nina could respond, an attendant came in with
a tray of breakfast for her, and she realized that she didn't
even know what time it was. There was a wristwatch on the
table by the bed: a sleek stainless steel model. She picked
it up. The crystal was smashed and the minute hand was
bent. The hands were stopped at 1:39. "It was like that
when they brought you in," Novalis said. "You must have
broken it when you fell."

He sat next to her on the bed. "The call came in at a
quarter to two this morning. You were in the hospital by
ten after, and you were out cold for about five hours." He
glanced at his own watch. "It's going on 9:30 now."

"Thanks." She nodded at him, grateful for some facts
with which she could anchor herself. Apparently he realized how disoriented she was feeling. Maybe he was not as
insensitive as he had seemed.

"You still don't remember anything about the shooting?" he asked. "Nothing leading up to it? Like what you

were doing in a deserted part of town in the small hours of the morning?''

So much for sensitivity. He made her feel defensive without knowing why. "No," she replied coldly. "If I knew anything I would tell you, wouldn't I?"

"Would you?" The blue eyes that met hers held a challenge.

"Hey, wait a minute. What the hell are you getting at? Do you think I have something to hide?"

"Lady, at this point I don't think anything. All I know is someone reported hearing shots. You were found unconscious in the street. A witness saw a car driving away without its lights, but we got no description." He raked a hand through his untidy hair and frowned. "There're three possibilities. One, it was a random shooting, maybe a drive-by. Just bad luck for you."

"Thanks a lot," she muttered.

"Two," he continued unperturbed, "you saw something you shouldn't have and someone tried to kill you. He blew it—but maybe he'll try again. Three, you were involved in something, I don't know what, and it almost got you killed. I don't know which of those is the right one, but I'm going to find out."

"Oh, are you?" Nina was seething. "I'm sitting here with no memory, no *life,* and you think I'm a . . . a criminal?"

"Like I said, Miss Dennison, I don't think anything. Yet. Make that four possibilities." He turned to face her. "Four, this whole amnesia thing is an act." Seeing her eyes flash ominously, he raised both hands, palms out. "Hold on. I'm just thinking out loud here. I can't overlook anything."

She turned her shoulder to him and regarded the breakfast tray with disfavor. Eggs, sausage, buttered toast, orange juice. She drank the juice and set the glass down with a thump.

After a moment Novalis said, "What's the matter? Aren't you hungry?"

"Not that it's any of your business," Nina told him, "but I happen to be wondering if I'm a vegetarian."

He hooted with laughter and she glared at him. "I'm sorry," he said. "You say some funny things, that's all."

"I'm so glad you're amused, Detective Lieutenant Novalis. This whole situation must be just a riot to you."

"Look, I really am sorry if I upset you. I don't think the situation you're in is funny at all, and I'm going to do my best to help you, if I can. And by the way, you might as well call me Mike. We're going to be seeing a lot of each other."

"We are?" The prospect was unsettling. The bed moved under her when he shifted his weight slightly; the tang of leather and his musky scent teased her nostrils. Once again Nina was disturbingly aware of his nearness and his overwhelming maleness. Not that Novalis looked like a movie star or a male model—far from it. He was much more real, and a whole lot more sensual. His shirt looked as if he'd grabbed it out of a laundry hamper. His eyes were bloodshot. Deep lines bracketed his mouth. But under the dark beard stubble the chiseled planes of his face were strong and rugged. His thick, dark hair was messy; Nina had noticed that he had a habit of running his hands through it. Yet despite the evident weariness in his face and his raffish, unkempt look, Detective Lieutenant Novalis was one very handsome man. Which, Nina told herself sternly, could only complicate the mess she was in. The last thing she needed right now was to be attracted to this man. Any man. She was going to have her hands full just finding out what kind of person she was.

He turned a little, and looked directly at her, and then he smiled. Nina was shaken by the wave of heat that flickered through her. She froze, determined not to react to him. *I cannot let myself trust this man,* she told herself fiercely. *He thinks I'm lying.* Then another thought came, one she had been fighting to hold at bay: *Oh, God, what if I really did do something wrong? He'll find out.* She forced herself to look away, trying to appear calm.

"Oh, sure, we're going to be spending a lot of time together," Mike was saying. "Think about it for a minute. You may have lost your memory, but you're still right in the middle of a police investigation. A while ago you told the docs that the only thing you want is to get your memory back. Fine. I understand that. But you've got another problem. Memory or no memory, someone tried to kill you. Don't you want to know why? And don't you want to keep him from having another shot at you?"

"Of course I do!"

"That's where I come in. I have to investigate you and everything about you. And, hey, you might be glad to have a detective around. You're trying to find out about your life, right? Well, that's what we're good at—finding things out. So what d'you say? How about cooperating with me?"

"Do I have a choice?"

"Nope."

"Then fine," Nina said, hoping she sounded confident. "I've got nothing to hide." *Have I?* She ignored the frightened inner voice. "I'll cooperate with you. I just wish I knew whether I'm a suspect, a victim or an innocent bystander."

He stood. "Believe me, lady," he said, "I wish I knew the same thing."

Chapter 2

Nina left the hospital half an hour later. She had written down the doctors' phone numbers and assured Dr. Tooley that she'd call him to make an appointment for counseling. If necessary, she had added silently. Somehow she didn't think that the answer to her problems lay in therapy. Detective work sounded like a more promising avenue—even if it meant being dogged by Mike Novalis.

He guided her to a dust-covered midnight blue car with one slightly crumpled fender. The floor in back was littered with fast-food burger wrappers and soda cans. "At least we know *you're* not a vegetarian," Nina said dryly.

He looked sheepish. "That junk's too easy," he said. "I keep telling myself to start eating better. How about you—do you like to cook?"

Nina looked at him exasperatedly. "Read my lips—*I don't know.* Do I have to get it tattooed on my forehead?" Even as she spoke, though, some part of her was taking stock of his remark. It sounded as though he lived alone. So what? she asked herself. You're in trouble, this is serious. *Stop thinking of this guy as a man!* But when his shoulder brushed hers and her senses leapt into startled life, she knew it wouldn't be easy.

They drove through the streets of Center City Philadelphia. "There's a great Italian restaurant on the next corner, I think," Mike said as they approached Washington Square. "What's it called? La Something?"

"La Buca," Nina replied without thinking. "Great seafood."

He shot her a swift glance. "Ever eat there?"

"I—I don't know," she faltered. "I guess I must have. I mean, I know about the restaurant...but I can't remember being inside it."

He was silent.

"You don't believe me, do you?" she accused him. "You're trying to trick me, to prove I haven't really lost my memory."

He kept his eyes on the street ahead. "Look, Nina, if you want to think I'm trying to trick you, I can't do anything about it. But maybe I'm trying to help you figure out what you know and what you don't know. Didn't the docs say you'd have to keep questioning everything, probing the limits of your memory loss?"

"You're right. Sorry. But I still feel as if you're suspicious of me."

"I am." He turned his indigo gaze on her briefly. "Nothing's settled. But will you please try to relax? I'm not out to get you just because I'm a cop, you know."

There was a hint of bitterness in his voice. *He's right,* Nina tried to convince herself. *I have nothing to be afraid of, nothing to hide. Do I?* She felt the fear stirring again. Her life was a mass of unanswered questions. She hoped she could find the answers. But what if she found them— and couldn't live with them?

She glanced sidelong at Mike Novalis. His hands rested easily on the wheel; they were tanned and capable looking, with a few small scars—hands that had known hard use. She wondered how long he had been a cop. *I'd better try to get along with him. Apart from a couple of doctors, he's the only person I know.* That thought was almost unbearably depressing. Surely she had friends, people who cared about her. Her memory just had to come back soon. She stared out the window, willing the streets and storefronts to burst into vivid familiarity. But the hoped-for memories failed to materialize; the picture remained stubbornly out of focus.

Mike pulled up to the curb near an intersection a few blocks from the Delaware River. Decades ago this must have been a busy, important part of town, but now it was shabby and rundown. Tall brick warehouses, some with cracked and broken windows, rose on either side. Lank grass and weeds sprouted in vacant lots. The street was potholed. Traffic was light. The few pedestrians, shabby men who looked as though they had nothing to do, stared at their car with mild curiosity.

"Why are we stopping here?" she asked, twisting in her seat to look around.

"Does any of this look familiar?"

She shook her head.

"Are you sure, Nina?" His voice was steady, unthreatening. "You were here last night."

"You mean . . . this is where—?"

"Yes. This is where you were shot. We found you right over there."

Nina stared at the bleak street and tried to imagine it late at night. The streetlights were far apart; the block must be dark and more than a little forbidding. What could she have been doing in this lonely place at two in the morning? Had she really been involved in some shady activity, something that made someone want to kill her? She shivered and touched the Band-Aid on her forehead. "Nothing. I don't remember anything," she said miserably.

Mike looked at her and felt a pang of compassion. Her face was drawn and she was huddled in her seat. He wanted to draw her into his arms and comfort her, to smooth the worried lines from her face with his fingertips. And his lips. A dangerous and unprofessional idea, he chided himself, even *if* she's completely innocent. And that's a damned big if.

She glanced up and he saw the look in her eyes, candid and sad, and his hands tightened on the wheel. If she was acting, she deserved an Oscar. "It's okay," he said, starting up the car. "I just thought it was worth a try. Don't worry about it. Hey, do something for me. Look in your coat pockets."

She shoved her hands deep into the pockets of her coat. She liked the coat: it was an olive green gabardine trench coat, long and full. It was dirty in back where she'd fallen—looking around at the dingy street, she could understand why. Otherwise it was spotless and new looking.

Her fingers encountered paper in one of the pockets. It was a sales slip from Bloomingdale's, dated yesterday, for the purchase of one coat, evidently the one she was wearing. She had paid by credit card. Her eyes widened when she saw how much it had cost. It seemed that she possessed either a comfortable income or extravagant shopping habits.

"There's something else in here," she said, feeling around at the bottom of the deep pocket. The object proved to be a plastic cardkey bearing the address of an office building in Center City. Nina's name and photograph were imprinted on the key. She showed it to Mike.

"It's the key to the place where you work," he told her.

"You knew it was there."

"Sure I did. I went through your things while you were unconscious."

Aware that he was watching her closely, Nina fought down her anger. She had bigger things than her privacy to worry about. He'd only been doing what any cop would have done. And maybe he really could help her. God knew she needed it.

He said, "We could go check out your job, or we could go to your apartment. What's it going to be?"

Nina took a deep breath. She wanted to know about her work, but she also felt nervous. Was she ready to face co-workers? They would be strangers to her now. Would they be avidly curious about her plight, or sympathetic, or incredulous? She thought tiredly of all the explanations she'd have to make, all the questions she'd have to answer. Anyway, she was much more curious about her home. There, if anywhere, she would find clues to the kind of person she was.

She glanced at Mike. "Home, please," she said.

Whistling softly between his teeth, he drove south along the waterfront, leaving the drab warehouse district behind. Soon they were passing through the cobblestoned streets of Society Hill, a riverfront neighborhood of gentrified town houses and chic apartment buildings, trendy restaurants and stylish boutiques. Mellow red brick glowed in the sun; the yellow-green leaves of ginkgo trees fluttered in the mild September breeze; bronze and gold chrysanthemums blazed in stone pots. Camera-laden tourists wandered about, gawking at the old buildings and historic landmarks: Independence Hall was less than a dozen blocks away.

"Jumpers," Mike said with a grin, nodding at one determined band of sidewalk strollers who were hopping in front of a tall, narrow colonial brick house. They were trying to see into the first-floor rooms, which were several steps above street level.

Nina laughed. "It'd be hard to have much privacy if you lived in one of those houses." A thought struck her. "I don't, do I? Where *do* I live?"

Now it was his turn to laugh. "Look at your driver's license. That's what I did. Never mind, we're almost there."

He found a space in front of a handsome building that had been created by knocking together two of the narrow old houses. There were four mailboxes and an intercom speaker next to the front door. A narrow driveway led into a tiny paved courtyard with four parking spaces. Three were empty; a shiny cocoa brown BMW was parked in the fourth.

"I live *here?*" Nina said, impressed. Rents and real-estate costs in this part of town were notoriously high.

"Yeah, this is a classy case."

Nina winced inwardly at the reminder that she was a "case." She pictured Novalis shoving a manila folder with her name scrawled across it into a bulging drawer in a dented old green police department filing cabinet. For a brief instant she had felt almost like any ordinary woman out for a drive with a man, a woman who could joke and laugh and enjoy the autumn sunshine. But didn't even know who she was. And Mike Novalis wasn't here to take her on a pleasure drive. He was on a case. Hers.

They walked up the worn white marble steps and scanned the mailboxes. Dennison, Apt. 4, said a discreet printed card on one. "There's a set of keys in your bag," Mike said helpfully.

Nina bristled a little. She was getting tired of the way he was always one step ahead of her, and she hated the fact that he knew more than she did about her own life. But she was secretly glad to have him with her now. It felt strange to be entering a home she didn't even remember, but it would have been much stranger, and maybe a little frightening, to be doing it alone.

"The outside pocket," he prompted.

She shot a peevish glance at him. "I'm getting to it." The keys, when she finally dug them out of the bag, dangled from an enameled metal BMW emblem.

He whistled. "Maybe that brown number in the lot is yours. Nice wheels."

"Wow. Do you think it might be?"

"We'll check it out later. Let's go on in."

He took the keys from her hand, unlocked the door and stepped through first. Suppressing a sigh at his rudeness, Nina followed him into a spotless, rather austere hall. The walls were white, the carpet was beige and doors on either side bore plain brass numerals: 1 and 2. A flight of stairs led to the second floor. Mike walked ahead of her. He acts as if he has more right to be here than I have, Nina grumbled to herself.

When they reached apartment 4, Mike motioned for her to stand back while he opened her door. But when he started to walk in ahead of her, Nina crowded impatiently forward to push past him. All at once he whirled, pulling her hard against him with an arm that felt like iron. He clapped the other hand firmly over her mouth.

"Quiet," he whispered in her ear. "Do exactly what I say. Don't make any noise. Do you understand?"

Nina's heart thundered in her ears, and her legs shook with shock and indignation. But she looked up and saw reassurance in Mike's eyes, and she knew that nothing was going to hurt her. She nodded, and he took his hand away from her mouth. "Good girl," he whispered. "Now go downstairs and wait for me by the front door. Don't come up until I call you. If you hear yelling or shots, run outside and call the cops. Got that?"

Nina nodded again, dry-throated with fear, and he squeezed her shoulder and gave her a gentle shove. She looked back from the top of the stairs. As Mike eased her door open, he reached inside his jacket and withdrew a small but wicked-looking gun. She hurried downstairs.

In the hushed hallway Nina could hear nothing. The whole surreal episode had taken only a few seconds. She strained her ears. What was going on up there? What was happening to Mike?

She tiptoed back up the stairs and peered around the corner of the stairwell. Mike was coming out of her apartment. "I thought I told you to wait downstairs." He wasn't whispering any more, and the gun was no longer visible.

"I did. And then I didn't hear anything, and I thought—"

"No, you *didn't* think. Next time just do what I say, okay?" But his smile took the sting out of the words. She knew he was right; he was the expert here, and she should have followed his instructions. From now on she'd gladly let him precede her through every doorway.

"Okay. Sorry. But what's going on? Is somebody in there?"

"No. But either someone has been here before us . . . or you're one hell of a housekeeper."

This can't be home. Nina stood in the doorway of her apartment, gazing at a complete and total mess. Pictures hung crookedly on the off-white walls. In front of a wall of oak bookshelves, books and cassettes lay in heaps on the sand-colored carpeting. Stuffing dribbled from shredded sofa cushions. Plants lay limply in little piles of dirt next to their overturned pots. Stepping gingerly through the debris, Nina looked into a bedroom. The bed was unmade—literally. Dove gray sheets and a matching comforter were strewn across the floor, and feathers from dismembered pillows were everywhere. Drawers gaped open, disgorging tangles of clothing. Back in the living room, Nina saw a small but streamlined yellow-tiled kitchen through an archway. Here, too, drawers and cupboards were open. Canisters of flour and pasta had been emptied onto the counter, and cereal boxes spilled their contents across the surface of a butcher-block table.

Nina was numb. She didn't know what she had expected, but it certainly wasn't this . . . this shambles. She had hoped that her home would tell her who she really was, that it would give her a sense of security. Instead, she had walked into something that looked like a hurricane disaster area.

She wanted to scream, or cry. Instead she made herself take a deep breath. Mike was watching her, looking apprehensive. "I really have to get a new cleaning woman," she said as lightly as she could manage, and he shot her a quick smile.

"That's the way," he said. "I know this is rough, but you can handle it."

"What is this? What happened?"

"Someone searched your place. Probably not long ago—those plants aren't dead yet. Whoever did it was in a hurry."

"Burglars?"

"I don't know." He combed a hand through his shaggy hair. "Might have been pros—they didn't break your lock. Either they used a lock pick to get in, or they had a key. But pros don't make this kind of mess just to rip off your jewelry or money or stereo equipment. And your CD player is still here. No, whoever did this was looking for something." He let that sink in. "Any idea what?"

"No. And before you ask, no, I don't know who had a key to my apartment. I have amnesia, remember?"

"Yeah, I remember." He was silent for a moment, then said, "Look, I know you must want to start going through your stuff, but it would be better if you didn't touch anything for a while. I need to get the fingerprint guys over here, just in case we get lucky and get some prints. How about having some lunch with me while they work? Then we'll come back here and I'll help you get this place in shape."

Nina took another look around. Her apartment, her life, her world—all turned upside down. Would they ever be right again? "Sure, let's get some lunch," she said dispiritedly.

Mike made a phone call, and within minutes half a dozen businesslike men and women were in Nina's apartment. Making no comment on the disorder, they proceeded to set up cameras and to dust for prints. Nina's own prints were taken—"So that we can eliminate them," as Mike soothingly explained—and she dabbed ruefully with an alcohol-soaked cotton ball at her ink-stained fingertips as they left the building. *Wonder if this is the first time I've done this?*

They picked the first restaurant they came to in Nina's neighborhood. Nina didn't think about the potential pitfalls of dining locally until they almost collided with a tanned blond woman about her own age who was on her way out. The blonde planted herself in front of them, waved a hand in front of Nina's face and said, "Earth to Nina—wake up! Hey, how're you doing?"

Nina stammered, "Sorry, I didn't see you. Uh, hi."

The blonde looked Mike up and down and the message in her eyes when she turned to Nina was clear: *Aren't you going to introduce me?*

Nina wasn't ready for this. She hadn't thought about running into someone who knew her. Should she try to explain about the amnesia, or should she bluff it?

Mike came to her rescue. "Mike Novalis," he said, extending his hand with that smile of his that could melt a glacier.

"Danielle Cole," the blonde said as they shook hands.

Mike turned to Nina. "I think I see a table, Nina. Are you about ready?"

"Yes," she said gratefully. Improvising, she said, "We've got to eat and run, Danielle. I'll see you later."

"See you Tuesday night." As Danielle left she grinned and made an enthusiastic thumbs-up sign, rolling her eyes toward Mike.

"Thanks," Nina said to Mike as they sat down. "That was a pretty awkward moment."

"You'd probably better decide how you're going to handle this," he advised. "You know, what you're going to tell people."

"I feel so strange. Hollow. That woman—Danielle—she could be my best friend, and I don't even know it. And what did she mean about Tuesday night?" Nina didn't mention the fact that Danielle had obviously thought she was on a date with Mike. *And* that she thought Mike was a hunk.

"Maybe we'll find some answers when we go through your place," Mike told her. He nodded at another table, where four businessmen were digging into large, colorful salads. "Those things look pretty good, if you still think you're a vegetarian."

"Actually...I'm kind of hungry for a cheeseburger. A big one, with fries."

Mike looked at her, his blue eyes dancing with amusement.

"I've decided I'm *not* a vegetarian," she told him firmly, and then added, "Well, if I was, I've changed." She wondered uneasily just how many other things would change before she got her life back.

Mike studied Nina during the meal. She had a way of looking at everything around her with a slight, puzzled frown; she seemed nervous and ill at ease. That didn't mean anything. It was probably exactly the way an amnesiac *would* feel. But so would someone with something to hide.

He remembered her white, bloodstained face against the dark pavement. Now he felt himself being drawn to the

living reality of her: her animated expressions, the shifting amber glints that warmed her green eyes, the irony that
could edge her voice—even the way her long, deft fingers
plucked at the edges of the paper place mat, absently rip-
ping off strips and rolling them into tiny balls.

He'd known plenty of women in his thirty-five years.
And he had always known exactly what he wanted from
them, exactly how much they could give him. He'd had his
share of relationships, pleasant ones for the most part,
with carefully limited expectations and demands. He'd
steered clear of women who wanted more than he was
willing to give easily. Dating and relationships became a
game, a highly enjoyable one, played by a set of well-
rehearsed, unspoken rules. Until he'd met the woman who
had made him break his rules. She'd made him believe in
trust and sacrifice. In the possibility of love. Well, he knew
better now. All the trust, all the love, had been blown away
when she pulled the trigger. But it hadn't been Mike who
died....

He tore his thoughts away from that dark path and
looked again at Nina. It had been a long time since Karen.
A long time since he'd felt desire. But he was feeling it
now, desire so strong that it hurt. And just as with Karen,
he knew it was dangerous. Too damned dangerous.

Nina felt the pull of his eyes on her. Finally she looked
up to meet them. She wished she could name their vivid
color. Aquamarine? No, they were a deeper blue. Lapis
lazuli? No, they were clearer, more brilliant. Sapphire?
Maybe, but the sparkle of a stone was a lifeless thing
compared with the changing lights in Mike Novalis's eyes.
In the few hours she had known him, those eyes had glimmered with humor, comforted her with their steady gaze—
and chilled her with their cool, remote assessment. She
wondered what else they could do. What did they look like
when they were hot with passion? Did he close them when

he kissed? She closed her own eyes briefly to drive away the unwanted images.

"Tell me about me," she said abruptly. "I know you've checked up on me. Tell me what you know about my life. It can't do any harm. If I'm lying about the amnesia—" here she looked up, and his heart gave a strange little lurch when he saw the hint of scorn and hurt on her face "—I already know it all, anyway. And if I'm not lying, I *need* to know. You can help me."

He nodded. Her request made sense. "Fair enough. Here's what we know. It's not much. First of all, you've never made the net." Seeing her quizzical expression, he shook his head slightly and gave her a crooked half smile. "Sorry. Cop talk. It just means you haven't been arrested for anything."

That's some consolation. Whatever mess I'm in now, at least I'm not a career criminal. "What else?"

"Somebody at the station talked to your landlord. You've lived in that apartment for just over four years. You listed a couple of college professors as references when you moved in. The building is run by a management company—they don't know anything about your personal life. You're not married."

He hesitated, and his voice was stiff and awkward when he continued. "I don't know whether or not you're involved with anyone. A boyfriend."

Nina nodded. "I guess I'll find out," she said, hoping her voice didn't reveal the aching emptiness she suddenly felt. It wasn't the thought of being alone. She could deal with that. Aloneness was a known factor. What hurt was the uncertainty, the strangeness of not knowing even the most intimate thing about her own life.

"Right," Mike said. "We'll find out." Nina pretended not to notice the change in pronoun.

"I can tell you another thing," Mike said. "That key in your coat pocket—to the building where you work. We checked it out. You work for an import company with offices there.'' There was a pause, then Mike dropped words into the silence like stones. "Zakroff and Duchesne." He looked at her with narrowed eyes, as if waiting.

Some indefinable emotion shivered along Nina's spine. She almost recognized those names, as though they had meant something once, a long time ago.... Suddenly Mike saw her face go pale. She squeezed her eyes shut and clutched at her forehead.

"Nina! Nina, are you okay? What is it?''

Comforted by the genuine concern in his voice, she opened her eyes and drew a shaky breath. "I'm okay. I just...I had a sort of mental flash when you said those names. It was, well, a sort of vision. I saw two men. One was blond, handsome, the other had darker hair, but he was bald on top. They were in some kind of tiny room, and...the room looked like it was *moving.*'' She went on eagerly, "It's got to be a memory, right? Maybe it's them—Zakroff and whoever. Maybe it's the start of my memories coming back!''

Mike looked into her glowing face and couldn't help feeling some of her excitement, despite his suspicions. *She could be telling the truth. Or is she setting me up to play the fool?* "I hope you're right," he said, and he meant it.

He took a bite of his grilled chicken sandwich and asked pleasantly, "The name Zakroff and Duchesne doesn't mean anything to you?''

She shook her head.

"Then how about this? Emeralds.''

She looked up sharply. "What about them?''

Mike knew he had gotten to her somehow. He saw it in the sudden tension of her shoulders and in her expression, at once eager and curiously guarded. The mention of emeralds had touched a nerve. She looked almost...afraid. Not much of a breakthrough, but it was something. He said calmly, as if it meant nothing out of the ordinary,

"Zakroff and Duchesne are gem importers. Right now they're specializing in emeralds."

Nina had put down her cheeseburger, and now she began turning her water glass between her fingers, frowning down at the flashing, swirling chips of ice. She had felt something, a jolt of tension, when he mentioned emeralds. It wasn't startlingly clear, like the visual flash in which she'd seen the two men; it was just a vague feeling of deep unease. Frustrated, she felt the impression fading away.

The ice sparkled in Nina's glass. She was sure that she'd seen something just like it before, a cascade of bits of ice that threw off dazzling flashes of light . . . but the background should be black velvet, not the dull red paper of a disposable place mat. And the ice should be green. Emeralds again. Suddenly she remembered waking up in the hospital, noticing the nurse's engagement ring. There was an elusive thread here, linking her to her former self, if only she could follow it.

"What do I do at Zakroff and Duchesne?" she asked.

Mike looked at her. Her face was averted; she was gazing down at her glass. Was she really struggling to overcome an amnesiac block, or was she planning her next move, deciding what to say to him? Manipulating him?

He wondered how she'd respond if he told her that her employers were being investigated by federal agents. *Idiot!* he snarled inwardly. *That's the last thing she should know—with or without amnesia.* What was it about this woman that threw his judgment out of whack? He realized that she was still waiting for an answer.

"I don't know what you do," he said flatly. "You were at work yesterday—that's all I can tell you. Are you finished? The forensics team ought to be through at your place by now."

Nina reached for her bag, intending to pay for her lunch, but he drew out his wallet impatiently. "It's on the department," he said. "Let's get going."

Back at Nina's building, Mike stepped aside politely this time to let her precede him up the stairs. Nothing had changed in the apartment. The forensics officers had finished their job; one of them had stayed behind to report to Novalis.

"Miss Dennison's prints were all over the place, as you'd expect," he said. "But we lifted a few others. We'll check them out and let you know if we get a match."

"Yeah." Mike wasn't going to hold his breath. Whoever had tossed Nina's apartment had probably worn gloves.

"Lieutenant, there's something else you ought to see," the policeman said quietly.

He led Mike to a desk in the corner of the living room. Like everything else in Nina's apartment, the desk bore signs of either remarkably bad housekeeping or a determined and destructive search. The policeman pointed to a half-opened drawer. "We found it just like that."

Across the room, Nina watched Mike and the uniformed policeman bend to look into the drawer. The officer handed Mike a pen, which he used to pull the drawer all the way open.

A moment passed, and then Mike said softly, "Nina, would you come here, please?"

She crossed the room slowly, almost reluctantly. Something told her she wasn't going to like what she was about to see. The look on Mike's face when he turned to her was coolly speculative. "Can you tell me anything about this?" he asked.

Nina peered into the drawer. There, on top of a thoroughly ordinary litter of papers, rubber bands, pens and

forward and put a finger under her chin, tilting her face up. "We'll find it," he repeated, and was rewarded by a shaky smile. He held his breath, watching the topaz lights shift in her jade green eyes. Nina was unable to move, held by his light touch and his piercing look as though by a spell. She felt a flush of heat creeping up her throat. Then, as if the spell were lifted suddenly from them both, she drew away sharply and his hand dropped as though burned.

They stood for a moment, looking anywhere but at each other, while silence hardened between them.

"Well," she said finally, "I guess I'll try putting my life back together." She walked toward the bedroom. Without looking back she added, "Feel free to look for clues or whatever it is you have to do."

He watched her go into the bedroom and close the door. "Don't you worry, baby," he said quietly. "I'm gonna do whatever I have to do."

Chapter 3

The bedroom was a mess. The first step, Nina decided, was to get her clothes up off the floor. She began folding sweaters and hanging blouses, trying not to give way to the anger and revulsion that swept over her every time she imagined some stranger handling her things, throwing them around. Gradually, though, the soft textures and muted colors of the clothes calmed her nerves. In fact, she decided, they were almost *too* soothing—Nina's entire wardrobe seemed to be beige, charcoal gray or navy. Everything was elegant and very conservative. *I've got to buy a red outfit,* Nina told herself. She pictured a scarlet leather miniskirt hanging in the closet next to the camel-colored wool suit and almost giggled. *Maybe just a sweater to start with.* When she finished tidying up the clothes, Nina looked around the room with satisfaction: chaos was beginning to give way to order.

Mike was moving around in the living room; Nina heard the muffled sounds of drawers opening and closing. She was sorry that she had closed the door between them with such finality. It had gained her some privacy, but now she was consumed with curiosity. What was he doing out there? She had a right to know—it was *her* stuff he was poking around in. Shouldn't he be asking her questions?

She couldn't stay in the bedroom all afternoon. It was time to remake the bed, and she refused to use the sheets that the searchers had ripped from the mattress. She had noticed a linen closet in the bathroom.

Nina opened the bedroom door to find Mike seated at her desk, calmly examining a stack of papers that obviously belonged in an open file drawer. She bit back an annoyed exclamation but couldn't keep all the tension out of her voice when she asked, "Find anything incriminating?"

He gave her a brief, dispassionate glance. "Not yet. Don't worry—when I do, you'll be the first to know."

Nina marched to the linen closet, which, she was happy to discover, held several clean sets of sheets, only slightly rumpled, as though someone had flipped hastily through them.

Back in the bedroom—with the door open this time— she remade the bed. *Not much I can do about these,* she thought, stuffing the slashed pillows into a trash bag. *But at least this room looks fairly normal now.* The bedroom did look orderly and sedate, with its cool colors and delicate floral prints. Just one thing still jarred—the drawer of her nightstand gaped crookedly open. No doubt the searcher had ransacked it.

The drawer wouldn't shut. Nina shoved it harder, but it was jammed. She scrabbled among its contents: a box of tissues, a package of throat lozenges, an emery board.... Something was stuck in the back of the drawer. It felt like a book. Nina grasped a corner and tugged, and the object that had kept the drawer from closing came free. It was a leatherbound book with the year and the word *Diary* stamped on the cover.

Nina's hands trembled with excitement. She realized that she was holding what might be her best clue to the mysteries of her past. Was this what the searcher had been looking for? She didn't stop to think. There was no way she was going to let Mike Novalis get his hands on her diary—not until she knew exactly what it contained. Until she knew whether she had something to hide.

Quickly she shoved the diary under the edge of the mattress, then closed the drawer. She was aching to read the diary, but she couldn't risk letting Novalis know that she had found it. Whatever secrets it held would simply have to wait. She took a final look around the bedroom.

"Nice job."

Nina whirled guiltily at the sound of Mike's voice behind her. How much had he seen?

She forced herself to look away from the corner of the mattress where the diary was hidden. Mike was gazing around the restored room. "Looks good," he said. "Did you find anything interesting?"

"No. Just my clothes and things." She was surprised by how matter-of-fact her voice sounded.

His gaze rested on her for a moment, and then he reached out and opened a large, carved wooden box that stood on the bureau. Inside was a clutter of jewelry. Nina examined the pieces one by one. A necklace of turquoise beads, two silver chains with charms, a dozen or so pairs of earrings, mostly silver. Several rings.

"So the break-in wasn't a jewel theft," Mike said.

"The truth is, this jewelry isn't worth all that much," Nina answered. "I like it—it's beautiful, all handmade craft pieces—but there's no gold. And look, all the stones are semiprecious, garnets and topazes and so on. No diamonds or rubies. These—" she indicated a pair of discreet pearl earrings "—are the most valuable things here, and they're worth no more than two hundred dollars."

"Maybe you had a lot of other, more valuable jewelry, and the perpetrator took it."

"Maybe. But wouldn't it have been easier just to grab it all instead of picking through it?"

"Sure it would. Like I said before, this break-in wasn't a robbery. But it looks like you know a lot about jewelry."

He was right, Nina realized. She had assessed her jewelry with authority. Once again, just as when she looked at the glittering ice cubes in the restaurant, she felt that sense of haunting familiarity, that feeling that she was on the verge of remembering something important—and once again it faded away.

"Come out here," Mike said, moving into the living room. "I've got a few things to show you." Nina saw that he had stacked the scattered magazines and books into piles. He led her to one pile and she knelt to examine it. There were issues of a magazine called *Gemologists' Quarterly* and a number of books dealing with gemstones, from an ancient and well-worn paperback called *Rocks and Minerals of the World* to *A Catalog of Gems in the Metropolitan Museum of Art* to a textbook titled *Advanced Gemology*.

"I'm no Sherlock Holmes," said Mike, "but I'd say you're some kind of expert in precious stones."

"Gemologist," corrected Nina absently, and then she looked up, eyes alight with excitement. "My God, that's right, I'm a gemologist! I recognize all these books, I know everything that's in them."

Mike couldn't help himself—the look of joy and hope on her face took his breath away. He'd never seen anything so beautiful. He dropped to his knees next to her and took her hands in his. "That's great, Nina. Do you remember reading them? What about where you went to school?"

Slowly the light in her face faded, replaced by puzzlement. She shook her head. "No. I—I remember the information, but I can't remember anything else, I can't—"

Her voice broke. Mike felt her hands, still grasped in his, clench into fists, and a rush of tenderness almost overwhelmed him. Pulling her closer, comforting her, would be the easiest and most natural thing in the world. Instead he did the smart thing. He let her go, and she turned away. When she spoke again, her voice was angry. "Damn it, it's my *life,* and I can't remember!"

Mike stood and looked down at her bent head, resisting an urge to stroke the tousled auburn hair. Now that he wasn't looking into her eyes, wasn't touching her, his wariness returned. *If this is an act,* he told himself, *she's another Meryl Streep. And if she's trying to do a job on you, fella, it's working.* His lips tightened. He wasn't going to get burned that way again.

He walked to the desk and picked up a small book. "Here. You might find this useful."

Nina got to her feet—and suddenly the room fractured into shards of light. She saw a swirl of movement that resolved itself into a dark, shining swath of fur. An instant later she realized that the fur was a mink coat. A blond woman was wearing the coat, twirling in front of Nina. The woman's hair was wound into a French twist, and she was smiling. Nina seemed to hear a light, musical voice say, "How do you like it?" Then once again came the flashes of light, and Nina blinked. She was in her living room, alone with Mike, who was staring at her.

"Nina, did you hear me? What is it?"

"Another memory, I guess. Like in the restaurant, when I sort of blacked out and saw those two men. The same thing just happened—a flash of light, and then I saw something. This time it was a blond woman. She was wearing a mink coat. And I think," Nina added, straining to recall every detail of that fleeting vision, "yes, I'm pretty sure she was standing right in this room."

"Did you recognize her?"

She shook her head. "Maybe it'll come back to me."

Despite his suspicions Mike was moved by her sad, empty voice. "Sure it will," he said.

Nina trembled. Mike's voice had held a familiar, cherishing note—it was the same voice he'd used to comfort her when she lay stunned in the street after the shooting. And she was shocked at just how good it felt when he spoke to her in that warm, caressing voice. The sound of it shivered across her flesh, raising goose bumps on the sensitive skin of her arms and neck. But in the next instant she brought herself back to reality: *I can just imagine how he'd sound if he discovered that diary under the mattress.*

"Maybe this will make you feel better," Mike said, and Nina saw that he was still holding out that little book. It was, she realized, an address book. It was open to the front page, labeled Important Numbers. There she had scrawled "Mom," followed by an area code and phone number.

"I already checked. It's a Florida code."

"Thanks." Nina held the book, staring down at the number through eyes blurred with unshed tears. Would her mother's voice trigger a return of memory, or would the woman at the other end of the telephone line be just another stranger?

"I don't think I'm ready to call her just yet." Nina's voice was unsteady. "I feel a little off-balance. Maybe after I work on this mess for a while—" She nodded toward the disaster area that was her kitchen.

"Sure, I understand. I'll give you a hand."

She shot him a swift, surprised glance. "You're going to help me clean up?"

He grinned, a flash of white against his dark stubble, and those boyish dimples reappeared briefly. "Sure, why not? Besides, there could be a clue in your oatmeal, and I wouldn't want to miss it.''

''Well, okay. As you can see, I need all the help I can get.'' *In more ways than one,* she thought.

''First, though, I'm going to see if I can save these guys,'' Mike said, pointing at the four overturned house-plants.

Nina went into the kitchen, found an apron and began cleaning up the worst of the mess: the food that had been carelessly strewn across the counters, the table and the floor. It looked as though someone had opened every container, searching for something that might have been hidden among the contents.

As she worked she stole glances at Mike. He'd gone down on his knees and was gently restoring the plants to their pots, scooping up the discarded potting soil and pat-ting it into place around their roots. Nina thought she heard him humming, and then realized that he was talk-ing as he worked—to himself or to the plants, she wasn't sure which. ''Philodendron, huh?'' she heard him mut-ter. ''You guys're pretty hard to kill. I think you'll pull through.'' She smiled. *Real tough guy.*

He finished his horticultural first aid, watered the plants and arranged them around the room. ''Hey,'' he called out to Nina, ''is this where they go?'' Before she could an-swer he said, ''Never mind, I know—you don't remem-ber. I'm sorry, I don't mean to keep putting you on the spot. I'll start over. Do these plants look all right?''

''They look fine. Thanks. Now how about looking for clues in here—with the vacuum cleaner.'' Mike groaned but lent a hand willingly enough, and for a time they worked side by side in companionable silence.

''You're going to have to restock your kitchen,'' Mike remarked as he sealed a garbage bag on an assortment of pasta, cereal and crackers that he had swept up from the floor.

"There are some frozen dinners in the freezer that haven't been opened," Nina said, "and some cans of soup and packages of tea and cocoa. But you're right, I need to go to the store. Maybe tomorrow. If I can remember where the store is."

Mike snapped his fingers. "That reminds me. That brown BMW is yours—I found the insurance papers in your desk. Want to go down and take a look at it?"

"Good idea. I could use a break," Nina answered, grateful for the suggestion. Her head was beginning to ache, and she felt tired and drained.

The fresh late-afternoon breeze felt good, though, and the gorgeous sports car would have boosted anyone's spirits. She watched while Mike quickly and expertly examined the car.

"Nothing in the glove compartment but the registration and insurance card," he reported. "Nothing in the trunk but a spare tire and a set of jumper cables. The car is spotless."

"No fast-food wrappers on the floor?" Nina said teasingly, just to see if she could make him grin.

"Nope," he answered. "Just a few lobster claws and champagne bottles." And then he grinned again, dimples and all, and the grin did strange, unsettling things to Nina's heartbeat. *Better hope he doesn't do that too often,* she warned herself. *I've got enough trouble without getting weak in the knees every time the cop who's investigating me smiles.*

At Mike's suggestion, Nina agreed to take the car for a short spin. He said that he wanted to be sure she remembered how to handle it. She couldn't find any fault with his reasoning, but with him sitting next to her, quietly watching her every move as she pulled out of the parking lot and into traffic, she felt like a sixteen-year-old taking her first driving test.

"Where do you want me to go?" she asked.

"Nowhere in particular. Just drive around for a few minutes. Maybe being behind the wheel will trigger some memories."

But it didn't. Nina had no trouble driving, and the car's control panel seemed familiar, but she had no actual recollection of ever being in the BMW. Her sensation behind the wheel was much like what she had experienced when she looked at her gemology books: the knowledge was there, but she couldn't remember acquiring it. The doctors had called this sort of knowledge "generalized memory." It was very different from those vivid, sharp flashes in which she saw people and scenes but did not know who or where they were. Nina could only hope that eventually she would begin to recognize the images that appeared in those blinding visions.

She drove aimlessly, and after a few turns she found herself on a ramp leading down to the riverside docks. She pulled into a parking area and looked out across the riverfront. The sun was beginning to go down; shadows stretched across the broad slate blue Delaware. Across the river the factories and warehouses of Camden glittered in the last of the day's light. Mike cracked open the sunroof, and the evening air stirred their hair.

"Feel any better?" he asked after a few moments.

"It's the strangest thing," Nina said. "I remember bits and pieces of my life—the names of restaurants, and who's president, and being a gemologist. But none of it seems to have anything to do with *me*." She drummed her hands on the steering wheel in frustration. "I feel as though my life before today didn't really exist."

Mike laid one hand on hers, stilling their restless motion. "It did, Nina." His voice and his touch were kind, but when she looked at him his expression was remote. She would have given anything at that moment to see warmth and reassurance in his eyes, but she sensed that he was holding back, reserving judgment. *That's right—it's all part of the job to him,* she thought bleakly. She started up the car and headed for home.

Mike shoved his hands into his jacket pockets and gazed unseeingly out the window. He glanced at Nina. Her face was set and she was staring straight ahead as she drove. His thoughts raced around and around in a tormented circle: She can't be faking. She's hurting. Her amnesia is real, I'd bet my life on it. But what if she *is* faking, having a good laugh at my expense?

Always, Mike ended up at the same bleak conclusion: Even if Nina were telling the absolute, unvarnished truth, he was dangerously close to stepping over the line with her. This should have been a simple open-and-shut investigation of a shooting, but his emotions were getting involved, and his control was slipping. He wanted to help her find herself, he wanted to protect her—and he had to find out if she was hiding something. And if she kept looking at him with those brave smiles and those sad eyes, he didn't know *what* the hell he was going to do.

Nina was quiet until they were back in her apartment. Then she took a deep breath and said, "I think I'm ready to make that telephone call now. To my mother."

"Would you like me to leave the room?" Mike spoke gently, and Nina almost nodded, grateful for his understanding—he was giving her a choice, when he could probably have insisted on listening in on all of her calls. Then she realized that she did not want to be alone. Mike Novalis was a lot of things—suspicious, moody, infuriating—but Nina was sure that above all he was strong. And right now she needed some strength, even if it was only borrowed.

"Please stay," she whispered, and dialed the number.

Her mother answered on the third ring, and Nina knew at once that she could not tell this woman what had happened to her. Her mother's voice was faint and frail; it was the voice of someone who needed comfort and attention—not someone who could deal with an amnesiac daughter, a bullet wound and a police investigation.

"How are you feeling?" Nina asked.

"Oh, you know how it is. The doctors say there's nothing at all wrong with me, but..." There followed a list of minor symptoms, as well as grievances about the neighbors' loud bridge parties.

"You said you had a problem, something you needed my help with," Nina prompted.

"Oh, yes, I'm so glad you remembered. I'm going to redecorate the living room. Do you think I should go with sea-foam green or teal blue?"

Nina blinked. This was not what she had expected. "Uh, blue, I guess. Yes, definitely the blue."

"Well, I'll think about it." Her mother sounded dubious.

Nina's mind raced. There was so much she wanted to know—but how could she ask questions without alarming her mother? "Mom," she ventured, "I was thinking about Dad this morning," and then she paused. Would her mother put her father on the line?

"Were you, dear?" Her mother's voice was tender. "I'm glad. You know, I think about him all the time. He would have been so proud of the way you and your brother turned out. It's hard to believe it's been ten years." Then, in a livelier tone, "I'm looking forward to having you both here at Christmas. I talked to Charley the other day, and he said that he and Lynn and the boys can't wait to see you."

"I'm looking forward to it, too," Nina murmured.

"Maybe you'd like to bring someone down here with you?" her mother suggested. "If you're seeing anyone, that is..."

"No. No one special." *As far as I know.*

She said goodbye to her mother, promising to call again soon, and hung up the phone.

"Any luck?" said Mike, behind her.

"No," Nina said, feeling flat and empty. "I didn't recognize her voice. I could pass her on the street tomorrow and not know who she was. And my father's dead." Disappointment and loneliness and despair tore at her; she couldn't hold back the tears any longer. Then strong, gentle hands took her shoulders. Mike turned her and drew her into the circle of his arms and held her while she wept.

He had acted without thinking, responding instinctively to her distress. At first he had wanted only to comfort her as he might comfort a hurt child, but as he held her body to his, burying his face in her hair, thrilling to the delicious yielding firmness of her breasts against his chest, his desire swelled. His grip on her tightened—only a little, but enough to pull her hips tight against the taut, aching pressure in his jeans....

She looked up, eyes wide and lips parted, and it took all of Mike's strength for him to step back from her and look away. He walked over to the bookshelves and picked up a handful of the fallen books, shoving them onto the shelves at random. He was trying to appear calm, but mentally he was lashing himself. *Are you out of your mind? Getting turned on—and letting her know it! If she's innocent, she could have your badge for what you just did. And if she's not, she could take a damn sight more than that away from you. Start thinking with your brain, not with what's between your legs, you idiot!*

Nina felt dazed. The grief that had driven her into Mike's arms was temporarily forgotten—her mind and senses were drugged by the surge of white-hot desire she'd felt when he pulled her close. He was across the room now, acting as though nothing had happened, and her legs were still shaking. But Nina knew that Mike had felt it, too; the touch of her hips against his, brief though it was, had seared her with the awareness of his hardness, his body's hunger for her. Nina felt an answering hunger. *It's only because you're hurt, vulnerable,* she told herself. *You're all mixed up—you don't know what you're doing.* But it was hard to think clearly when what she most wanted to do was to run across the room to where he stood with his back turned to her, wrap her arms around his waist and ask him to hold her again. And this time to lower his mouth to hers and kiss her until she was breathless.

"I think," she began, and started over, sternly banishing the tremor from her voice, "I think I'll take a shower."

"Fine," he said without turning around, still mechanically shelving books. Even from across the room Nina could see that he was putting cookbooks in with mystery novels. "I'll be here when you get out."

That's what I'm afraid of, Nina thought as she closed the bathroom door behind her.

A few minutes later, Nina was willing to admit that the shower hadn't been such a great idea, after all. She'd been looking for an excuse to get away from Mike Novalis for a little while so that her emotions could cool down. But the silky touch of the warm water as it flowed through her hair and cascaded down her body served only to make her thoughts more overheated than before. Every inch of her body seemed alive with tingling sensation, as though the brief embrace she and Mike had just shared had wakened some sleeping force within her that would not be quieted. As she soaped herself, she imagined Mike's hands on her arms, her breasts, her thighs. What if he were here in the shower with her, slick and hard and ready? Even as she tried to drive the image from her mind, her body betrayed her: Her nipples hardened, an ache was building at the core of her womanhood—

Nina pounded her fist against the cool, hard tiles of the shower wall. *This has got to stop!* She gave the tap a savage jerk, and the warm water turned cold. Shivering in the sudden chill, Nina spelled out the details of her predicament as she quickly rinsed. Even if she were innocent of any wrongdoing—*and I've got to believe I'm innocent!*—someone had still taken a shot at her and searched her apartment. And even if the shooting was purely random and the break-in a wild coincidence, she still had amnesia.

All of which, Nina pointed out to herself as she stepped out of the tub and grabbed a towel, added up to the fact that she had no business being attracted to the detective who might end up arresting her. Or to anyone. *I don't even know what kind of person Nina Dennison really is. And until I know who I am, how can I even think about being with someone else?* She dressed quickly, combed her wet hair straight back and resolutely refused to put on any makeup. *It doesn't matter how I look to him. He's the detective, I'm the suspect—remember?* Recalling the fire that had raced through her veins when Mike held her, Nina squared her shoulders and braced herself. She would act as though it hadn't happened. And she would make certain that it didn't happen again.

Mike listened to the water running in the bathroom and tried not to think about Nina in the shower. He was still hard and aching from the feel of her in his arms, and now he couldn't stop picturing the water streaming over her smooth, wet body. He imagined himself in the shower with her. He would soap her back, and then she'd turn to him, glistening like a mermaid, and he knew just how she would feel against him when she drew him close—

Belatedly Mike noticed that he'd been putting Nina's books onto her shelves upside down. "Better let her finish this," he muttered. He needed a distraction, and there was one desk drawer he hadn't yet been through.

A few moments later Mike was deep in thought, but he wasn't thinking about sharing a shower with Nina. He was staring down at the passport in his hand, remembering his department's first and only briefing on the Zakroff and Duchesne case.

Morris Hecht hadn't been in a good mood that day. He wasn't exactly cheerful to begin with, and having to start the day with a 7:30 meeting hadn't helped. That meeting had been with the senior FBI official in charge of the Zakroff and Duchesne investigation, and Hecht was now ready to pass on to his staff the few morsels of information that the FBI had deigned to share with him.

Hecht had stomped into the detectives' squad room and snagged a doughnut from the box by the coffeemaker. After one bite he looked at it in disgust, put it down on someone's desk and lit a cigar, ignoring the pained expressions of his detectives.

"Once again we have the honor of hosting an FBI investigation," he said dourly. "I'm authorized to tell you just enough to keep you from screwing up the feds' case. There's a Philadelphia company involved. Gem dealers called Zakroff and Duchesne. There's an international angle. The firm does a lot of importing. From Colombia. It seems that country is a major source of emeralds—as well as another expensive luxury item. Somebody thinks the Médellin cocaine cartel could be branching out into gem smuggling, maybe using emeralds as a way to get their funds out of Colombia. The FBI is checking out this firm."

"They need any help from us, Chief?" Detective Sarris's mocking question provoked derisive laughter from her fellow officers.

"Hell, no." Hecht puffed on his cigar. "As far as the guy in charge of this case is concerned, we're just glorified traffic cops. But you're on notice. If any of you turn up anything involving this Zakroff and Duchesne outfit, or any new Colombian connections, or if you hear anything on the street about emeralds, report to me and I'll pass it on to the feds. Got it?"

"If we get a tip, do we win a prize?" Sarris called out.

"Yeah." Hecht stood and ground out his cigar in a plate that held a half-eaten bagel. "You win a free vacation in sunny Colombia."

Mike caught his breath when Nina came out of the bathroom. Her hair was slicked back, wet from her shower, and for an instant he remembered the seductive image of her that had filled his thoughts as he listened to the drumming of the water. Then he caught sight of the small Band-Aid on her temple and felt a surge of anger. *If the bastard who did that tries again . . .*

Nina's fresh-scrubbed face, bare of makeup, was anything but deliberately seductive, and yet its effect on him was powerful. She looked touchingly pure. Innocent. *Hold on,* he cautioned himself. *Let's see how she explains this.*

"Come here." He motioned to her to sit next to him on the sofa, and she perched warily, as if ready for instant flight. He couldn't blame her, after the way he'd practically jumped her. Keeping his tone carefully neutral, he said, "I've found your passport."

"Oh. Have I been anywhere wonderful?"

"Take a look." Mike handed her the dark blue folder and watched her brow crease in bewilderment as she leafed through it.

"I don't remember any of these trips," she said.

"One to Switzerland," he remarked. "And five to Colombia. All in the past eighteen months. You must like it there."

Nina felt him watching her again, studying her as though she were under a microscope. *He's waiting for me to give myself away,* she realized. *Only I don't even know what it is I'm supposed to be hiding!* She looked doubtfully at the passport. "Maybe they were business trips."

"That's a possibility. A lot of business comes out of Colombia these days."

Then it hit her. Colombia—cocaine. "You think I'm mixed up with drugs!"

"Nina, I told you before, I don't think anything yet. I'm just trying to pick up enough pieces to form a picture. And you've got to admit, one thing does come to mind at the mention of Colombia. You thought of it yourself."

She looked into Mike's eyes. The warmth, the connection, between them was gone. Those blue eyes were not exactly hostile now, but they were guarded and cool, all business. Yet blue fire still glinted in their sapphire depths.

"Wait a minute!" she exclaimed. "I think I've got it. Didn't you say that this company I work for imports emeralds?" He nodded, and she continued, "Well, I'm a gemologist, right? So I probably went to Colombia on buying trips. Buying stones, not drugs."

It was amazing, Mike mused, the way her eyes picked up glints of golden light and her expression came alive when she was excited. He forced himself to focus on what she was saying; it made sense so far.

"Most of the top-quality emeralds mined today come from Colombia," Nina went on. "There are huge open-pit mines in the interior. People come from all over to work in them, desperate for the chance to make a fortune. The mines are pretty wild and lawless—anyone who finds a stone has to smuggle it out of the mine or else he'll be robbed or killed by someone with a bigger gun."

"You sound as though you've been there."

"Maybe I have been, or maybe I just read about it, or saw it on television. How many times do I have to tell you—*I don't remember!*"

"Relax, Nina, please. I wasn't accusing you," Mike said, and in fairness Nina had to admit that his tone had been conversational rather than confrontational. "I was just interested in what you were describing, and I wondered whether any of it felt familiar."

She sighed. "Not really. I mean, it felt like something you just know, not something you've actually experienced."

"From the sound of it," he said dryly, "I'd say it's just as well if you haven't experienced it firsthand. Sounds like the wild West, only with automatic weapons."

She shuddered. "Not necessarily something I'd want to remember, even if I'd been there."

"Your idea about business trips makes sense, though. We'll find out tomorrow."

She looked up, startled. Somehow in all the confusion she hadn't really thought about tomorrow.

"I'll pick you up at eight o'clock," Mike informed her. "We'll go to your office and talk to the people there, and then maybe we can interview some of the people in your address book. That ought to help you fill in some of the blanks."

So she was to spend another day with Mike Novalis. Nina didn't know whether to be relieved or apprehensive. She wouldn't be completely on her own in this strangely alien existence. But she would have to deal with Mike's suspicions of her—and with the fact every time he ran his hand through that messy black hair her fingers ached to do the same thing.

Nina looked around for a clock. "Hey, you reset my VCR clock," she said. "Thanks."

"All part of the service." He flashed her that devastating grin—and then tried, with no success, to hide a huge yawn. It was much later than Nina had expected, nearly nine o'clock. Mike's eyes looked raw and red, and he was pale under his beard shadow. He must be exhausted. Come to think of it, she was exhausted, and she'd had a few restful hours of unconsciousness at the hospital. It had been a long day for both of them.

Mike rose from the sofa and stretched. Nina watched fascinated, unable to drag her eyes away, as his T-shirt stretched tight over his broad chest and muscular shoulders. He lifted his arms higher, and his shirt came out of the waistband of his jeans, revealing a few inches of flat, hard stomach. An arrow of dark hair ran down the center of it, straight toward the zipper. Mike finished stretching and the shirt came down. Nina swallowed and looked away. She was sure that he'd noticed her ogling him. *So what?* she told herself defiantly. *I was just getting even for his peek inside my hospital gown.* Still, she wasn't quite ready to meet his gaze.

"Are you sure you want to be alone tonight?"

Nina gasped at the boldness of his question. Her surprise must have shown on her face, because Mike stepped back from her so sharply that it was almost a jump. He raised both hands, palms out, and said sheepishly, "I'm sorry, I didn't mean that the way it sounded. I just meant that if you *don't* want to be alone, I can get a policewoman or a nurse to stay with you."

Nina shook her head. His question had been innocent, after all. *But it's a darned good thing you don't know that the idea of spending the night with you was the first thing that came into my mind.* "No, thanks, I don't need anyone to stay with me. I'd really like to be alone for a while. I'll be ready when you come by in the morning."

He picked up his jacket and went to the door. "There's a couple of things I have to tell you," he said, looking her squarely in the eyes. "First of all, I put a tap on your phone line. And before you blow up at me about your rights, it's legal, and it's standard procedure in a case where your life may be in danger."

"It's also a nice way for you to check up on me," Nina said bitterly, torn between anger and fear. "It's because you think I'm a suspect, not because you think I'm a victim."

He turned away. "Have it your own way," he said tiredly. "But I'm going to protect you whether you want me to or not. The other thing you need to know is that there's going to be an officer watching the house all night. For your protection. Whether you want it or not. If you leave, he'll follow you." He paused, expecting an indignant outburst, but she was silent. "His name is Simms."

"Is he your partner?"

Mike whirled. "What did you say?" His gaze was piercing and glacier cold.

"You know—your partner. I thought police and detectives always worked in pairs."

"You watch too much TV," Mike said, and he opened the door. "I'll see you tomorrow." And then he was gone, leaving Nina to wonder what she had said to earn that icy glare.

Mike cursed his hair-trigger temper as he descended the stairs of Nina's building. He shouldn't have lashed out at Nina like that. It was natural for her to resent being spied on. And she had no way of knowing that *partner* was one word that nobody used in his presence.

The truth was, Mike admitted, that Nina Dennison unsettled him in every possible way, threw him off his stride. Half the time he suspected that she was making a fool of him, and the rest of the time he could barely keep his hands off her. He stepped outside and took a deep breath of the cool night air. All he needed was a good night's sleep, and then he'd do his best to help her—or to bring her in.

As ordered, there was Simms on sentry duty in a police car parked behind Mike's. Mike crossed the street, and the young cop rolled down his window.

"Got plenty of coffee, Simms?"

"I'm not a coffee drinker. Don't worry, I'll stay awake." Simms held up a six-pack of diet colas. Mike shuddered.

"Whatever turns you on. Get someone to relieve you if you have to—I'll be back at eight in the morning. She's in apartment 4, top left, and she knows you're out here."

Simms nodded. "Just one thing, Lieutenant. Am I doing surveillance on a suspect, or am I a bodyguard on protective duty?"

"Both, Simms. Both." Mike nodded good-night and made for his own car. He looked up at Nina's windows before driving off, but all the blinds were down.

As soon as Mike was gone, Nina took out the diary. At last, she thought, I'll get some insight into who I really am.

But as she paged through the diary, looking for clues to her past, she found only disappointment. Day after day, week after week, went by with nothing more than brief, businesslike notes in her tidy handwriting: "Meeting with Armand and Julien D.," "Called Mom," "Meet Danielle at gym." There were plenty of references to people she couldn't place, but none of them jogged a memory. "Movie Carl 7:00 p.m." Who was Carl? What movie had they seen on June 28? She riffled through the pages, but Carl's name didn't appear again.

Comparing the diary with her passport, Nina checked the dates of her trips to Colombia. The diary contained flight numbers and hotel reservations in Bogotá, along with notes of times and addresses that apparently referred to a series of appointments, but no hint of what Nina had been doing in South America. Nina pored over the pages leading up to yesterday's date—the date of her shooting—but found only more short entries about tasks she had performed or meetings she had scheduled. "Pick up dry cleaning." "Call Louis M. at ASPG."

As Nina closed the diary, something further ahead in the book caught her eye. On the page devoted to next Tuesday she had written "Talk to Julien D.?" The writing was larger than the rest of the entries and, uncharacteristically, she had drawn a big circle around the words. That was all. Nina flipped through the rest of the book, but the pages were blank.

''Not much of a diary,'' she said aloud. She'd been hoping for a journal that would reveal the inner life of Nina Dennison—*her* life, her passions and secrets and dreams. Instead she'd found a singularly uninformative appointment book. *Might as well have given this to Mike,* she thought with a wry smile. *No secrets here.*

She almost wished Mike were still there. At least he'd be someone to talk to. On impulse she picked up a pen and wrote ''Mike Novalis 8:00 a.m.'' under tomorrow's date. Then she turned back to today's page and scrawled, ''Not much of a diary!'' She looked at it for a moment, and then she started writing:

Today is the first day of the rest of your life. How often have I heard that silly phrase, I wonder? Well, today really *is* the first day. Today is the day I woke up in the hospital with amnesia. They say I'll get my memory back. *When?* And what do I do in the meantime?

Nina wrote for nearly an hour, filling up pages and pages without regard for the fact that the diary allotted her one page per day. She scribbled the things she wished she'd been able to say to her mother. She wrote about the fears that had lurked just beneath the surface of her thoughts all day—the fear that the shooting had been not random but a deliberate attempt on her life, and the fear that she was mixed up in something criminal. She wrote a prayer. And last of all she wrote, ''There's a cop outside right now, watching my house. I guess I'm glad he's there. But I wish it were Mike.''

Finally, stretching her cramped fingers, Nina set her pen down. *I can't show this diary to Mike now.* She took a last look at the book as she put it in the nightstand drawer. Up to the middle of September, the diary contained sparse, concise notes. But from there almost to mid-October was a single turbulent, passionate entry, full of underlinings and exclamation marks. It was hard to believe that both parts of the diary had been written by the same person. *Has the amnesia changed me?* Nina wondered. *Or was I this emotional all along, and just didn't show it?*

Late that night, as she tossed and turned restlessly in bed, Nina had another of those sharp, clear mental flashes. It was a lot like the vision she'd had of the two men in the tiny room, and the one of the blond woman wearing the mink coat. Except, she realized afterward, this one couldn't be a memory. For what she had seen in this brief moment of vision was Mike Novalis coming toward her, laughing and gloriously bare chested. She couldn't quite make out where he was; the background looked like trees. Too tired to figure out how she could possibly have a memory of someone she'd met for the first time that morning, Nina finally fell into a deep, dreamless sleep.

Chapter 4

When Mike picked Nina up in the morning, he was determined to remain cool, professional and detached. But his detachment almost deserted him when she answered the door in a cream-colored silk blouse and a navy blue skirt. The outfit was far from provocative; some would even have called it demure. The V neck of the blouse revealed only the faintest hint of cleavage, and the skirt came modestly to the middle of her knee. But somehow, on Nina, it all looked damned sexy. The dark circles had vanished from under her eyes, and her gaze was clear. *Looks like she slept a lot better than I did,* Mike thought sourly. His own slumbers had been disturbed by frequent thoughts of Nina, many of them blatantly carnal.

"Have you thought about how you want to handle this?" he asked her on the way to the Zakroff and Duchesne offices.

"I think I'm just going to tell them the truth—that I got wounded by a gunshot and lost my memory."

Mike nodded approvingly. "That's what I figured, too. After all, I'm going to be asking a lot of questions. They'll need to know why I'm there."

"Do the police go to all this trouble for every amnesia victim?"

"Nope. I'm not here because you have amnesia. I'm here because you're the victim of a violent crime. I'll try to find out whether anyone at your job had the motive or the opportunity to take a shot at you."

Mike didn't add that the chances were pretty good that he wouldn't even be doing that much if her job hadn't linked her to the hush-hush federal investigation of Zakroff and Duchesne. The feds would probably take over the case any minute. And maybe there *was* no link. The shooting could have been purely random, a drive-by. The break-in at Nina's apartment *could* have been coincidence, or maybe someone with access to information from the hospital had tossed the place, knowing that she wouldn't be home. Nina *could* be completely honest, and completely safe. Stranger things had happened. He'd been trying to convince himself of that all night.

The cardkey from Nina's coat pocket let them into a downtown office building. On the ninth floor they found a black door bearing a shiny gold Z and D logo; Nina's cardkey opened this door, too. It led to a suite of offices, but before Nina could take in her surroundings, a jovial voice bellowed her name.

"Nina! At last you appear!" A tall, heavyset man in his mid-sixties bustled up and took Nina's hands in his, kissing her cheek. Everything about him was flamboyant, from the theatrical waves of his silvery hair and his upturned mustache to the canary yellow silk of the vest that was stretched snugly across his ample paunch. He cocked a quizzical eye at Nina. "Where were you yesterday, *liebchen?*" His gaze rested speculatively on Mike. "And who is your handsome friend?"

"He's not my friend," Nina blurted out. "Not exactly—oh, never mind that now. Oh, hell, this is awkward!" She looked into the stranger's eyes and saw only friendly concern. "I'll just get it over with—I'm not sure who you are."

His eyebrows rose in surprise. "If this is a joke, Nina, I'm afraid I have missed the point."

"It's no joke. I was...injured the night before last, and I have amnesia. I woke up in the hospital. I don't remember anything. This is the police detective who's investigating the case."

The silver-haired man looked at her for a moment, as though to determine whether she were serious, and then said, "You'd both better come into my office."

He ushered them into a large, well-appointed office and closed the door. "Perhaps I'd better introduce myself," he began, but Nina interrupted him.

"Are you...Armand?"

"I am," he replied delightedly. "So you remember me, eh?"

"No," Nina confessed, and his face fell. "But you called my apartment and left a message on my machine, and just now I recognized your voice. The accent."

"Austrian," he informed them. "I am Armand Zakroff, one of the owners of this firm. And your employer, Nina."

Mike introduced himself, and Zakroff examined his police ID closely before handing it back.

"Now, *liebchen,* tell Armand everything," he said.

"There isn't much to tell." Nina gave him an quick summary of the events of the past twenty-four hours. "So now I'm just trying to pick up the pieces," she concluded.

"But...but this is terrible," said Zakroff. "Someone shoots you! That such a thing should happen, right on the street. And you," he said, turning to Mike, "you are here to find who did it, yes?"

"Maybe," Mike corrected. "It's more than likely that the attack on Miss Dennison was a random shooting, not aimed at her specifically. If that's the case—" he shrugged "—we'll probably never know who did it. But I've got to check out the people in her life, ask the questions that we always ask in cases like this. Just routine, you understand."

"Of course," Zakroff said expansively. "Anything I can do to help...."

"As a matter of fact," Mike said smoothly, "you could help by telling me where you were between 1:00 and 2:00 a.m. on Thursday morning."

Zakroff stared at him, frowning. "You think that I would hurt Nina? What nonsense! But if you must know, I was at home, with my wife and family."

"Is there someone who can confirm that?" Mike asked quietly.

"Any other night, no. I would be asleep, my wife would be asleep. But Wednesday night my daughter became engaged to marry her young man, and we all stayed up celebrating—my wife, her sister, the sister's husband, my two girls and Edward, who is to marry Katherine. The guests left our house around two-thirty in the morning. So you see—" he smiled, spreading his hands "—I have witnesses."

"So you have," said Mike. "Sorry I had to ask. And congratulations. One more thing. I think you said 'one of the owners of the firm'?"

"That's right. My partner is a young man named Julien Duchesne." Zakroff glanced at Nina. "Surely you remember Julien?"

"No, I'm afraid I don't." But Nina recalled the note she'd found in her diary: "Talk to Julien D.?"

"I'd like a few words with him," Mike was saying.

"He's in Switzerland right now. Julien is Swiss, by the way. He comes and goes quite a lot. I don't have a phone number for him, but perhaps he will call."

"When will he be back?"

"Let's see. Today is Friday...Julien will be back next Tuesday."

That fit, Nina thought. The note in the diary was on next Tuesday's page.

"I'll talk to him then," Mike said. But the voice inside his mind said, *You're just going through the motions. You'll be off the case by then. If there is a case.*

"Nina," Zakroff said, "you must have a thousand questions. I have some, too. What can we do to help you get your memories back?"

Where should she start? "First of all, what's my job here?"

Zakroff shook his head sadly. "Oh, Nina, how can you have forgotten so much?"

"Well, I know I'm a gemologist. I seem to know an awful lot about gems. But what do I *do?*"

Zakroff brightened. "Maybe all is not lost. Wait—I have an idea. Try a little experiment for me." He took a key from his vest pocket and opened a desk drawer. "What's this?" he demanded, handing Nina a small black box with the Z and D logo stamped on it in gold.

She opened the box and held out one hand absently; Zakroff placed a jeweler's loupe in her outstretched hand and winked at Mike, finger to his lips to ensure silence.

The box contained a diamond. Nina picked it up, examined it and declared, "Blue-white diamond, brilliant cut, good fire. Hard to be sure of the weight without scales, but I'd say it's about 80 points. It would be worth about two thousand dollars, except for the fact that there's a tiny chip on the girdle. The best thing would be to have the stone recut—a perfect new stone would be worth more than this miscut one, even if it's a bit smaller."

"Again," Zakroff urged, handing her another little box.

Nina was exhilarated. At last she'd found something that she knew, a foothold of certainty in the midst of doubt. Her confidence soared as she assessed the second gem. "Kunzite, emerald cut, about seven carats. Not very valuable, but what a beautiful stone." She held it up, admiring its pale rose color.

Zakroff chuckled. "One more, please."

"No problem. I could do this all day."

"You usually do, *liebchen.*" He handed her a third box.

Nina opened it and stared at the contents. Watching her from across the room, Mike saw her shoulders tense and wondered what was going through her mind. *Something* had happened when she opened that box, he was positive of it.

This time Nina hesitated for a few moments before picking up the stone. "Green beryl," she finally said, turning the gem to catch the light from the north window. Rays of green fire wavered around the room. "Better known as emerald. Not a perfect stone—lots of inclusions. The cut's very crude. But it could be cut down into three good baguettes, each a couple of carats." She paused, glanced at Mike. "It's just a guess, but I'd say this stone comes from Colombia."

"Of course it does," Zakroff assured her. "You brought it back yourself. Bravo, Nina! Your skill has not deserted you." He turned to Mike. "Nina is a brilliant gemologist, you know. One of the best I've worked with, and I've been in the jewelry business all my life. She has the instinct, something that cannot be taught—she can read the stones and tell the good ones from the bad, and the great ones from the good. That is why I send her on buying trips. Her eye never fails. Especially with rubies and emeralds, which are the hardest of all stones to assess properly."

Mike saw that Nina was beaming as she drank in Zakroff's words of praise, and in that instant he understood what she had been going through. It wasn't her vanity that was being fed—it was her need to have an identity. Zakroff had given her back part of herself. Then Mike realized something else: Without quite realizing it, he had begun to assume that Nina was telling the truth about her amnesia. *Stay sharp,* he cautioned himself. *This could still go either way. And you've been wrong before.*

"Nina's a funny one, though," Zakroff continued, looking fondly at her. "She never wears fine stones—she loves little gimcrack bits of turquoise and coral and amethyst. I think she'd rather look at spodumene than at a perfect blue diamond."

"Spodumene?" Mike said. "I never heard of it. Sounds like some kind of Eastern European vegetable."

Nina laughed, a burst of full-throated merriment. Mike realized that it was the first time she'd laughed like that in all the hours they'd spent together. "Or a pasta dish," she said.

"Or a tropical disease."

"Or a toilet bowl cleanser—New Spodumene, now with superactivating bubbles." Nina paused. Armand Zakroff was turning from one to the other of them like a spectator at a tennis tournament. "Actually," she continued more soberly, "it's a very pretty pink semiprecious gem. That piece of kunzite, the second stone I looked at, was a form of spodumene."

"Nina, Nina, you may have amnesia, but you haven't really changed," said Zakroff. "You're always talking about the semiprecious stones, how we don't do enough with them, how dollar value isn't everything. Your fights with Julien—" He broke off in midsentence and fiddled with his necktie.

Mike couldn't let this pass. "You say there were fights between Miss Dennison and your partner?"

Zakroff looked rueful. "I shouldn't have spoken."

"But you did," Mike said in a level voice. "Now I think you'd better explain what you meant."

"Please, Armand. I need to know everything you can tell me," Nina added.

"They weren't really fights. Just disagreements. You see, Nina, you've been wanting us to branch out into other areas of the business, working more with semiprecious stones and new designers, even teaching jewelry making. You had a vision of Z and D becoming a real design studio. But Julien feels very strongly that the firm should continue to do what we've always done—import high-value gemstones. Period. That's where the maximum profit lies. So the two of you have had . . . disagreements, if you will. But such things happen in every business."

"What about you?" Nina asked. "Whose side were you on?"

He met her gaze directly. "I haven't taken a side yet. Julien is my partner, his father helped me start the business. You are my most valued employee. I have been thinking about what both of you have said—but I have made no decisions about the future of the firm."

"I see. And what about me? Are you willing to let me go on working here, now that you know I can't even remember when you hired me."

Zakroff got up from behind his desk and crossed to Nina's side, placing a hand on her shoulder. "January, six years ago," he said softly. "*I* remember. God gave me two daughters, Nina, but you are like a third daughter to Therese and me. Let you stay? I would not permit you to leave."

"Thank you." Nina felt dizzy with relief, as though a great weight had been lifted from her shoulders. Some part of her life, at least, was salvageable. Her professional knowledge was intact. She still had her job. And if Armand Zakroff was what he seemed to be, she also had a friend.

"We'll get through this, *liebchen*, with the help of the good detective here."

Mike stood. "I think Miss Dennison and I should look over her office now. After that I'll want to talk with your other employees."

"Of course, anything." Zakroff opened the door and pointed out Nina's office, on the far side of the reception area.

"Armand—" Nina said excitedly. "Is this Julien Duchesne?"

She was looking at one of the many photographs on Zakroff's office wall. This one showed Armand and a tall, slender, fair-haired man with their arms around each other's shoulders. As soon as Nina had seen the picture, she had recognized the blond man from the vision she'd had yesterday in the restaurant.

"Yes, it is indeed Julien. Why? Do you recognize him?"

"Not exactly. I had a sort of memory, yesterday, just a quick image of him and another man. I thought at the time that the two men might be Zakroff and Duchesne. But the other man I saw wasn't you. Oh, one more question. Do you—do we keep the gems, the emeralds in particular, in a metal box?"

Zakroff's eyebrows rose. "Well, we keep everything in the safe, of course. Is that what you mean?"

She shook her head. "Never mind. I want to look at my office now. I'll be back to talk with you soon." Impulsively she leaned forward and kissed Armand on the cheek. "Thanks."

"Do you want to tell me what that was all about? The business about the metal box, I mean?" Mike asked when they were alone in Nina's office. He sat casually on the edge of her desk, and in spite of her interest in exploring her workplace Nina could not help but notice how the material of his slacks tightened across one muscular thigh.

Mike was dressed much more formally than yesterday, but he looked just as masculine in khakis and a sport jacket as he had in leather and denim. In fact, Nina couldn't imagine any outfit in which Mike wouldn't look all male—and just a little rough around the edges. *This guy would look sexy in a clown's suit.* But she had to admit that the orange wig probably wouldn't do as much for the sapphire brilliance of his eyes as the light blue shirt and deeper blue tie he was wearing today. He was clean shaven, too, and for the first time she noticed a slight cleft in his chin. His face looked a little gentler without the beard stubble, she decided, but no less attractive.

"The metal box?" he reminded her.

"Oh, right. Well, when I opened the third box Armand gave me, the one with the emerald, I had another of those flashes—like the two men I saw when we were in the restaurant, and the woman wearing the mink coat." She didn't mention the third vision she'd had: the image of Mike himself, wearing a smile and no shirt. She still hadn't figured out how he had managed to work his way into what had to be her memory. Maybe she was simply getting a bit too obsessed with him.

"So what did you see?" Mike asked.

"This time it was a bunch of emeralds, dozens of them, some of them just raw stones, not even cut. They were in a box about the size and shape of a cigar box, but it looked as if it was made of steel."

"Anything else? Anyone holding the box?"

"Nothing."

"Well, it's probably something that you saw on one of those buying trips." Mike was relieved; the memory flash was what had spooked Nina when she had looked into the third box. *No big secret, after all.*

Nina paced restlessly to the window. Like Armand's, it faced north. *Sure, north light is the best for looking at gems.* But it didn't offer much of a view: just another office building across the street. "What now?" she asked Mike.

"I'd like to talk to the other people here, see if anybody knows anything about your movements Wednesday night or Thursday morning, possible enemies, that kind of thing. And if it's okay with you, maybe I'll talk to a few people from your address book, too."

Nina hesitated. On one hand, she still hoped that somehow she could recover her memory without letting everyone in on the fact that she'd lost it. On the other, it had been a relief to tell Armand the whole story, and she had no doubt that everybody in the office would soon know the details. Why try to keep the shooting a secret? Or the amnesia?

"Sure, go ahead," she said resignedly. "I'm going to go through the book and talk to people, too. We have to ask questions if we're going to find any answers."

"That's the attitude," Mike said. "I'll meet you here this afternoon and take you home."

Nina was still looking out the window, and in its surface she saw Mike's reflection behind her. It came closer.

"I know this isn't easy," he said in a low voice. "You've got a lot of courage, Nina." She turned to thank him, but he was already on his way out the door.

That afternoon Mike and Nina compared notes. No one at Z and D had offered any information about what Nina was doing in northeast Philly in the small hours of Thursday morning. No one admitted to possessing a key to Nina's apartment. No one had any ideas about who might have wanted to harm Nina. Nina's secretary had told Mike that Nina seemed to have something on her mind for a few days before the shooting—"kind of quiet, like she was worried about something," was how she put it. But, Mike cautioned himself, that might mean nothing at all.

The pattern of Nina's life had begun to emerge: work-outs at the neighborhood gym with her friend Danielle, vacations to California once a year to see a college room-mate who lived in San Francisco, visits to her mother's home in Florida two or three times a year. In the past year Nina had dated three men, but none of the relationships had amounted to anything serious. Nina's secretary de-scribed all three of them as "nice guys—but the kind who turn out to be friends, not boyfriends, if you know what I mean." Mike was having their backgrounds checked out, but on the surface none of them looked like a likely can-didate for a would-be murderer. As far as Mike could tell, Nina hadn't seen any of them for several months.

Nina had learned more about her work at Zakroff and Duchesne. Her job consisted of appraising stones offered for sale and bidding for them on the firm's behalf. Since Z and D had been specializing in emeralds, she had been traveling to Colombia for the quarterly gem auctions, which were attended by buyers from all over the world. Although she was much younger than many professionals in her field, she was regarded as one of the top gemolo-gists on the East Coast; once a year she taught a course on gems for the mineralogy department at Princeton Univer-sity.

Nina also discovered that she earned a very good sal-ary—"and worth every penny," Armand had assured her. All her bills were paid up and she had some savings. The luxury sports car, bought earlier this year, appeared to be her only extravagance; before buying it, she had driven a no-frills compact that she'd had since college.

Mike had examined Nina's finances, too, and had failed to come up with anything suspicious. No big sums of cash from unexplained sources, no expenditures that didn't match her income, no known debts. If she did have a se-cret, something connected with drugs or gambling or smuggling, she'd managed to keep every last trace of it out of her everyday life—and that, Mike knew, was no easy trick.

"In short, no leads on the shooting," Mike summed up for Nina as they compared notes.

"Same here. I haven't found out anything about what happened Wednesday night or Thursday morning. But I've learned a lot about my life."

"Feel better?"

"Yes," she said, a bit surprised. "I do. At least I feel like I belong somewhere now, and I have something I can do. I'll just have to wait for the rest of it to come back."

Mike drove Nina home and dropped her off. He checked the street—yeah, there was Simms, on the job just like he was supposed to be. Mike gave him the high sign as they drove past his car, and then, to his surprise, Nina leaned over and waved. Bemused, Simms waved back. Mike grinned at Simms's startled expression. This was no ordinary surveillance job.

"So what's the plan for tomorrow?" Nina asked as she prepared to get out of the car.

Mike didn't want to tell her that he didn't really have a plan. There weren't any solid leads to follow; he just didn't want to let this case go. To let Nina go. And it wasn't just that he liked being around her—although that was beginning to be a big problem in itself. But how could he tell her that he had a feeling in his gut that kept warning him that things weren't what they seemed? How could he tell her that he was afraid her life might still be in danger? So he told her the simple truth.

"There's no plan, but I'll be in touch. This evening and tomorrow morning I'll be at headquarters—you call me if you need anything, all right? I've got to put in some paperwork. You're not my only case, you know." This last was said jokingly; Mike didn't want to leave her, but he didn't want it to show. *Keep it light.*

"Yeah, I know," Nina replied as she got out of the car, legs flashing. Before closing the door she leaned in and said, "But I'll bet I'm the only amnesiac gemologist shooting victim you're working on right now."

"What d'you know?" he exclaimed in mock surprise. "You are." *And the only long-legged, green-eyed redhead.* "See you."

Mike watched Nina's slim form slip inside her front door and waited for the lights to come on in her apartment before he drove away. He wished he'd met her in some ordinary way, some way that had nothing to do with his job, so that he could have gone upstairs to that lighted room with her. He wished it even more half an hour later, when he found a note from Hecht on his desk: "1:30 p.m. tomorrow, my office, re Dennison." Reading the note, Mike had a sinking feeling that he was about to be pulled off Nina's case.

That night Nina called her brother Charley in Chicago. He sounded glad to hear from her, but it was clear from the first minute of the call that he was distracted, all wrapped up in his wife and kids. Nina chatted brightly for a few moments and ended the call without telling him about her amnesia. His voice had triggered no recollections, and after the call she felt more alone than she had before.

Her hand hovered over the dial. Mike had said to call him if she needed anything. She couldn't tell him what she needed; she wasn't even sure herself. All she knew was that she craved the sound of his voice. And if she called him, his voice wouldn't be enough. She'd want to see him, and if she saw him, she'd want to touch him....

"Get over this," she said aloud. "You're drawn to him because he's the only guy you know. It isn't real. Pretty soon you'll get your life back on track and forget all about him." But the words had a doubtful, unconvincing sound.

Got to get to work. Nina sat at the desk and began scanning the papers that Mike had read yesterday. Armand had urged her to spend the weekend with his family, but she had turned him down, telling him that she needed to continue with the task of sifting through her things, hoping to awaken memories. Now she was doing just that, examining the bits and pieces of her life, and she was finding them depressing.

There was no evidence of any wrongdoing in her past. That was a relief. But she didn't find much evidence of fun, either, or of passion. She read dozens of letters and cards from friends, both men and women, dating back to her college years. None of them were truly intimate. None hinted at love—or hate. All of her relationships seemed to have been careful, sensible and controlled.

Like her apartment, with its tasteful, understated furnishings in neutral colors. Like her diary, with those terse, businesslike entries. Like her clothes, so professional and so...so *beige.* The only excitement in her wardrobe was her underclothing, which was surprisingly lacy and colorful. *But it doesn't look as though anyone else ever sees it.*

Nina hated to admit it, but her existence looked a little cold and empty. She was getting the impression that hers had been a life lived from the sidelines. It was the life of a cautious spectator, not that of a player. *Well, I'm having an adventure now. It doesn't get much more adventurous than being shot at and losing your memory.*

After an hour or so, Nina made some chamomile tea and propped herself up in bed with the diary to record her impressions of the day. This time she only used up a week's worth of pages, although her words ran out beyond the neat lines into the margins. She ended with, "What next?"

Only after Nina closed the diary and turned off the light did she admit to herself that when she wrote those final words she hadn't been thinking about her amnesia. She'd been thinking about Mike Novalis and wondering what "I'll be in touch" had meant.

Chapter 5

When Mike walked into his chief's office the next day he found Hecht with a short, saturnine man who looked about fifty. Mike pegged the stranger right away: only a fed would wear a gray flannel suit on a Saturday. Sure enough, Hecht introduced him as David Irons, the senior FBI supervisor in charge of the Zakroff and Duchesne investigation.

Irons was holding a copy of the report Mike had put on Hecht's desk last night, summarizing the status of Nina's case. "It's come to my attention," he said, with a hard look at Mike, "that you've been investigating a shooting that took place at about 1:30 a.m. Thursday morning."

Mike leaned back in his chair, folded his arms across his chest and nodded.

"The victim was one Nina Dennison, an employee of the firm Zakroff and Duchesne."

Another nod. Mike didn't mean to be a hard-ass, but guys like Irons rubbed him the wrong way. Sometimes they

seemed more concerned with their turf, with who out-
ranked whom, than with getting a job done.

"And have you found out who shot Dennison, Detective Novalis?" Irons asked.

"No."

Hecht glared at Mike, so he elaborated. "I didn't turn
up any leads among her co-workers or in her personal life.
Her story of amnesia seems to check out."

"Well, then, Detective Novalis, you'll be glad to know
that you don't have to pursue this unrewarding case any
further." Irons made a note on the report and slipped it
into a thick file, which he snapped shut. "As you know,
my task force has been working on Miss Dennison's firm
from another angle for some time. We've determined that
her shooting was a simple drive-by. Case closed."

"How do you know it was a drive-by?" Mike said chal-
lengingly.

Irons smoothed his short, thinning dark hair with the
palms of both hands and said, "I'm not at liberty to discuss the federal investigation at this time. Trust me, we
have good reason."

"Damn it, we're all on the same side here, aren't we?"
Mike burst out, exasperated. "Why can't you federal guys
ever throw us cops a bone?"

Irons smiled briefly. "As I said, I'm not at liberty—"

"Yeah, yeah," Mike interrupted. "What about the
search of Dennison's apartment?"

Irons shrugged. "A break-in. It happens. Probably a
junkie who trashed the place when he didn't find any drugs
or cash."

"The gun in her drawer?"

"Ballistics traced the registration. It was one of a batch
stolen from a gun shop in Jersey a couple years back. It's
probably been on the street ever since."

"But how'd it get in Dennison's apartment?"

Irons sighed. "People own guns, Novalis. You know how easy it is for even a law-abiding citizen to get hold of an unregistered firearm. She probably bought it herself."

Mike shook his head. "She's not the type."

Irons shot him a sharp look.

"Anyway," Mike continued, "we found it sitting right out in the open. A thief would've seen it and taken it. The way it looks to me, that gun was put there to set Dennison up, make it look like she's implicated in something, and that doesn't look good for her." Mike rose to his feet and looked down at Irons, whose smooth face and sharp eyes gave nothing away. "I think Dennison's life may still be in danger," Mike said. "I want round-the-clock protective surveillance on her."

"Your own report contains no evidence of a continued threat. And your theory about the gun is just moonshine, Novalis. Chances are she bought the gun, and the guy who broke into her place was so high he didn't know what he was doing. I can't assign protection just because you don't think she's 'the type' to own a gun." Irons's tone was tinged with sarcasm. "Give me some real proof."

Mike's jaw tightened. "I've got no proof, nothing concrete."

"Well, my task force *does* have good evidence," Irons responded. "I'm sorry I can't discuss it with you, but you'll just have to leave this matter in our hands."

"The department could keep a watch on her," Mike suggested. "At least when she's at home."

Irons glanced at Hecht, who scowled but said, "Novalis, you're off the case. Period."

"I want to know what we're gonna do in case the shooter has another chance at her," Mike insisted stubbornly.

"We're not doing anything," Hecht said with exaggerated patience. "I pulled Simms off surveillance. Like the man said, it was a drive-by. The shooter won't be back."

Every instinct Mike possessed after years on the force was screaming that this was wrong. "I still think—"

"Look, Novalis," Irons interrupted brusquely, "I've read your file. I know you used to be an outstanding undercover vice cop. I know you had a reputation for blowing off the rules from time to time, doing things your own way. Nothing wrong with being an unorthodox cop—until something explodes in your face. And you have, shall we say, a history of going off the rails when there's a good-looking woman involved in a case."

Rage surged through Mike's veins, but he didn't speak. He forced himself to remain expressionless as he stared back at Irons.

"I don't want you screwing up my task force, Novalis," Irons said. He smiled thinly, but there was steel in his voice. "Nina Dennison has nothing to do with my case, but I need a clear field. Stay away from her, stay away from Zakroff and Duchesne." Without waiting for an answer he nodded to Hecht and strode out the door.

Hecht reached into his desk drawer for a cigar. "Smooth-talking bureaucrat," he muttered. "Might as well be a politician."

Mike was still standing, staring at the spot where Irons had been; his fists were slowly unclenching.

"That was a little rough," Hecht said, and cleared his throat. "The guy's an uptight jerk. But he's right—he calls the shots on this one. So do yourself a favor and forget this shooting. Get back to work on your other files."

Mike turned and stared cold eyed at his boss for a moment. But all he said as he left the office was, "You got it. I'm off the case."

Mike spent a couple of hours trying to work off his anger. A session on the pistol range and another in the weight room of the police gym didn't do much to help. But his innate honesty forced him to admit that he didn't know whether his anger stemmed from Irons's air of superiority and his refusal to discuss the case, or from the thinly veiled contempt in his voice when he'd referred to Mike's past. *Don't be too hard on Irons,* he told himself. *You've said worse than that to yourself. A million times.*

One thing was clear to Mike: He had to tell Nina that his case was closed. He owed her that much. An odd sort of bond had formed between them over the past few days, a partnership, and there was more to it than the undeniable sexual attraction that crackled in the air between them. Although he'd never been able to banish all traces of his initial suspicion and skepticism, Mike had come to admire Nina's spirit. Without memory, she was as alone as anyone could be, yet she hadn't let fear or pain crush her.

All right, he decided, I'll call her now. Maybe it'll make her day to hear that she's no longer under police investigation.

But when he left the gym, Mike didn't go to a phone. He headed for his car.

Nina didn't realize that things had changed until the early afternoon, when she went to the grocery store. Last night she'd peeked out of her bedroom window just before going to bed. The blue-and-white police car had been parked in its usual spot, across the street from her building. Now it was gone. On the way to the store she kept checking her rearview mirror. Nothing.

Her first reaction was a heady feeling of relief: She was no longer under police investigation. Then she felt a pang of disappointment. Why hadn't Mike Novalis called to tell her what was going on? Surely he wouldn't just walk out of her life without a farewell? She tried to convince herself that she had no reason to be surprised or hurt. *So the two of you shared a few sparks—big deal! To him you're nothing but routine police business. Get over it.* But the words didn't ring true, and Nina simply couldn't bring herself to believe them. There had been some connection between Mike and herself, of that she was certain. But what it meant, or whether it was a good thing, she could not say.

It was only later, after she had put away her groceries, that another thought, a slightly ominous one, occurred to Nina: *If I'm no longer under police investigation, does that mean I'm no longer under police protection? Should I be scared?*

She dismissed the thought at once. Mike would never have let them drop the surveillance if there were the slightest danger to her. On no evidence at all other than the two days they had spent together, Nina knew he would never let her get hurt. He was too good a cop for that. But she wished she had heard from him one last time. And still she couldn't quite believe that he wouldn't at least call to say goodbye.

So she was not altogether surprised when Mike turned up on her doorstep later that afternoon. When he asked her if everything was okay, she replied with a question of her own, lightly phrased but serious in intent: "Is that an official inquiry?"

And when he looked down at her with an oddly helpless, searching expression and said, "No," Nina knew that something important had shifted in their relationship. Mike hadn't come to her because of his job. He was there because he wanted to be. The knowledge both exhilarated and frightened her. *Now what do I do? What do I want?*

Mike had wrestled with the question of what to tell Nina, and he had finally decided that his only option was to give her the official line as laid down by Irons and Hecht. Without alluding to the FBI's interest in Zakroff and Duchesne, he explained to her that the investigation into her shooting was over. This didn't mean that the police had found the shooter, he told her—only that they had found nothing to suggest that the incident was anything but a random drive-by shooting, one of the street crimes that had become all too frequent in the city. The fact that the shooting had resulted in amnesia only complicated the case, but ultimately the amnesia was not a police matter.

"What about the gun you found here?" she asked.

"Well, it's not registered to you, so I can't give it back to you."

She shuddered. "I don't want it. That's not what I meant."

"I know. It's a street gun, stolen from a gun shop in Jersey a few years ago."

"But how did it get here?"

Mike sighed. "I don't know. But I've got no leads to follow on the gun or anything else. I'm closing the file."

"Does this mean that you finally believe I really do have amnesia?"

"I've got no reason not to," he replied, and then he reached out and brushed her long bangs back from one temple. "Hey, you've taken off your Band-Aid," he said. "I can hardly see the mark. You won't have much of a scar." He let his fingertips linger for a moment on her smooth skin; he'd been wanting to touch her for so long that he could not deny himself the feel of her.

Nina's pulse began to race when he touched her hair. So she hadn't simply imagined the attraction—on his side or on hers. It was there, and stronger than ever. She was so absorbed by the sensation of his fingers grazing her skin that she didn't realize until much later that he had failed to answer her question.

Mike hadn't decided what he was going to do after he told Nina that her case was closed. But when she had opened her door and smiled at him, so shyly and yet so happily, he'd made up his mind without realizing it. And now, after seeing the way her eyes turned smoky and a flush rose in her cheeks when he touched her, he didn't hesitate. The police department and the FBI would have

his head on a platter if he had anything more to do with
Nina Dennison. But he was no longer even thinking about
walking away.

"Come on," he said abruptly. "I want you to meet
someone."

At first Nina thought that Mike was taking her back to
the street where she'd been shot. He hadn't said a word
since bundling her into his car, leaving her to watch the
chic streets of her Society Hill neighborhood give way to
the dismal warehouse district north of the Old City. She
was almost positive that the intersection they had just
passed was the street he'd pointed out to her as the shooting site. In the next block Mike pulled up in front of an
old, seemingly empty factory building. Its windows had
been filled in with cement blocks, and graffiti adorned the
rusted metal door to which Mike escorted her.

"Watch your step," he said, and took her elbow to
steady her as she circled some broken glass. He produced
a heavy key ring and went to work on the door; Nina noticed that despite its apparent decrepitude the door boasted
several shiny new locks.

"This is a lovely spot to visit, and don't think I'm not
grateful," she said, "but what the heck are we doing
here?"

He flashed her a mischievous grin over his shoulder.
"You'll see."

The interior was a dusty, empty, echoing cavern of a
place, as rundown as the building's exterior—with one
exception. The freight elevator was clean. It carried them
smoothly to the factory's top floor. When the elevator
stopped, Nina became aware of a scrabbling, thumping
sound, as though something large were running across a
wooden floor and throwing itself against the other side of
the elevator door.

"It sounds like a giant rat," she said dubiously. "You're not going to open this door, are you?"

Mike opened the door and stepped out of the elevator, greeted by joyous barking. When Nina followed, somewhat tentatively, she found him having his face thoroughly licked by a very large, sleek black dog whose front paws reached all the way to Mike's shoulders. Sighting a new face, the dog abandoned Mike and lunged toward Nina, tail wagging and pink tongue lolling. Instinctively she knelt down to hug it. "Good dog," she crooned, rubbing its floppy ears. "What a beautiful doggy you are."

"Well," said Mike, "looks like you like animals."

"You know, I think you're right." She knuckled the dog's head and he grinned at her foolishly. "What's his name?"

"Sig."

"Oh. Named after Freud, I suppose."

"Not exactly. He's named after the first gun I had when I joined the force. A Sig Sauer pistol."

Nina nodded, not looking up. *This is his world,* she told herself. *He's a good man, but he still lives in a world of sudden violence and guns. Like the gun that shot me.* She stroked Sig's smooth coat, admiring the sheen of the slick black fur that shaded to seal brown on his muzzle and paws. "What kind of dog is he?" she asked.

"Doberman."

Of course a cop would have a Doberman. That or a German shepherd. Then she took a more critical look at Sig, who, sensing an easy mark, had flopped over onto his back so that she could rub his belly. Sig didn't have the intent, almost ruthless look that she associated with the typical Doberman pinscher; instead, he looked sweet and floppy, like a cartoon dog. "Hey, wait a minute. Aren't Dobermans supposed to have no tails and those little pointy stand-up ears?"

"Yeah. They're born this way—" Mike waved at Sig "—and later their tails are docked and their ears cropped at the vet's. But when the time came to do it, I just didn't have the heart."

"I'm glad," Nina said softly. "I like his silly ears." She tugged them gently, winning a look of adoration from Sig.

"I think you've got a fan there," Mike observed. "If you don't mind, he can keep you company while I take a quick shower."

Nina had been so preoccupied with the dog that she had paid no attention to her surroundings. She took a quick look around, and for a moment she had the illusion that she was out-of-doors. The top floor of the building was a huge room bathed in light from the high, slanted ceiling, which was all glass. The place was a wilderness of greenery: trees and shrubs grew out of big tubs, and vines hung from the pipes and ducts that crisscrossed the space overhead and snaked down the walls.

"What is this place?" she called out to Mike.

"My apartment." He vanished through a doorway in the far wall.

The dog nuzzled Nina's hand, and when she looked down he picked up a rubber ball and gazed up at her hopefully, tail wagging.

"You want to play, big guy? Well, why not?" Nina winged the ball into the wide-open spaces of Mike's living room, and Sig bounded after it. She soon realized that she had made a mistake, for Sig was so overjoyed to have found a playmate that he kept bringing the ball back for her to throw again. And again. And again. But each time he galumphed off in pursuit, Nina had a chance to look around at the place where Mike Novalis lived.

The floor was of wood, worn and faded with long use. Nina saw that a kitchen had been built against one wall. Nearby stood a table and chairs, and a battered blue sofa and easy chair on a big red rug. Opposite the kitchen was a low wooden platform that held a bed and a shelf for a TV and a stereo. Except for this corner, the rest of the loft was empty, a big, slightly dusty playground for Sig. It was an unconventional, rough-and-ready place. Not the easiest place to live in, Nina mused, but maybe it was worth the effort. Mike's furnishings seemed humble, almost Spartan, but the light filtering through the vast vaulted room gave the place the feel of a cathedral, and the plants gave it life.

Paws scrabbled across the floor and slithered to a stop at her feet. Sig carefully placed the ball in her hand and waited.

"All right," Nina told him. "One more time."

"Fat chance," she heard Mike say. She turned. He was emerging from the bathroom, wreathed in whirls of steam. Nina knew that she was staring, but she couldn't take her eyes away. It wasn't just the fact that Mike was wearing only a pair of tight jeans, or that his broad shoulders, his tautly muscled arms and his flat, hard belly were bare and still damp, or that droplets of water were falling from his wet black hair, running down the sculpted curves of his chest and glistening in the dark swirls of hair that dusted his pectorals. Raw masculinity, unselfconsciously rubbing at his hair with a towel. All of that would have been hard enough to handle, but what rooted Nina to the spot was a powerful feeling of déjà vu. The picture that Mike made at that very instant—laughing, half-naked, framed by potted fig and palm trees—was exactly like the image of him that had flashed into her mind on Thursday night. Down to the last detail.

The moment was broken: Mike came farther into the room to take the ball from Sig, and Nina tried to gather her scattered wits. She had known that the flash of vision in which she'd seen Mike was not a memory, of course; she couldn't be remembering someone she'd just met. She'd assumed that the "memory" was something her mind had made up on the spot. After the shock and exhaustion of that first long day, starting with the hospital and ending with the diary, she had been tired and overly imaginative. Mike had appeared in the "memory" because she had spent the whole day with him and had gotten used to seeing him. The reason he had appeared bare chested and smiling had been pretty easy to figure out, too—she'd been all too aware of his physical attractions. But it was strange that her subconscious mind had cooked up a scene that was so much like reality, right down to the plants that she'd seen as a forest.

Nina shook her head. *I guess it's just a coincidence. Weird.* She felt a tiny, niggling doubt, as though something were not quite right with that explanation. Yet she could not come up with a better one. She put the matter out of her mind.

Mike had crossed to his sleeping area and, arms over his head, was putting on a T-shirt. There was something touchingly intimate in the sight of him putting his clothes on. *This is what he would be doing if we had made love,* Nina realized with a jolt. She watched in silence as he finished dressing, half wanting to cross the room and stop him.

"Why did you bring me here?" she asked when he joined her.

"I wanted you to meet Sig. I thought you might like to take him home with you for a couple of days. He likes you, obviously, and he's a good protector." Seeing her eyes darken with apprehension, Mike berated himself for his lousy choice of words.

"You think I need protection?" The question was almost a whisper.

"No, of course not," he lied. "I only meant that you might feel better if you had some company at home. Something to keep you from being alone."

She gazed at him for a long minute, and he wondered whether she had bought it. He didn't want to frighten her needlessly, but he couldn't shake the hunch that there was more to the case of Nina Dennison than he had been told. He'd been flamed in the past for following his hunches, but he wasn't going to let that stop him from doing whatever he could to protect this woman. Even if she was still lying to him about the amnesia, he didn't want to see her hurt. Or worse.

"Okay," Nina decided. "I'll take him home with me." Maybe it would be nice to have some company in that empty apartment. And maybe, just maybe, it would come in handy to have Sig looking out for her. She chuckled. She'd be willing to bet that the next person who tried to break into her apartment would get a hell of a surprise. But she didn't quite acknowledge that there was another reason for accepting Mike's offer. As long as she had the dog, she could be sure that she would see the master again.

They took Sig back to Nina's apartment. The big dog looked a little out of place at first; he roamed anxiously from room to room, as though he missed his cavernous loft, but then he settled down comfortably on the floor, chewing at one of Nina's sofa pillows. "Oh, let him," she said when Mike started to take the pillow away. "It was already ruined, anyway." Whoever had searched Nina's apartment had slashed the pillow open, and the stuffing had begun to spill out. Sig was only speeding up the process of disintegration.

Nina felt a new tension. She was no longer Mike's case; he was no longer her cop. They were a woman and a man, and she wasn't sure how to act toward him now. Or what to expect from him.

Both of them were silent for a moment. Nina didn't want Mike to leave. She was about to offer him some coffee when he asked, "How would you like to have dinner?"

She looked at him and nodded, suddenly shy. "I'd like that," she forced herself to say, knowing that she was blushing. When he helped her on with her jacket, she tingled with excitement. *Like a teenager on her first date,* she chided herself. Then she laughed. It *was* a first date—sort of. After all, she couldn't remember any others.

"What's so funny?" he inquired, looking down at her. The coldness was gone from his eyes; their blue was warm and inviting.

"I'll tell you sometime," she responded lightly.

He ushered her into his car, and she noticed that the burger wrappers and coffee cups had vanished from the floor.

"How about South Philly?" he asked. "Does Italian sound good?"

"Pasta sounds fabulous."

"Who knows? Maybe we can find a place that serves spaghetti alla spodumene."

Ever since he'd first seen Nina, Mike had wondered what might have happened if he had met her somewhere ordinary—maybe over broccoli at the grocery store. Now he was no longer assigned to investigate her, and here they were. Unfortunately, even the most casual contact with Nina Dennison was off-limits. Hecht and Irons had made that crystal clear.

He shouldn't have walked into DeFazio's feeling proud to have someone as radiant as Nina on his arm. He shouldn't be sitting across from her at a cozy, candlelit corner table, drinking in the sight of her, making her laugh with anecdotes about police academy and stories of Sig's exploits. He shouldn't be with her at all. But she was like a fire, and he was a man who'd been cold for longer than he had realized. He needed to warm himself in the glow of her company for just a little longer.

She was so easy to be with. Mike found himself loosening up, relaxing in a way that he hadn't for a long time. They talked all through dinner and all the way back to her apartment. Unwilling to let the evening end, pulled by his feeling for Nina yet uncertain where that feeling was leading him, Mike walked up to Nina's apartment with her "to check on Sig."

Nina made coffee, and as they sat at the kitchen table, cradling the warm mugs, she said, "You know, you have an unfair advantage. You know a lot about me, but I don't know very much about you."

"What do you want to know?" He stirred milk into his coffee and gave her a lazy smile.

Everything. What you taste like, what you feel like, how you think. "Well . . . have you ever been married?"

His eyes changed then. Nina felt that suddenly he was looking at something a million miles away from her, something not very pretty.

"No. I came close once, a couple of years ago, but it didn't work out."

There was a long, strained silence. The comfortable companionship was gone. To restore it, Mike knew, he had to offer Nina a part of himself. And to his amazement, he was ready to do so. He didn't know why he felt like baring his soul to a woman he'd known for only two days, but suddenly he knew that he wanted to tell her something about himself. *But not everything,* he warned himself.

"I owe you an apology," he began abruptly. "The other night, when I was leaving, you asked about my partner. I snapped out at you. You deserve to know why."

He put his hands on the table, facedown, and took a deep breath. "I used to work undercover, on the vice squad. I had a partner, a guy named Jack Renzo. We worked together for four years. He was the best friend I ever had.''

The memories Mike had tried so hard to repress were surging back, and for a moment he was afraid he would cry. Then he went on. He tried to make his voice flat and impersonal, as if he were reading a report about someone else, but he knew he was failing; he sounded ragged. ''Three years ago Jack and I spent months setting up a big drug bust, working with the DEA. We infiltrated the local end of a drug ring that was bringing coke and heroin up from Texas. It was gonna be the biggest bust in department history, it was gonna make us all heroes.'' He tasted bitterness. ''When it came down, everything went wrong. The stuff had been moved, and they were waiting for us.''

He closed his eyes. Darkness brought him no relief—he saw another darkness, the inside of a deserted warehouse in the middle of the night. Suddenly the darkness was pierced by the red flares of gunfire, the silence shattered by shots and cries. The loudest cry was ripped from his own throat. He opened his eyes. ''Jack was hit. He was wearing a vest, but they blew both his legs off with a machine gun. He bled to death in ninety seconds.''

Mike looked at the table and saw with a distant sort of surprise that his hands were shaking. And he hadn't even told her the worst of it. Not by a long shot. ''Since then I haven't worked with a regular partner. I don't like being reminded of Jack, and that's why I reacted the way I did when you asked about my partner. That's enough—I don't want to talk about it anymore.''

Mike fell silent, but his anguish echoed in Nina's heart. In the past few days she, too, had become intimate with loneliness and loss. She wanted to look away from that bleak, ravaged face, but she could not. She reached out, as if by her touch she could lighten the burden he bore. Something flamed up in the azure depths of his eyes. Was it a warning? Or a plea?

Nina's hand dropped. For a long moment she simply looked at Mike, at his tense expression, his intent gaze, his lips half-parted as if he wanted to speak but could not. His grief and introspection had vanished, to be replaced by other emotions: doubt, wariness, longing. And, she saw with a thrill of purely primitive need, desire.

Am I going to spend the rest of my life afraid to reach for what I really want? The question sounded so clearly in Nina's mind that for a moment she was afraid she'd spoken aloud. She raised her hand again, and this time she did not let it fall. Gently, tentatively, driven by a force deeper and more real than her fears, she touched Mike's face, tracing the line of one jet black brow with a fingertip and then, more boldly, stroking his cheek with her open hand.

All the while Mike watched her eyes, and she could not look away from that fierce, penetrating gaze. Nina had crossed a line, and she knew it. There was no room between them now for pride, or politeness, or pretense. She saw naked hunger in his look and knew that it was mirrored on her own face, there for him to see. A delicious melting warmth spread from the core of her throughout her whole body. She was weak with longing and yet, paradoxically, knowing how much he wanted her, she exulted in her power.

Mike rose to his feet and pulled her up with him. They were next to each other, lightly touching along the whole lengths of their bodies. Nina felt electric, alive, every particle of her reaching eagerly toward him. He tilted her face up and lowered his mouth to hers.

His kiss explored her mouth with breathtaking gentleness. His lips brushed across hers, lightly at first, almost teasingly, and then a little harder. He captured her full lower lip, gently nipping it in his teeth and sucking it. The tip of his tongue traced the contours of her mouth and then slipped between her lips.

Nina ached to be pressed tightly to him, but his hands gripped her waist and held her in place, close enough to feel his body barely touching hers, but not as close as she wanted to be. She wrapped her arms around his neck, tangling her fingers in the glossy thick hair that she'd been wanting to touch for so long, and tried to draw him nearer, but still he held his distance.

Mike nearly groaned when his tongue slid between her parted lips and found hers. Her lips were soft and yielding, but her tongue thrust ardently against his, driving him wild with the desire to taste more of her, to see how much hotter he could make her. His need for her raced through his blood; it filled his mind and all his senses. Already, just from kissing her, he was rigid and ready. But he wanted more from this woman than to spend himself in her. He needed to pleasure her, to touch every part of her. As she answered his kiss with her own, nibbling his lips, sliding her tongue into his mouth, he forced himself to pull away. Her whimper of dismay almost broke his resolve, but he made himself draw back.

Her mouth felt cold without his lips on it. Nina shook her head, dazed. Passion had swept over her as wild and hot and sudden as a brushfire—and she didn't want the fire to go out. Why had he taken his lips away from hers? Why was he looking at her so seriously?

"Nina." Mike's voice was hoarse. "I have to go. Because if I don't go now, I won't go at all."

She didn't have to think it over. This time she knew with unshakable clarity just what she wanted. Not a man, any man, but *this* man, right now. She met his earnest gaze. "Don't go."

He looked at her, and she could tell that he was exerting all his strength to hold himself back. "Are you sure?" he asked softly.

For answer she stepped forward and took him into her arms.

This time his kiss was anything but gentle. Head bent back, neck arched, she surrendered her mouth to him, and he kissed her hard and long. He thrust his tongue deep into her mouth and shivered with pleasure when her lips tightened around it. He backed her against the wall, took her wrists in his outstretched hands and ground himself against her so that he could feel every curve of her.

Nina was on fire. Her breasts were pressed to Mike's chest, her thighs were parted around his legs, and still she wanted more of herself to touch more of him. His sex, hard and erect beneath the tight denim, rubbed against her, and the yearning inside her intensified. He kissed her and held her like that until she thought she would burst with need, and then he released her hands and in a single motion pulled her sweater off.

Her full breasts were almost spilling out of her lacy pink bra; he could see the darker pink nipples through the lace. They were taut, eager to be touched. "Oh, God, Nina, I want you," he said thickly. His hands and his mouth and his loins were aching for her, but he wanted to go slow, to savor every touch, every sensation.

Very slowly, he reached out one hand and touched her breasts just above the lace. She gasped, and he saw her tremble. Her skin was as soft as silk and very, very warm. He went on touching her, watching her face, forcing himself to go slowly. Her eyes closed and she moaned softly as he teased her, brushing first one, then both breasts with his palms. He cupped them, willing his hands not to close on them urgently. Finally he lightly stroked the stiff pink peaks, and she breathed, "Oh, yes."

He toyed with her nipples, tugging them gently. But he needed more. The waiting was torture; he couldn't hold back much longer. "Tell me what you want, Nina," he murmured.

There was no sound in the world but Mike's voice, no sensation other than his fingers on her breasts and the waves of pleasure they sent rocketing through her. "Kiss me there," she said dizzily, and nearly fainted at the exquisite pleasure of his mouth on one erect nipple, kissing and licking her through the lace.

Mike's self-control cracked. He couldn't bear to have even the thinnest barrier between them now. Hands shaking, he removed her bra and buried his face in the warmth between her breasts. He covered the swelling mounds with kisses and sucked the taut nipples. Then he scooped her up easily and headed toward the bedroom.

Cradled in Mike's arms, Nina trailed kisses along the line of his jaw and down his neck. "I'm gonna drop you if you keep doing that," he warned her.

"All right, how about this?" She ran the tip of her tongue around his ear and then nipped the lobe between her lips.

Mike nearly stumbled. "That's not a whole lot better."

"I'll just leave you alone, then."

"Not necessary." Nina felt herself being lowered to the bed, and a moment later Mike was beside her, shirtless. "We've reached our destination," he said into her ear. "Now you can do anything you want."

She looked up at him. "Anything?"

"Anything," he said, and his voice was no longer playful. It was the husky, hungry voice of a man on the verge of being consumed by desire. Nina pulled him on top of her, exploring his shoulders and back with eager hands. The weight of his body, the feel of him against her, the scent of his skin and hair—all were exactly right. Passion was raging within her, but beneath it ran a deeper current of something else: happiness. She and Mike were about to become one, and that was how it should be.

Mike eased her slacks off. The lacy panties followed. He stroked her thighs, her hips, her sleek belly, and then he slipped his fingers into the soft, damp folds beneath the auburn curls.

Nina cried out when he touched her, but it was a cry of delight and discovery. She felt herself moving uncontrollably, surging against him like the waves beating again and again against a rock. Mike kissed her deeply while his gentle but insistent caress urged her on toward ecstasy. Something inside her was very close to giving way when she suddenly squirmed away from him and said, "No, not yet."

Mike froze. He hadn't dreamed that she would stop him at this point, but not for the world would he so much as touch her against her will.

"Not like that," she whispered against his chest. "I want to feel you inside me."

He held her against him, kissing her hair. Then he looked into her eyes and saw there a depth of passion and need that matched his own. He touched her lips with his. "I'll be right back."

Nina heard the rustle of foil, and a moment later Mike was stretched out next to her again. She felt the welcome weight of his arousal in the place where he had been touching her, and she opened herself to him.

He entered her with a groan, and for her there was only an ecstatic pleasure as she stretched to hold him. He filled her and completed her, and as their bodies moved together in a rhythm older than time she felt herself rising up and up until, with a convulsion that shook her to her core, she passed into a realm of timeless joy. And Mike was there with her, murmuring her name into her mouth as he kissed her, his arms and legs tangled with hers, shuddering as he exploded into her.

They lay together for a long time afterward, drifting slowly back down to earth but not loosening their hold on each other. When they did separate, it was only for a little while. Mike lifted himself off her and lay next to her, pulling her close.

She tilted her face up to his and they kissed, each feeling the other smile through the kiss.

"Wow," Nina murmured. "That was—"

"Incredible," he suggested.

"Yeah," she replied, snuggling still closer to him, wrapping her arms more tightly around him. "The best."

A laugh rumbled in his chest. "How would you know, sweetheart? You've got amnesia." His voice was teasing, but tender, and Nina was pierced by a pang of joy. For the first time she felt that he really believed her.

Later, much later, Nina woke up from a dark and disturbing dream. She couldn't remember much, only a feeling of dread and the swift-fading impression that she was trying desperately to run away from something, or someone. She lay with her head pillowed on Mike's chest, but the calm beat of his heart against her cheek could not soothe her troubled thoughts. His closeness was a reminder that she had added a new complication to her already confusing situation.

Nina did not regret the choice she had made—for a moment her arms tightened around Mike as though she would never let him go, and he murmured gently and stroked her hair—but she was shaken by the depth of her feelings for him. *What if he doesn't feel the same way?* Even worse, what if her own feelings weren't real? Maybe they were a side effect of her amnesia: Perhaps she was drawn to Mike because he was a source of strength, the one rock she could cling to in a frighteningly uncertain world? All she knew at this moment was that she wished the night would never end.

Mike gazed unseeingly up at Nina's ceiling, forcing himself to be gentle as he stroked her hair and eased her into sleep. He wanted to crush her to him with all his strength, to lose himself in her again, to forget all his doubts in the haze of passion. Something had happened to him tonight, something that went far beyond the simple satisfaction of desire, and it terrified him. Nina had aroused a tenderness and a longing unlike anything he'd ever felt—but he would keep those feelings under control. Not because Irons and Hecht had ordered him to stay away from Nina; he'd defied orders before, and he'd do it again. But because he couldn't be sure of Nina herself. *She's alone, she's vulnerable. She needs someone, and right now you're all she's got. Maybe there's nothing more to it than that.* And all the while, lurking at the back of his mind, was what he tried not to think about: *She could be lying to you. Remember the last time.*

At last Mike fell asleep, only to dream that it was Karen he held in his arms. He jerked awake, the nightmare gunfire echoing in his mind, and it took him a moment to realize that the sound he was hearing was real. It was a dog barking—Sig, in the next room. Nina was awake, too, clinging to his arm. "What's wrong?" she cried.

"Sig," Mike answered tersely. "Someone's at your door." He was already out of bed, climbing into his jeans. He threw a quick glance at the illuminated clock on Nina's night table; it was five-thirty in the morning.

Nina slipped into a robe and started for the living room. Sig had stopped barking and was crouched with his eyes fastened on the door, growling low in his throat with a steady intensity that boded ill for whomever was on the other side of the door.

Mike hurried past her. "Get back," he ordered, pushing her into the bedroom. He took a position flat against the wall, next to the front door, one arm cocked; Nina stole a quick peek into the living room and saw that his gun was in his hand. He threw the front door open.

A tall fair-haired man in a camel overcoat burst into the room. "Nina, Nina, where are you? Are you all right?" he called. The sight of Sig, crouched and snarling balefully,

brought him up short. Then he turned and saw Mike, who
had him covered from behind. The blond stranger scowled
and said, "Who the devil are you? And what are you doing in my fiancée's apartment?"

Chapter 6

Mike's years as a cop had prepared him to deal with surprises, often unpleasant ones, but nothing had prepared him for this. Still, for a man who felt as though he'd just been kicked in the stomach with a steel-toed boot, he stayed pretty cool.

"Police," he said tersely, reaching into a back pocket for his badge and holding it out. His other hand, the one holding the gun, never wavered. "Now it's your turn. Can I see some ID, please?"

The request was nothing more than Mike's attempt to make the situation seem halfway official. He already had a pretty good idea who the stranger was, and his guess was confirmed when Nina spoke from behind him.

"Julien?" she said, in a faint, disbelieving voice, and then, more definitely, "Julien Duchesne."

The blond man's eyes widened. "You remember me," he said. He spoke with a slight European accent. "My dear, I am so relieved. Armand said that you had lost your memory."

"I *have* lost my memory." Nina's voice was flat. "I don't remember you at all. I recognized you from a picture I saw."

"I—I see. Well, clearly we have much to talk about. And now, Officer," Duchesne said, turning back to Mike, "perhaps you'd be good enough to take that gun out of my face. And I believe I asked you a question." His voice sharpened. "Just what are you doing here in my fiancée's apartment?"

Julien Duchesne was looking coldly at Mike, but it was Nina who spoke. She burst out, "Your fiancée? You and I are . . . *engaged?*"

"That is correct," Duchesne replied, with a look at her that was both fond and sad. "You don't remember even that? My sweet, this is most distressing."

Nina sat down suddenly. "You're telling me. Look, I can't quite take this in. I'm sorry," she added, as Julien's handsome features twisted in a sudden grimace of pain, "but you've got to understand, I didn't have a clue about this. It doesn't seem real."

Nina's head was spinning. For the first time in several days, she felt as though she were about to lose control. The shock of waking from the warm circle of Mike's arms to find that she was engaged to marry another man, a man who was virtually a stranger, had left her feeling sick and shaken. Worst of all was the icy, stunned look on Mike's face. She ached to run to him and take him in her arms. Yet what had been possible last night no longer seemed within reach. In the space of a few moments, a gulf had yawned between them. Apart from a single stricken glance at Julien's first reference to "my fiancée," Mike hadn't once looked at her. And now Julien Duchesne, eyes narrowed speculatively, was looking from Nina to Mike and back again, his expression leaving little doubt of the conclusions he was drawing.

"Miss Dennison and I spent some time combing her personal records and interviewing her co-workers and friends," Mike said to Julien. "She's right—there wasn't a clue about your engagement. It seems odd that nobody mentioned it, not even Armand Zakroff. Can you explain that?"

"Look here," Duchesne flared, "I don't have to answer your questions. Furthermore, I'm still waiting for an explanation from you. Why the hell are you here?"

"I'm investigating Miss Dennison's case," Mike said woodenly.

"And this is what you call 'investigating'?" Julien's voice crackled, and he glared angrily at Mike. "I find you here at an ungodly hour in the morning, barely dressed, alone with a woman who was in the hospital just a few days ago. You've clearly been forcing your attentions on a sick, confused woman, and," he added contemptuously, "I'm going to see that you pay for it."

"Stop it!" Nina's exclamation cut like a knife into the tension between the two men. "Just stop it, Julien. Mike's here at my invitation."

Julien's expression changed at that, but Nina carried on, determined to say what she had to say. "Get this straight, both of you. I'm not sick, I'm not confused. I've lost my memory. Period. Julien, it seems that you and I have a lot of things to talk about, but I don't need someone to take care of me. And I wish you *would* explain why no one mentioned our engagement."

Julien crossed the room to the sofa and sat next to Nina. Sig, now sitting still as a statue at Mike's feet, followed Julien's every move with unblinking eyes. So did Mike.

"I'm sorry, my dear." Julien rubbed his hands across his face and then took one of Nina's hands in both of his, patting it gently. "You must understand, this is all very difficult for me. I was in Geneva, I spoke to Armand and he told me of your—your accident. I flew back at once.

And now I find this...situation.'' Julien cast a pained glance at Mike.

"But this is between us," he said, looking into Nina's eyes. His own were a light, clear gray. "I know we can work this out, Nina. Whatever you've done, we can get past it. After all, if you truly do not remember me..." He gazed searchingly at her. "Nothing? Nothing at all?"

Nina looked away and shook her head. "I still don't understand," she said stubbornly. "Why didn't anyone know about our engagement?"

Julien smiled. "That was your idea, Nina. You wanted us to keep our relationship a secret from Armand and the others at Z and D. I kept telling you that secrecy was unnecessary, but you felt that it wouldn't look right for an employee of the firm to be dating one of the partners. We became engaged the night before I left for Switzerland and agreed that we would tell everyone when I returned."

"I see. How long were we, um, dating?"

"Oh, it was a whirlwind courtship." Julien laughed. "Just a few weeks. Don't you remember, darling—you said that true love can happen in the blink of an eye."

"Did I?" Nina's voice was hoarse. She couldn't keep from darting a swift, tormented glance at Mike. His eyes were a wall of blue ice, holding her at a distance. Behind the wall she thought she glimpsed a hint of some passionate entreaty—and then he looked away. Without a word he walked into the bedroom. Nina heard the bedsprings creak and realized that he was putting on his shoes, getting ready to walk out of her apartment. And out of her life.

Get up, she ordered herself. *Stop him, don't let him leave. Don't let things end this way.* But Julien's hands tightened on hers, and he uttered his own entreaty in a low voice. "Nina, I am truly sorry if I came on too strong at first. This has been a shock to me, too, you know. But, please, give me a chance. Give *us* a chance. I know you love me. I can make you remember—if you'll let me." He leaned forward as if to kiss her, and Nina could not keep from flinching.

"I'm sorry," she stammered, "but don't you see? It's as though I don't know you at all."

Julien smiled. "I understand," he said tenderly. "I promise you, I will be patient."

Just then something cold and wet intruded on their handclasp. It was Sig's nose. The big dog was shoving his face into Nina's hand, whimpering. She extricated her hand from Julien's grasp and began to stroke Sig, murmuring, "It's all right, fella."

Perfect timing, boy, Mike thought bleakly. He was back in the living room, fully dressed and wearing his jacket. *I'd roll over and play dead if I thought she'd tell me that everything's gonna be all right.*

"Nina," Julien said suddenly, "that beast has destroyed your sofa cushions."

Sig bristled, almost as if he understood and resented Julien's remark, and Nina said with a sigh, "No, that wasn't the dog, Julien. It was a prowler—oh, never mind, I'll fill you in."

Suddenly Nina was weary to her very bones. She wanted only to crawl back into bed and pretend that the past half hour had never happened. The thought of bed reminded her of Mike, of the feel of his body on hers and the taste of his mouth, and her flesh began to tingle. An alluring image rose up: Mike, naked and warm in her soft gray sheets, welcoming her into his embrace. She looked up, and reality drove that image away. Mike was dressed to leave. His expression was remote and impersonal.

Thinking that she would have the chance to exchange a few words with him if she walked him downstairs to the front door, Nina started to rise. Then she sank back with a low groan, hand pressed to her forehead.

"Nina, what is it?" The voice was Mike's. So was the arm around her shoulders. Nina drew strength from his presence, but she was too absorbed in the now-familiar flashes of white light to respond. The flashes cleared, and Nina saw a vivid little scene: Julien Duchesne's profile, silhouetted against some sort of flapping white sheet. His fine, fair hair was blown back from his forehead and there was a feeling of motion, and then a glimpse of dark waves flecked with white foam. The image faded, and Nina became aware that Mike was holding her protectively from one side while Julien, on her other side, looked daggers at Mike and clutched her hands. She felt like a football being tugged between two little boys.

"Oh, stop it," she muttered crossly, and stood. "Julien, do you have a boat?"

Julien shot a keen glance at her. "Why, yes, a sailboat. The *Diamantina*. I keep her at a marina on Long Beach Island. Why do you ask?"

"Just a memory flash. I've been on the boat with you, haven't I?"

A look of surprise crossed his features, and he paused for a moment before answering. "Yes. Of course you have. In fact," he said, "that is where we got engaged."

Mike interrupted, his voice sounding harsh and rusty. "I'd think you'd be likely to remember a big event like that. But you hesitated just now, as if you weren't quite sure."

Nina looked curiously at him, not sure what he was getting at, but Julien bit back an exclamation of annoyance.

"If I hesitated, as you say, it was only because I see no reason to discuss our intimate affairs in your presence, Officer. And now I believe your business here is finished, is it not?"

Mike swept the room with a single glance. Did Nina only imagine it, or did his gaze linger on her for a moment? If his eyes held a message, she could not read it. She wondered what he could read in her own face; she felt her lips trembling and her eyes filling with tears. Why didn't he reach out to her? If only he would cross the room to her side, hold her, kiss her. Then everything would be simple. Then Nina wouldn't have to choose, wouldn't have to take the risk of reaching out to him—

"Yes," Mike said. "My business here is finished." He nodded curtly. "Miss Dennison. Mr. Duchesne."

"Good day, Officer," Julien said, politely dismissive. Nina opened her mouth to speak, not knowing what she wanted to say, but Mike was gone.

He pounded down her stairs and out onto the street in a cold fury. At Julien Duchesne, for being the one who was still upstairs with Nina. At Nina, for letting him go. And most of all at himself. Not just for leaving Nina, but for letting himself care about her. For letting her matter so much that his guts were twisted into a knot that grew tighter with each step away from her.

"Damn it!" He pounded a fist on the roof of his car, and Sig woofed gently in sympathy.

Mike looked down at Sig. The dog's absurdly long ears were cocked, his head tilted at a hopeful angle.

"You wanna go back upstairs, don't you, buddy?"

Sig's tailed wagged.

"Yeah, me, too. But forget it." He threw the door of the Grand Am open and, with a resigned snuffle, Sig clambered into the back seat. There he unearthed a rawhide chew toy and immediately settled down, mangling it contentedly.

"Got an extra one of those?" Mike asked him. "Ah, forget it. It wouldn't do any good."

Sig looked up from his slobbery toy, his brown eyes gleaming in the early-morning light. All Mike could think of was how Nina's eyes would look in that light, how they'd sparkle with golden lights as he pulled her to him—

His hands clenched on the steering wheel and he felt close to tears. "You screwed up again, Novalis," he whispered. "Big time." From some dark place buried deep in his memories he seemed to hear a woman's mocking laugh.

After Mike's departure, Nina tried to relieve the strained atmosphere in her apartment by making coffee and offering a cup to Julien. He sat at the kitchen table, watching her, and she realized that she felt uncomfortable in just her bathrobe. Although the terry-cloth robe was by no means revealing, his gaze was somehow assessing. Or was it possessive?

"I'm going to change," she said abruptly. And then, knowing that she would sound ungracious but not knowing how else to say what had to be said, she added, "Please stay here."

He nodded courteously. "Of course." His tone was gentle and understanding; Nina felt a little churlish as she pointedly closed the bedroom door between them.

The rumpled bed seemed to fill the room, reminding her of what had passed between her and Mike. Was it really only a few hours since he had carried her to this room and laid her on the bed? As she moved to straighten the tangled sheets and tossed pillows, the scent of him rose up from the bedclothes. Burying her face in the bed, she breathed in the mingled musk of their lovemaking and shuddered to the memory of his touch, his lips on her throat, the feel of him entering her. For a moment it was as if he were there in the room with her, strong and comforting.

"Oh, Mike," she whispered in a broken voice.

Then she heard Julien stirring in the kitchen: the scrape of his chair against the floor, the rattle of his cup in the saucer. Who was this fair-haired, gray-eyed stranger, this intrusive, insistent presence who had laid such sudden claim to her? How much of herself had she given to him? Nina gritted her teeth in frustration. Trying to reassemble the fragments of her life was like trying to put together a jigsaw puzzle without ever seeing the picture on the box. New pieces kept turning up, but she had no idea what to make of them.

Hastily she plumped the pillows and drew the comforter over the sheets. Then she dressed quickly in plain tan slacks and a beige sweater. No makeup, no jewelry. She felt almost defiant about it. *I don't need to try to impress him,* she told herself. *We're already engaged.* The notion of being someone's fiancée was utterly strange to her—as outlandish as learning that she'd been shot, or that she had amnesia. But one thing she'd learned from her time with Mike: The way to find answers was to ask questions. And now there were some questions she had to ask Julien.

She went back into the kitchen. "I think we have some things to talk about," she said carefully.

"I agree." Julien was sitting on the sofa. He patted the cushion next to him, but she perched on a chair instead.

"You say that we had a whirlwind courtship, that we've only been dating for a few weeks," Nina continued. She looked him straight in the eye. "I don't know how else to ask this: Were we lovers?"

Julien smiled, a slow, confident smile that Nina supposed must once have kindled an answering spark in her. Now she felt nothing, only a vague discomfort under his lingering gaze.

Swiftly he crossed the room to kneel next to her chair, capturing her hands in his. "You really have forgotten everything, haven't you, darling?" he said. "Don't worry, we'll get your memories back. Or make new ones." His voice was intimate, caressing. It sent a shiver up Nina's spine. But the shiver, she realized, was one of uneasiness. The whole situation gave her the creeps. In fact, she admitted to herself, she hated it. This man knew her intimately—and she knew nothing about it. It was as though it had happened without her knowledge or consent. It felt like a violation.

She was about to snap out a rebuff when she caught herself. *Take it easy. It's not Julien's fault. This situation has got to be hard on him, too.* So she merely withdrew her hands and said in a milder tone, "Look, Julien, you have to understand. Things aren't like they were before. I don't remember us being together. It's going to take some time for me to feel comfortable with you—with everyone in my life," she added hastily, seeing the hurt in his eyes.

Julien sighed and returned to the sofa. "Yes, I see that. But now I must ask you a question."

Nina tensed. She knew what was coming. Ever since Julien had burst into the apartment, she had been wondering how she was going to answer this question.

"Please don't take offense," he continued, "but I must know what has occurred between you and that policeman."

His tone was almost that of a parent chastising an erring child. And something in his voice—the hint of possessiveness, perhaps—strengthened Nina's resolve.

"Julien," she said firmly, "whatever happened between Mike and me is between Mike and me. It has nothing to do with you."

He gaped. "Nothing to do with me? But... but we are betrothed. And I find him in your apartment, both of you half-dressed! What am I supposed to think?"

"Think whatever you like, Julien," Nina said evenly, "but remember, as far as I'm concerned, I didn't even know you until an hour ago. And as for Mike, the subject is closed."

He stared at her, white-faced, his thin lips pressed tightly together. She met his eyes and didn't look away. Gradually the anger faded from his features. He shrugged, smiled ruefully and said, "What choice do I have?"

"None." For the first time since Mike's silent departure, Nina's spirits lifted a bit. Standing up to Julien had felt good. Not only that, she recognized with surprise, it had felt almost...familiar. The moment of confrontation had carried a haunting echo of memory, as though she and Julien had faced off that way before. *Of course,* she reminded herself. *Armand said we've had disagreements in the office.* And at the same time they had been dating and falling in love outside office hours.

She studied Julien for a moment. Tall and slim, clad in a beautifully tailored gray suit, he looked about thirty-eight years old. *My fiancé,* Nina thought, *and I don't even know how old he is!* His features were fine and regular, his whole appearance urbane and refined. He fit right in with Nina's subtle, tasteful decor. Suddenly a vivid image of Mike swam before her eyes: his messy hair, his wrinkled T-shirts, his dusty loft. Surely anyone looking at Nina's life would see that Julien was a much better match for her than Mike was. Then why was the thought of Mike like a hand wringing her heart? Why did she ache to be with him now? She was afraid that she knew the answer to that one.

Julien was looking at her, unspoken questions in his eyes, and she turned away, feeling guilty. She owed this man something, although she wasn't yet sure what it was. Somehow they had to decide how they were going to proceed.

As if following her thoughts, Julien said, "Nina, I realize that your amnesia has been a terrible shock to you. I suppose that learning of our engagement came as something of a shock, too, although I hope not an unpleasant one." He smiled. "I don't want to force myself on you. All I ask is that you spend some time with me, that you get to know me again."

"I guess that's fair," Nina said slowly.

He gave a sigh of relief, and Nina realized that he hadn't been certain of her response.

"Good," he said, leaning forward. "Now I know that everything will be all right. You fell in love with me once. You'll fall in love with me all over again."

Nina looked at his handsome, earnest face, glowing with pleasure and attentiveness, and felt only weariness. And a great emptiness, as if she'd lost something inestimably precious.

At Julien's urging, Nina spent the day with him. He arranged a perfect day for her, starting with Sunday breakfast at the Fairmont: smoked salmon omelets, flaky croissants and fresh-squeezed fruit juice. Then they went for a long, leisurely walk in the park around the Museum of Art, admiring the first hints of fall colors in the oaks and maples that lined the wide boulevards. Nina continued to feel awkward with him, but nonetheless there were moments when she found herself enjoying his company. *I must have been in love with him,* she told herself more than once. *After all, I'm engaged to marry him.*

There was a lot to like in Julien, she decided. His tastes were elegant and cosmopolitan; apparently he had always had plenty of money. Yet he was not flashy or showy—he simply seemed at home with wealth and style. His manner toward Nina was solicitous and polite. At first she stiffened instinctively when he took her arm to guide her down a flight of steps or help her out of his car, but he appeared to respect the limits she had set and did not attempt any greater intimacies.

He proved to be a polished raconteur, full of amusing stories about his travels and his adventures bargaining for fabulous gems in the remote corners of the world. The name "Marta" popped up in several of these anecdotes, and Nina said, "You'll have to get used to me asking a lot of questions. Who's Marta?"

"Of course," Julien exclaimed, "I keep forgetting that everything is new to you. Marta is my sister. She will be astonished to learn that you do not remember her. Marta is quite memorable, as you will see. And, of course, she is your closest friend."

Nina blinked. "She is?"

"Indeed. Like me, she was deeply distressed to hear of your accident. She had to take a later flight, however, so she will be here this evening."

"That'll be nice," Nina said weakly. Once again she was feeling overwhelmed. In a single day she had acquired not only a fiancé but also a new best friend.

"Marta is the only one who knew about our engagement," Julien was saying. "Of course we couldn't keep it a secret from *her*."

"Of course," Nina replied mechanically.

"We were planning to tell Armand this week," he said, "and then—"

"Armand! That reminds me," Nina said, snapping her fingers. "He said something about how you and I had been having some trouble."

Julien frowned. "What sort of trouble?"

"Arguments about the direction the firm should be taking. I wanted to branch out into teaching and design, and you wanted to stick with high-value importing."

Julien's face cleared. "Oh, that," he said with a light laugh. "I'm afraid you mustn't take what Armand says too seriously, my dear. As you know, he's a very emotional man, and now that he's getting older, I fear he begins to exaggerate. We had some differences of opinion on purely professional matters, but they were nothing serious. And," he said, looking fondly down at her, "I believe you were coming around to my point of view."

"I was, was I?"

"Oh, yes. I assure you, I can be very...persuasive." This was said with a look that teasingly hinted at past closeness. Nina moved away slightly. No matter what her relationship with Julien had been, Nina felt no physical attraction to him now. Julien seemed to accept her need to create a distance between them; his attitude betrayed no frustration or impatience. She wondered how long his patience would last.

Later in the afternoon, after they had returned to Nina's apartment and were sipping tea in her kitchen, Julien asked her to tell him all about the shooting. She told him what she knew. It wasn't much. He pressed her for details about everything that had happened in the past few days; he was especially interested in the fact that her apartment had been searched by unknown perpetrators. Armand, it appeared, hadn't mentioned that incident in his phone conversation with Julien.

"You've no idea what they were looking for?" he asked for the second or third time. "Or whether they found it?"

"They were probably just junkies, looking for cash," she retorted wearily. "Why are you making such a big deal of it?"

"I'm just concerned. Maybe whoever broke in here will come back. It's not safe for you to stay here. I think you should—"

"I think I should just forget about it and try to get on with my life," Nina said firmly. "I'm not moving out of my apartment, Julien."

"All right, all right," he said placatingly. But he couldn't seem to stop thinking about what he persisted in calling "the accident."

"You really don't remember anything at all?" he probed a few minutes later. "Not who shot you? Nothing about why it happened?"

"Not a thing."

"Amazing. What do the police think?"

She glanced quickly at him, but his face reflected only sincere interest. She reddened; apparently she had been too quick to imagine a veiled reference to Mike.

"They figure that it was just a random shooting. A drive-by."

Julien shook his head. "It's unbelievable that such a thing could happen. And the doctors—what do they say about your memory?"

Nina shrugged. "No one really knows. They say I'll probably recover my memory, but they don't know when. Maybe I'll start remembering more bits and pieces, or maybe it will all come back at once."

"I hope I'll be there when that happens," Julien said fervently.

Nina looked at him, eyebrows raised.

"So that I can see your face when you remember— about us," he explained.

"Oh. Listen, Julien, I don't want to be rude, but it's been a long day for me, and I'm tired. Perhaps you should go home now. I'll see you at the office tomorrow."

His face fell. "But Marta will be here any minute."

"She's coming *here?*"

"Naturally. She wants to see you. I promise you, we'll leave as soon as she's had a chance to see that you're all right."

Nina agreed wanly and excused herself. In the bathroom, she rummaged in the medicine cabinet for aspirin and swallowed two. She gazed into the mirror and realized that, with dark circles under her eyes and a glum expression, she didn't look much better now than she had in the hospital after the shooting. *Back where you started, huh?*

All at once she remembered how Mike had supported her, there in the hospital when she'd been afraid that she was going to fall. She was weak with yearning to feel him holding her again. Thoughts and memories of him that she had battled all day to suppress came flooding into her mind, and she closed her eyes to keep her tears at bay. She wondered where Mike was just then, and what he was doing. And whether he was thinking of her.

* * *

Mike shifted irritably in his seat, trying to get comfortable. After six or seven hours, any car could feel as if it had been designed by the Spanish Inquisition. It wouldn't have been so bad if he'd been moving, going somewhere, but he was just sitting. And, he admitted, his mood didn't help much.

He'd been in a lousy frame of mind when he left Nina's apartment that morning, and the intervening hours had done nothing to cheer him up. Now it was the tail end of a pretty decent Sunday afternoon. He could be knocking back a cold beer somewhere, watching a ball game on TV. He could be taking Sig for a run; he reached into the back seat and knuckled the dog's head, and Sig snorted, scratched an ear with a hind paw and went back to sleep. At least Sig didn't seem to mind the fact that they had spent most of the day in the car.

He'd been unable to drive away from Nina's building. He'd sat outside for hours, staking the place out, calling himself every kind of fool. He'd followed Julien and Nina when they went out to eat. He'd watched them from a distance, two slender, long-legged figures, as they strolled along Ben Franklin Boulevard and sat chatting on the art museum steps. He'd followed them back to Nina's apartment. Now he was sitting and waiting—for what, he didn't know. *Are you a cop or a stalker?* he asked himself disgustedly.

He knew one thing—he was jealous as hell. But it wasn't just jealousy of Julien Duchesne that was gnawing at him. All right, he disliked the guy's smooth good looks and his air of superiority. Julien Duchesne wasn't the kind of man Mike Novalis was likely to warm up to. And the fact that Duchesne had laid claim to a place in Nina Dennison's life didn't make the guy any more likable. But none of that explained why Mike was watching Nina's apartment. He had no official reason to do so—in fact, he had been given clear orders to stay away. So it had to be personal, right?

Mike sighed. His feelings about Nina and about this case were so tangled that he was having a hard time sorting them out. He had no claim on her, even though his body still throbbed with the memory of her. What had happened between them had been more than just the hungry coupling of two lonely people, of that he was sure. Nina had touched him in a way no one else ever had, not even Karen. And he had thought he loved Karen. So what did that say about his feelings for Nina?

He shook his head angrily. Better not to think about that. No matter what he felt for Nina, she had a past with Julien Duchesne—her memory of being on his sailboat proved that. Maybe she had a future with him, as well. God knew Duchesne had a lot to offer. What did Mike have? A dump of an apartment, a goofy dog, a beat-up car, a dangerous job. A battered heart. Too battered, perhaps. All things considered, maybe he'd better keep it to himself.

Grimly Mike forced his thoughts back into a more professional track. *Go back to the basics,* he ordered himself. *Look at the facts. You know something's going on at Zakroff and Duchesne. You know someone took a shot at Nina Dennison. You know someone searched her apartment. And that's all you know. Anything else is guesswork.*

As much as he hated to admit it, even after making love with Nina Dennison, Mike couldn't prove that she was telling the truth about her amnesia. Any more than he could simply accept Irons's assurances that the attack on Nina was a random shooting and that she was in no further danger. To Mike, the equation looked the same now as on that first morning in the hospital: Nina could be completely clean, or she could be up to her neck in something dirty. Either way, she might be in danger. Guilty, in-

nocent—Mike wasn't sure that that mattered any longer.
He just wasn't going to let anything happen to her. Not if
he could help it.

What're you gonna do? he jeered at himself. *Stake her
out all week?* The answer was clear: *If I have to.* Of course,
there was the problem of his caseload, which had been
suffering from neglect since the middle of the week. Hecht
would have his hide. For the first time Mike felt the full
burden of the isolation that had enveloped him since Jack
Renzo's death and the debacle over Karen. He had grown
used to feeling ostracized, but now for the first time he
wondered whether some of the isolation had been self-
imposed. Had others drawn away from him, or had he
drawn away from them?

Mike was jerked out of his uncomfortable reverie by a
flurry of activity on the street. A red sports car swept up
in front of Nina's building, and out of it stepped one of the
most gorgeous women Mike had ever seen. She was tall,
model-slim, blond and chic, with a mink coat draped over
her shoulders. She tripped up Nina's front steps on high
heels and a moment later was admitted to the building.
Mike recalled that one of Nina's memory flashes had involved a blond woman in a mink coat. *Must be one of her
friends.* The blonde didn't match the description of anyone who had turned up in his brief investigation into the
life and times of Nina Dennison, but then he'd only been
on the case for a couple of days.

Not long enough, he thought, watching the door
through which the blonde had disappeared. *Not nearly
long enough.*

Nina was relieved when Marta buzzed her from the
downstairs intercom. Her nerves were shrieking with exhaustion and tension. Julien was being scrupulously polite, but nevertheless his very presence was a burden. Nina
wanted to be left alone with her thoughts. Maybe she'd

take a nice, hot bath. Or maybe, she thought tiredly, she'd climb right into bed, pull the covers up over her head and cry.

There came a quick, impatient knock at the door. Nina opened it and was engulfed in a cloud of perfume. A fastidious, beautiful woman stepped into the apartment.

"Nina, darling!" cried Marta. Leaning forward, Marta took Nina by the shoulders and planted a kiss on her cheek. In the air near it, actually. A long blond tendril that had worked loose from Marta's chignon tickled Nina's nose and made her sneeze. Or maybe it was the perfume. Marta appeared not to notice.

"Sweetie," she was saying in a light, swift voice with a slight accent, like her brother's, "I have been so worried. And Julien—he was a wreck when he heard the news. You should have seen him. Devastated! But now all is well, yes?" She brushed aside Nina's bangs. "Oh, lovely. Not even a scar, I hope. Good! And what is this about losing your memory? I hope you remember *me.*"

Suddenly Marta seemed to notice that Nina was not listening. Instead she was staring at Marta's glossy dark brown mink coat as if she had never seen one before.

"Oh, my new coat," Marta said. "I got it in Geneva." She pirouetted to show Nina the back of the coat. "Do you like it?"

All at once it hit Nina, and she simply couldn't take any more. "Oh, this is just too much," she said. She backed up until the sofa hit her behind the knees and then collapsed into it, ignoring Julien's and Marta's quizzical expressions. "As if I didn't already have enough trouble—!" She buried her face in her hands. Her shoulders heaved.

"Nina, what's wrong?" Julien rushed to her side. "Tell me."

He drew her hands away from her face. Nina was laughing helplessly, and at the look of baffled surprise on his face she laughed even harder.

"I'm sorry." Nina gasped. "I can't help it." She gulped and tried to control herself.

"But what *is* it?" Julien said. There was a hint of peevishness in his voice.

"Look, I can't explain. It wouldn't make any sense. But, please, both of you, I'm exhausted and I really need to be alone. Could you just leave? Now? Please?"

Julien and Marta exchanged glances. Their identical worried expressions heightened the family resemblance between them.

"Julien," Marta said, low voiced, "something is wrong here. I think she's hysterical. Do you think the sight of me upset her in some way? Triggered a memory, perhaps?" She looked doubtfully at Nina, who had crossed to the door and was holding it open.

"I don't know." Julien was equally concerned. "Nina," he said winningly, "maybe Marta should stay with you—"

"No!" Then, abashed at her vehemence, Nina said with as much patience as she could summon, "Please, I just want to be alone. Julien, I'll see you at the office tomorrow. Marta, it was nice of you to come, but I have a headache."

Julien opened his mouth as if to utter a protest or a suggestion, but at the sight of Nina's unyielding countenance he closed it again.

"Very well, my dear," he said mildly, and he ushered Marta toward the door.

"I understand, Nina," Marta said sympathetically as she left. "There has been a lot of excitement for you today. Rest now, and we'll talk tomorrow."

Julien tried to kiss Nina goodbye at the door, but she avoided the kiss by sticking her hand out for him to shake. He did so, and then, with a wry smile, lifted it gently to his lips.

"Goodbye, goodbye," Nina called, practically dancing with impatience. She slammed the door, bolted it and felt like sinking to the floor with relief. But although she had pleaded exhaustion to speed the Duchesnes on their way, her tiredness had vanished. Her mind was humming with a new and unexpected mystery. "Just what the *hell* is going on?" she demanded to the empty room.

She went into the bedroom and took her diary from the bedside table. Sitting in the kitchen, she went over everything that had happened to her since she had woken up in the hospital on Thursday morning, trying to remember each and every one of the vivid "memory" flashes she'd had. She made a list:

1. Thurs. (in restaurant)—Julien and another man (dark hair) in small room (cabin of boat?)
2. Thurs. afternoon—blond woman in mink coat in my apartment
3. Thurs. night—Mike N., no shirt, plants
4. Fri. (in Armand's office)—metal box full of emeralds
5. Sun.—Julien D. aboard sailboat

Nina studied the list, satisfied that it was complete. Then she put a check mark next to number three. On Thursday night she'd had a vision of Mike Novalis, bare chested and smiling, framed by a backdrop of plants. At the time she'd been unable to figure out how she could possibly be remembering something that had never happened. She'd decided that the vision was something cooked up by her own imagination, stoked by the simmering desire for Mike that had been building inside her throughout the day.

Then, on Saturday, she'd visited Mike's loft and seen her "vision" come true in every detail. There was no explanation; she'd chalked the whole thing up to coincidence. Eerie, sure, but still just possibly a coincidence. Now she was almost certain that there *was* another explanation, after all. She didn't want to believe it, but—

Slowly she reached out and made another check mark, this one next to number two. The blond woman she had seen in her flash of vision was Marta Duchesne. There was no room for doubt. Everything matched: the face, the voice, the hair. It might have made sense for Nina to have a memory of Marta, as the woman was apparently her best friend. But there was a kicker, and it was a big one. The vision could not have been a memory. For in the vision Marta spun around, modeling her new mink coat, and said, "Do you like it?" Exactly as she had done upon arriving at Nina's apartment not fifteen minutes ago.

It *couldn't* be coincidence. The alternative seemed impossible, yet Nina could see no way around it. Those brilliant scenes, framed in flashes of white light, weren't memories at all. She was seeing the future.

Nina paced around her apartment for hours, trying to figure out what had happened to her. The only idea she could come up with was that the gunshot wound that had caused her amnesia had somehow, unbelievably, also given her the ability to glimpse events before they happened.

Apparently there was no particular order to the process. Nina's third vision had come true before the second one. As for the other three, she had no idea when—or even if—they would take place. She had no control over her newfound ability. "I always thought seeing into the future would be more practical," she muttered. "Do I see next year's stock market results? No, I get a woman in a fur coat and a guy in a sailboat."

Her first thought was to call Mike. But what would she say? "Hi, I just thought you should know—I'm psychic"? She didn't know how she could make him believe her. *Especially when he didn't believe me about the amnesia,* she thought, remembering how his skepticism had riled her.

Nina wouldn't admit to herself that the real reason she didn't want to call Mike was that she didn't know what she would tell him about Julien Duchesne. Everything was so mixed up! Maybe Mike didn't even want to hear from her. She wouldn't be able to stand it if she called him and his response was merely polite. Or, worse yet, cool and distant.

At last, worn out with speculation, Nina washed her face and brushed her teeth. It was only eight o'clock in the evening, but she felt as if she could sleep for a month. She undressed, dropping her clothes in a heap on the bedroom floor. *I'll pick them up tomorrow,* she thought, and then caught herself wondering whether the neat and cautious Nina Dennison had ever in her life tossed her clothes carelessly on the floor. *Always room for new habits.*

She left her flannel nightgown on its hook in the closet and slipped naked between the sheets. Their cool caress against her skin awakened sensations that she had tried all day to forget. She shivered, thinking of the way Mike's hands had moved on her. Her body was taut, alive, on fire. The need that filled her had nothing at all to do with the man she had agreed to marry. No, this urgent need that gripped and tore at her like a wild thing was for Mike.

You've known him for less than a week! she raged at herself.

Yes, she answered, *and that's my whole life. He's the very first thing I remember. The only thing I need to remember.*

She tossed restlessly on the sheets that still smelled of him. Facedown, she clenched her fists in the pillow that he had used. But even as she felt the ache of desire in her breasts and in the warm cleft between her legs, she knew that what she wanted from Mike was more than sexual pleasure, more even than the ecstasy they had shared when they found the pinnacle of release together. What she wanted was to be enfolded in his arms, to feel his gentle hands stroking her hair and his kiss closing her tired eyes. And the fact that she yearned for gentleness and tenderness from Mike Novalis frightened her, for she did not know whether he would let himself give them.

Just before she tumbled into a deep well of sleep, Nina remembered the way Mike had looked just before he walked out of her apartment, his eyes as chill and forbidding as a wall of blue ice. Perhaps, she thought sleepily, that icy wall was not so much to keep her out as to keep his own pain locked away from the world.

Chapter 7

Nina's week got off to a rocky start. She woke on Monday morning after ten hours of sleep, feeling completely unrefreshed. As she ate breakfast and dressed for work she kept hoping that the phone would ring and that she'd pick it up and hear Mike's voice. But it didn't ring.

When she arrived at the Z and D offices, everyone from her secretary to Armand Zakroff converged on her, twittering with excitement. "Congratulations!" cried Debbie, her secretary. Debbie's eyes were bright with curiosity as she surveyed Nina. The office manager and the other appraisers and buyers crowded around Nina to pat her on the back and shake her hand. Bewildered, Nina scanned the group. There stood Julien, beaming with pride.

"You lucky dog!" Phil, one of the buyers, dug Julien in the ribs.

And Debbie said to Nina, "I can't believe you really kept it a secret!"

Then Nina understood. Julien had arrived at the office before her and had announced their engagement.

Her first reaction was outrage. How could he have done this to her without so much as a hint of his intentions? She was tempted to jump up onto a chair and shout, "Forget it, everybody! Just a joke. Back to your offices!" Then she saw that Julien's eyes were anxiously fixed on her. Her fury died down a little—to the level of anger and frustration. There was no point in causing a scene in front of the whole office. Both she and Julien had to work with these people, after all. A public argument would only embarrass everyone. The only thing that really mattered right now was getting a few things straight with Julien.

She pasted a smile onto her face and hoped it looked sincere. "Thanks, everybody," she said.

"Hey, Nina," Phil called out, "when're you guys getting married? When's the happy day?"

Getting further away all the time, she thought grimly. She caught Julien's eye and nodded toward her office.

"I'll keep you posted," she replied. "Right now I need a few words with Julien."

With laughter and teasing, the little crowd broke up. As Nina was about to follow Julien into her office, Armand laid a hand on her arm. "I'd like to see you in my office for a few minutes when you're free," he said quietly. Nina nodded. Armand walked off toward his own office, leaving her alone with her fiancé.

She went into her office and closed the door. Julien was lounging in her visitor's chair; she sat behind the desk.

"You look lovely today," he said.

Nina was in no mood to listen to compliments. She stared at him unsmiling and asked, "Just what the hell was that all about?"

Slowly the smile faded from his face. "I don't understand."

"Why did you tell everyone that you and I are engaged?"

He sighed. "I told you yesterday, darling, that we had already agreed to announce our engagement as soon as I returned from Geneva."

"Yes, you told me that. And I told you that things are different now. For God's sake, I have amnesia! You can't expect me to go on as if nothing has happened!"

He stared at her, his expression starkly bereft. "You say that things are different. Does that mean you no longer consider yourself . . . bound to me?"

Nina buried her face in her hands for an instant, trying to frame an answer. "Julien, I don't know what to say. I only know that I feel like you put me on the spot by telling everyone that we're engaged. Don't you see how unfair that was? Remember, as far as I'm concerned I met you for the first time yesterday!"

He was silent for a moment; he walked to her window and stood looking out at the sunny day. When he spoke, his tone was contrite. "You're right, of course. I do see that now. But I thought it would be pleasant for you to have something to celebrate with our friends here. And I thought it would be easier to have our relationship out in the open now. We'll be spending a lot of time together. People might as well get used to it."

Nina sat back in her chair and looked at Julien. He still didn't seem to realize that she wasn't at all sure what their "relationship" amounted to. He was gentle, agreeable—and damned persistent. Every time she carved out a little distance between them, he came right back, pressing against the boundaries she had drawn. He was not an easy man to discourage. For the first time it really sank in: *He's in love with me.*

"Okay, Julien, there's no point in arguing about it now. But just don't do anything else that involves me without talking to me about it first, all right?"

He smiled. "Does that include picking out your engagement ring?"

He can't be serious! Nina decided that the only way to deal with this query was to treat it as a joke. "Oh, I've got that all figured out," she said flippantly. "You can get me a great big emerald."

Julien had been leaning negligently against the window. Now he whirled to face Nina and bent over her chair, placing his hands on the arms and thrusting his face close to hers.

"What did you say?" he demanded.

Nina shrank back a little in the chair. Julien's sudden intensity was startling, as though his usual polite geniality were a mask that had slipped an inch or two.

"You heard me," she said. "I asked for an emerald." She saw that Julien's knuckles were white; he was gripping the arms of her chair almost hard enough to raise bruises. "It was just a joke," she added. "Relax."

He looked at her for a long moment before stepping back and releasing his grip. "Sorry," he said. The intent look was gone and he was smiling sheepishly. "I didn't mean to overreact."

"What got into you?"

"You really don't know?" She shook her head impatiently, and he said, "You caught me off guard when you mentioned an emerald for your engagement ring."

"Why?"

He gave a sad little laugh. "When I asked you to marry me and you said yes, we talked about your ring. You said you'd pick out an emerald on our next buying trip. So when you mentioned an emerald just now, I—well, I thought maybe you remembered that. It would mean so much to me if you remembered something, anything, about us."

"No," she said gently. "I don't remember anything. I'm sorry it upset you. The bit about the emerald was just a joke, because I know that we've been bringing in so many of them lately."

His gaze searched her face. "Yes, I see. Do you know—" he paused, then went on slowly "—when you spoke about a big emerald, I almost thought that..."

"That what?" Nina prompted.

"I don't wish to make you angry, but I wondered if perhaps you had not forgotten as much as you would have me think. If perhaps you were teasing me. Or testing me."

"I don't understand. Do you mean that you think I'm *faking* my amnesia?"

"Well... yes. The thought crossed my mind."

"But why?" Nina exploded. "Why would you think that?"

Julien threw his hands into the air. "I don't know. I'm sorry I mentioned it. But I wondered whether you were afraid of something. Trying to protect yourself, maybe, or keep a secret. It was just a silly idea, you see, but it occurred to me that no one could really know whether you had lost your memory or not."

"You, too, huh?" said Nina.

"I beg your pardon?"

"You're not the first person to have that idea. Mike—Detective Novalis—thought I was faking it, too. He thought I might have something to hide."

"Really?" Julien's tone was casual, but his expression grew thoughtful. "Now I wonder what made him think that?"

"I don't know," Nina declared, "and I don't care. I'm sick of the whole subject, and I'm tired of being under a microscope. Get this straight—I have amnesia. And I also," she added, glancing at the pile of paperwork on her desk, "have work to do. I have to get into the strong room and verify these appraisals."

"Of course," Julien said, rising and going to the door. "Don't forget, I'm a partner. The last thing I want is to interfere with the work of our star gemologist."

But he lingered in the doorway until she looked up.

"Let's have dinner together after work," he urged. "Please. We have so much to talk about."

Nina hesitated.

"Nina, please," he said imploringly, "don't fight me. Just give me a chance to make things right between us again. Don't you think you owe me that much?"

"When you put it that way," Nina said, touched by his earnestness, "I suppose I do."

It was only after he had left that Nina remembered something that had occurred the previous evening while she was writing in her diary, making the list of her visions. Leafing through the book to the first blank page, she'd caught sight of an earlier page and paused for a second, bemused. She had forgotten all about it in the excitement of discovering that she had become psychic—even if only fitfully so. Now, however, it came back to her: the diary page set aside for tomorrow, the day on which Julien had been scheduled to return from Europe. On that page she had written, "Talk to Julien D.?"

What had she been going to discuss with Julien tomorrow? And why was that entry the only mention of her fiancé in the entire diary? Even Armand had rated a few references—

Armand! He wanted to talk to her, and something told Nina that the subject wouldn't be gemstones.

When she entered his office, the big man was examining a small chess set, turning the pieces over in his large, surprisingly delicate fingers, squinting at them under his bright desk lamp. He greeted Nina with a quick smile. "Come and see, *liebchen.*"

Nina gave a soft cry of admiration. The black-and-white chess board was made of alternating squares of onyx and mother-of-pearl, perfectly fitted together inside a border of turquoise and coral mosaic. The pieces were magnificently carved from chunks of light and dark soapstone. The two turbaned kings sat on tiny, regal thrones. The queens reclined on divans. And the knights were mounted on elephants whose ears and trunks seemed to have been captured in midwave.

"It's lovely, Armand," she exclaimed.

"From India. A sample from a workshop there. Not terribly valuable, of course, there are no precious stones. But—" he waved one bearlike paw "—it is beautiful nonetheless. Fine craftsmanship." He heaved a sigh. "It's growing rarer."

"We could sell this and a hundred more like it," Nina said positively.

"Well, maybe. It doesn't fit in with our current inventory. But we'll see. That's not why I asked you to come see me. Please, sit."

Nina took a chair and waited. Armand looked kind but solemn.

"This business with Julien, this betrothal," he began, "came as quite a surprise to me."

"To me, too," said Nina wryly, and Armand smiled.

"I had no idea that you and Julien were...fond of each other," he continued. "To be quite honest, Nina, I always fancied that perhaps you, well, disliked him a little bit. I did not think he was your type."

"I don't even know what my type is," she said, thinking, *Oh, yes, I do. Mike Novalis is just my type.* She focused again on what Armand was saying, trying to banish the thought of Mike.

"Perhaps I shouldn't be telling you this," said Armand, looking worried, "but I feel that you need a friend right now, Nina. And although I know you don't remember me, I assure you that I have always been your friend."

Nina felt a rush of gratitude toward Armand Zakroff. He hadn't questioned her, hadn't doubted her or suspected her of anything fishy; he'd simply accepted the fact that she had lost her memory. And he had tried to help her.

"I'm sure you have, Armand," she said softly, and was touched by the pleasure in his warm brown eyes.

"Then I will tell you this. It is not a secret, exactly—I'm sure it is something that you knew quite well before your accident. It is about Julien. I have known him since he was a boy. He has always been rather high-strung. Excitable. And lately he has been under some strain. The Duchesnes were a wealthy family, but Julien and his sister have lost a considerable sum on the stock market in the past few years."

Armand spread his hands, palms up. "I don't know the details. I don't want to know. But I do know that both Julien and Marta have begun to feel the pinch—I fear that neither of them knows very much about economizing." He looked at Nina and gave a small shrug of his heavy shoulders. "I tell you this not to gossip but because I think you should know how things stand. Julien is experiencing some pressure. I did not want you to blame yourself if he seems moody or unhappy. I hope I have not done the wrong thing."

"Thank you, Armand. You haven't done the wrong thing." Impulsively, Nina crossed the room and gave him a hug. "I appreciate your concern. And to tell you the truth," she continued, feeling that here was someone in whom she could safely confide, "the whole situation with Julien is pretty strange. I don't know if I can explain it—I feel as though I don't know him at all, and at the same time he has so many expectations about me...."

"I think I understand, *liebchen*. I wish I could help you. But I know that you will figure out what is best for you. I will tell you just two things. First, if you ever need a friend, to talk to or for any other reason, come to me or Therese. And second, don't let Julien rush you. He's an impetuous fellow, but you take your time. Be sure of what you are doing. And don't worry," he added, "whatever happens between you and Julien, you need not worry about your position at Zakroff and Duchesne. You see—" he patted his ample stomach— "*I* am the majority partner."

Nina laughed. "That's good to know, Armand. Thank you. And now I'd better get back to work."

She was almost out the door when he called out, "Oh, Nina, one more thing. What have the police found out about the nogoodnik who shot you?"

"It was just a random shooting, Armand. It's unlikely that they'll ever know who did it—it was probably just some drugged-up kids in a car. The police have closed the file on my case."

He gave her a shrewd glance. "And that nice policeman—what was his name?"

"Novalis," said Nina through lips that felt stiff and wooden saying his name.

"That's right. What does the good Detective Novalis think about this?"

"I really don't know. The case is closed, so I haven't talked to him." Fatherly though Armand was, there were some things Nina wasn't ready to discuss even with him.

"I see." Those shrewd eyes were watching her closely, and Nina wondered just how much he *did* see. Did some wistful look appear on her face every time Mike Novalis was mentioned? Could Armand sense how much she felt for Mike—and how hurt she was that he hadn't called her?

Stop being paranoid. Get over this. Nina hurried back to her office and grabbed her bundle of appraisal forms. With any luck they would keep her busy all day long. Too busy to think or feel or hurt. And if she were very, very lucky, she thought, she'd be swamped with work for the next couple of decades.

Mike found that, with a little creative reporting, he was able to juggle his schedule just enough to let him keep a highly unofficial eye on Nina Dennison during the week that followed. He figured that as long as she was in the

Zakroff and Duchesne offices, surrounded by co-workers, she was probably pretty safe; in addition, he knew that somewhere, somehow, Irons and the feds had an eye on Z and D, maybe even an inside informant. The federal interest was an extra layer of protection for Nina, but it also meant that Mike had to steer clear of her while she was on the job. The last thing he needed was to get nailed for trespassing on Irons's turf.

So he did his best to stay on top of his regular caseload by day, and when he left the station house he concentrated on Nina's life outside the office. He followed her at a discreet distance on her way to and from the office, and he staked out her apartment building every night, careful to park in a different, inconspicuous spot each evening. He saw no evidence that Nina was under any surveillance but his own. If there was a federal agent watching her, the agent was damned good. Mike could only hope that his own activities were equally invisible to any other watcher.

Mike's only companion on his lonely nighttime vigils was Sig. He took to bringing the dog with him, partly so he wouldn't have to leave Sig alone in the loft all night as well as all day and partly because the dog was good company in the early-morning hours when Mike found himself alone with his soul. "C'mon, partner," he'd say, and Sig would hop into the back seat of the car, carrying the remains of his chew toy. A couple of times Mike thought about bringing a bottle of vodka for company instead, but he knew that wasn't the answer. He'd tried that once before, in the dark months after Jack Renzo bled to death in his arms, and he knew that after the easy sedation wore off he'd be left with more self-loathing than before. He decided to stick it out with only his dog and his thoughts.

A lot of those thoughts were about Karen Kurtzmann. For the first time in a long while, Mike found himself remembering how it had been with Karen in the early days. He'd been working undercover vice when they met, sporting a long ponytail, designer clothes, a diamond ear-ring—the whole small-time drug dealer look. He had managed to fool most people, but somehow Karen had seen right through his slick cover and recognized him for what he was: an honest cop trying to do his job. She had made him feel proud to be who he was. She had made him want to help her and take care of her—and she had prom-ised to be true to him.

He recalled the excitement of those first few meetings. Everything had to be top secret, of course, to protect Mike's cover. Now he wondered whether maybe the se-crecy and the intrigue had turned him on as much as Karen herself. Oh, she was desirable, no doubt about that, with her long ebony hair and her big soulful eyes. And the lush body that had posed so seductively in a string bikini the first time they met, while she eyed him over the tops of her designer sunglasses. *She read you like a book in that first glance,* Mike told himself now. *And all she had to do was reel you in.*

He was wild for her after their first time together, ready to break any rule, take any risk to be with her. Jack Renzo had loyally covered for him. But he'd also given Mike hell, warning him not to get emotionally involved with Karen. "Don't cross the line with this one, buddy," he'd said. "Don't let her get her hooks into you. She'll tear you apart." But Mike had been so sure that he could handle it. What he had with Karen was so good—how could it hurt him? Looking back, he realized that he'd been completely out of control, running on adrenaline and plain old-fashioned lust, throughout their short-lived relationship. And in the end Jack had been right.

"Good old Jack was no fool," Mike said aloud in his car. Sig looked up alertly. Mike patted the dog and then realized that for once he'd been able to think of Jack Renzo without rage and self-hatred. He felt loss, sadness, regret—but he could live with those feelings. He didn't know what had caused the change, but he was grateful for it.

The night work took its toll, of course. Mike snatched sleep in small doses, a few minutes at a time behind the wheel of his car, an hour or two in the morning or late afternoon while Nina was at work. His haggard appearance and irregular hours didn't go unnoticed. On Wednesday, Morris Hecht pulled him aside and gave him the once-over.

"You look like hell, Novalis."

"You're looking great, too, Chief."

"Never mind the wisecracks. What's going on?"

"What d'you mean?"

"I mean you look like you haven't slept in days, and you've got three case reports a week overdue."

Mike struggled to stifle a yawn. He didn't completely succeed. Hecht's eyes narrowed. "Look, Mike, you're running yourself ragged. Maybe it's none of my business, but it looks to me like whatever you're doing at night, it isn't sleeping."

Mike nodded. "You're right." Then, when Hecht looked at him expectantly, he explained, "It's none of your business."

Hecht sighed and expelled a cloud of cigar smoke; Mike stepped back a pace.

"Yeah, yeah," growled Hecht, and made a token gesture toward waving the smoke away. "Listen, Novalis, stay on the job. Try to show up for a morning briefing session once in a while." Mike nodded, and Hecht stumped off toward his office.

"And," the chief called as Mike walked away, "I don't care who you're doing the horizontal tango with, but it better not be that Dennison dame."

Mike kept walking, willing himself not to stiffen or break stride. Hecht was a wily one; Mike hoped that his remark was just a wild guess.

Four days later, Mike was almost ready to give it up. He'd seen nothing to indicate that Nina was up to anything surreptitious, or that she was in any danger: no suspicious characters following her or lurking around her building, no mysterious midnight errands or furtive visitors. And he had seen all he ever wanted to see of Julien Duchesne and of the woman he had IDed as Duchesne's sister, Marta.

Day or night, it seemed that the Duchesne siblings couldn't get enough of Nina Dennison's company. Julien took her to dinner several times; Marta took her on a shopping trip; the three of them went to a movie together. On nights when Nina didn't go out with them, one or both of them dropped by her apartment. He wondered how Nina could stand the constant attention.

Most galling of all were Julien's visits. Mike could just about stand to see Nina and Julien Duchesne together in a public place, a street or a restaurant. But the sight of Julien trotting eagerly up Nina's steps made Mike's hackles rise. Something about the guy bugged Mike: Julien was too attentive, too pushy. Mike kept telling himself that there was more to it than simple jealousy, although the thought of Julien and Nina together in her apartment, behind drawn blinds, was almost more than he could stand. His only consolation was the fact that Julien never spent the night at Nina's; he never stayed later than eleven o'clock, and most evenings he left earlier than that. And when Mike tailed Julien and Nina, he saw no sign of physical intimacy. She never took Julien's hand or slipped her arm around his waist. Julien's attitude toward her appeared unfailingly courtly and affectionate, but her body language showed stiffness and constraint. Mike took some comfort from that.

He still couldn't explain exactly why he was watching Nina. Sometimes he thought he had simply lost it over a woman once again. At other times his police instincts kicked in, telling him that something was going on. There were just too many things that didn't fit—little things, but they added up to enough to make Mike uneasy. Why wasn't Julien's number listed on the Important Numbers page of Nina's address book, if they were engaged? Why didn't she have any pictures of him in her purse or apartment? And even if Nina had wanted to keep her relationship with Julien a secret from their co-workers at Z and D, why didn't Danielle or any of her other friends outside work know about it?

Mike knew that he didn't have much of a reputation left, but he was willing to stake what was left of it on one thing: Nina Dennison had never agreed to marry Julien Duchesne. But he had no proof, nothing that he could take to Hecht or Irons, or even to Nina. They would say that he was accusing Duchesne out of jealousy—and maybe they'd be right.

Hell, maybe Duchesne was just a lovesick idiot who had gotten nowhere with Nina before her accident and now was using her amnesia to try to worm his way into her affections—a slimeball stunt, but Mike didn't know what he could do about it. There was another possibility, too, one that he shied away from thinking about. Nina could be running some deep game of her own, playing both him and Duchesne for suckers. Each time that thought occurred to him, he'd remember the way Nina had surrendered herself so trustingly to him, and he'd be ashamed of his suspicions, knowing that Nina was innocent. And then he'd be assailed by insidious memories: *You were sure about Karen, too.*

Mike didn't trust his feelings, and he didn't trust his instincts. Still, he hung on through a long week and most of the weekend. A hundred times he'd thought of calling Nina, but each time he was stopped by the memory of her stricken expression when Julien had burst into her apartment. If she'd only come to him then, if she'd spoken to him or made some gesture, Mike might have been able to believe that he meant something to her. But Julien had practically ordered him out of the apartment, and Nina had let him go. And now pride kept him from reaching out to her. Once before, a woman had cost him his self-respect and made a fool of him. He couldn't take a chance on that happening again, even though every glimpse and thought of Nina filled him with a longing unlike anything he'd ever known. *You've gotten through worse things,* he told himself. *You'll ride this out.* But in his heart he doubted if he'd ever stop wanting her. And wanting to believe in her.

The week seemed years long to Nina.

Work wasn't bad at all. She didn't have much trouble picking up the strings of her job at Z and D. Everyone from Armand Zakroff to Debbie was more than helpful, filling her in on the details of office routine and answering her questions. To her relief, she'd found that her professional knowledge was intact. She'd been afraid that her amnesia would impair her ability to do her job, but after a week at Z and D she felt confident that she wasn't going to be a liability to the firm. The only real surprise was learning that she and Julien were scheduled to go on another buying trip to Colombia the following Monday afternoon. Plans for the trip had been made weeks ago.

"You don't have to go, you know," Armand told her on Friday afternoon. "It's so soon after your injury. Perhaps you'd rather pass up this trip."

"But it's a major gem auction," Nina objected. "If I don't go, we won't have another chance to pick up good-quality uncut emeralds for months."

"Julien can handle it alone."

"Come on, Armand, I'm a much better spotter than Julien, and you know it." Nina had discovered that she did indeed have "the eye," as Armand called it. She read gems easily, seeing their weaknesses and strengths; to her, each stone was as distinctive and individual as an old friend.

"Julien will spend more and come back with less," she continued. "Don't worry, I'm up to making the trip. In fact, I'm looking forward to it."

Nina was telling the truth; she was excited about the trip. Using her skill exhilarated and empowered her. It felt good to have *something* in her life that wasn't confused, uncertain or mysterious. And she was eager to repay the trust and confidence that Armand had shown by doing an outstanding job for him at the auction.

"And being with Julien—?" Armand asked delicately.

"It will be fine," Nina assured him. Privately, however, she wasn't quite so sure.

She would have been happier to have a break from Julien's company. He seemed to have been constantly at her side, all week long. At work he kept popping into her office unannounced until she suggested, only half-jokingly, that he should start making appointments with Debbie if he wanted to see her. He cajoled her into having lunch with him every day; three times he surprised her with restaurant reservations for dinner.

"It's too much," she told him when he brought her home after dinner Saturday night. "I feel like you're crowding me."

"I'm sorry," he said. "I know it's foolish of me, but after what has happened, I can't help worrying about you. I want to take care of you, to be there for you if you need me."

"That's sweet, but—"

"There's more, you know." He touched her face, lightly. She stiffened and turned her head; Julien dropped his hand and sighed. "I've lost so much," he said in a low voice. "It hurts me to be a stranger to you. It's hard to be like this, when what I want is to make love with you, to have things be the way they were...."

Nina tried to imagine herself with Julien. Undoubtedly he was attractive, with his clear gray eyes, his perfect features, his long lean body. Yet she felt no desire for him, and no true affection. Only pity, and a sense of obligation that was growing increasingly burdensome.

"Julien," she said as gently as she could, "perhaps that will never happen."

"Don't say that!" He turned her face to his and kissed her. Nina didn't resist, but she didn't respond. The kiss was expert and assured, but his lips felt alien on hers; the pressure of his body against hers aroused nothing but a feeling of distaste. Finally he let her go and looked at her, breathing hard.

"You've made up your mind, haven't you?" His voice held anger, and something else, as well—regret, Nina thought.

All at once she was sure. "Yes, I have. Julien, I'm sorry, but I don't believe we'll ever regain the feelings we must have shared before I was shot. I can't be engaged to you now. You'll have to consider our relationship over."

His face was pale except for the two spots of color that burned on his cheekbones. "I can't do that!" he burst out.

"Julien, it's over. I've tried to be as fair to you as I can be, but there's just nothing there. I don't want to hurt you, but I won't pretend to feel something that I don't feel. And now I think you'd better go."

He took a deep breath. "We'll talk about this later."

"There isn't any more to talk about. I'm terribly sorry, Julien, truly I am. But if you do care about me, you'll see that I need to take care of myself now."

"This is about that cop, isn't it?"

"No, it isn't." Nina marveled at how level and unemotional her voice sounded. Not a trace of pain or hurt pride. She wasn't about to reveal to Julien that she hadn't heard from Mike in the week since they'd slept together. "It's about you and me. I'm not in love with you. I'm not going to be in love with you. Please accept that."

"I see." He crossed to the door with quick steps. "I suppose the appropriate sentiment is, 'We can still be friends,'" he said, making an effort to smile.

"I hope we can be," Nina said softly.

"Of course. And please, Nina, don't worry about us working together. There will be some awkward moments, I'm sure, but I'll try not to make you uncomfortable."

"Thank you, Julien. You really have been a gentleman about this."

"I try to be," he said with a crooked smile. Then he bowed and left.

Nina woke on Sunday feeling as if a weight had been lifted from her shoulders. For a week she'd tried to be fair to Julien Duchesne; she'd wrestled with her sense of obligation. She'd even felt guilty for betraying him with Mike, although she knew that the guilt was totally unfounded— she'd had no way of knowing she was promised to Julien when she fell in love with Mike.

Suddenly Nina realized just what she was thinking. Was she really in love with Mike Novalis? She knew that the answer was "yes." But she had no idea what to do about it—

The phone shrilled, cutting into her thoughts, and she ran for it. She was sure that it was Mike; she'd been thinking of him, she was finally free of Julien.... She picked up the phone and breathlessly said, "Hello."

"Nina, I have the most wonderful idea," Marta said. "I'll pick you up this afternoon and we'll work out at the gym, and then we'll have supper together, just us girls. And I have a surprise for you."

Nina nearly said no. She'd been looking forward to spending the day alone, catching up on her diary or maybe taking a long walk. But just because she had ended her engagement to Julien didn't mean that her friendship with Marta was at an end. During the past week Nina had genuinely enjoyed Marta's company. Perhaps Marta was a bit superficial and materialistic, but she was also cheerful, warm and supportive—easy to be around. Nina agreed to join her for a workout and supper.

While they were on their way to Marta's apartment to change their clothes after working out, Nina said, "I suppose you know what happened last night with Julien."

Marta shot her a sympathetic look. "Yes, he called me. He feels terrible, of course. And I'm sorry, too—I was so happy to think that my brother and my best friend were to be married. But don't worry—" she patted Nina's hand "—if you didn't feel good about being engaged to Julien, then you were right to break it off. I understand, believe me. This won't affect our friendship. And Julien will be all right, I'm sure of it."

Then Marta sprang her surprise. She had decided to accompany Julien and Nina to Colombia. "I thought it might ease the tension between you two if I came along," she said, adding with a laugh, "Besides, I could use a few days in a hot climate to work on my tan."

Nina realized that her first trip with Julien *would* be made a lot easier by the presence of a third party. "That's great!" she said. "I'm glad you're coming."

Marta smiled at her. "Oh, we'll have fun."

It was only after Nina stepped into Marta's bathroom to take a quick shower that she began to regret accepting Marta's invitation. Working out at the gym had been fun, but . . . she had spent so much time with the Duchesnes in the past week. She really needed a solitary evening before the trip to Colombia, which was bound to be hectic. Surely Marta wouldn't mind if she canceled their plans for dinner.

She stepped out of the bathroom and heard Marta talking in low tones. There was a hard, urgent note in her voice that Nina hadn't noticed before.

"Here or there, it doesn't matter where," Marta was saying. She was speaking into the telephone, her back to

Nina. "I tell you it's the only way to be sure. Yes, we'll take care of it. In fact, Julien may already have done it." She glanced up and saw Nina standing in the doorway. "Look, I have to go now, I have a guest," she said. "Yes, I'll let you know. Goodbye."

Marta hung up the phone and made a gesture of annoyance. "Sorry about that," she said. "Some trouble with our stockbroker."

"I see," said Nina, who didn't. She had no desire to pry into the Duchesnes' financial affairs. "Marta, I'm sorry, but I think I have to take a rain check on dinner. I just need an evening to myself."

Marta laughed. "I suppose we Duchesnes *can* be rather overwhelming," she admitted. "You've had a long week, I know. No problem. I'll run you home."

"Don't bother, I'll grab a cab. And, Marta, thanks for the rain check. I've got some things to do tonight. For one thing, I have to pack for Colombia."

"Don't forget to take that nice green raincoat," Marta advised. "The rainy season is about to start down there."

"I appreciate the tip. See you tomorrow."

"Tomorrow afternoon, at the airport," Marta called out gaily.

The first thing Nina did when she reached her apartment was check her answering machine. Nothing.

She packed quickly and efficiently. One business suit, two blouses. One pair of slacks and two of her most colorful T-shirts. Jeans, sneakers and a light jacket—Julien had said that they might have to make a visit to one of the mines. She took her trench coat from the closet and draped it over the suitcase. There. Now she was ready for the trip. It had only taken her fifteen minutes to pack. The empty evening stretched out in front of her. What next?

There was really only one thing she wanted to do. She had hoped for a week that Mike would call or come to see her. Oh, she had kept busy with Julien and his sister, but maybe, she now admitted to herself, she had let herself be persuaded to spend so much time with them because it was easier than facing up to the loneliness she felt without Mike.

She couldn't accept that things were over between them, that Mike could simply walk away from her without a backward glance. True, they had only spent one night together. She had taken him into her bed willingly and without conditions. He owed her nothing.

Then the demons of doubt began whispering: *What makes you think it was so special for him? Maybe it was just a fling, a casual release of tension. There's no reason to believe that he cares for you.*

Yet even when she was shaken by doubts, Nina couldn't help remembering the look in Mike's eyes when she reached out and touched his face. It was the look of a man who'd seen a revelation he hadn't dared to hope for. She remembered the tremor in his voice when he said, "Nina, I want you," the way he called her name as he climaxed inside her—she remembered everything, and she ached with the need to experience it again. Most of all she remembered the way he had cradled her in his arms afterward, murmuring to her and touching her gently, as though he could scarcely believe that she was real.

I'm not sure of much anymore, said Nina to herself. *But, amnesia or not, I know one thing. That night meant something to Mike.* Then why was he keeping his distance from her? Maybe if he knew that she had ended her engagement to Julien—? She dismissed that idea at once. She couldn't go to him and say, "I'm free now," as if she expected him to step in and fill the vacancy. She had too much dignity for that. And she thought better of Mike. If he had wanted to see her, he wouldn't have held back out of some men's-club notion that she was Julien's property. He would have come to her and said whatever he had to say.

That left only two alternatives. Maybe Mike still didn't trust her. Perhaps he still suspected her of scamming him about the amnesia or being involved in something crooked. Or maybe something inside him was holding him back; maybe he couldn't or wouldn't let himself act on his feelings. Nina didn't know which of those two possibilities she feared more. Either way, the outlook wasn't good.

All week she had hoped for another of those mysterious psychic flashes, some image that would make her believe that she'd see Mike again. Yet she had seen nothing. The visions were beyond her power to summon. If the inexplicable phenomenon were linked to her injury, as she suspected, perhaps it was fading as time passed. Yet something troubled her slightly: If the visions *were* glimpses of the future rather than memories of the past, why had she seen two visions of Julien aboard his boat? Given the break-up of their engagement, she didn't think she was likely to go sailing with him in the future. Perhaps not all of the visions were destined to come true. Or maybe the glimpses she'd had of Julien were connected with some future Z and D party aboard his boat. They weren't really important right now. What was important was Mike Novalis and what she was going to do about him.

She couldn't be sure of Mike's feelings for her—but she couldn't deny the strength of hers for him. She felt empty and incomplete without him. Was this love? She didn't know, but she had to have the chance to find out. Maybe she'd never thought that love could happen so swiftly, that life's deepest passion could bloom in just a few short days. But a lot of surprising things had happened to her lately. If she'd learned one thing, it was to expect the unexpected.

A voice in her mind was telling her to play it safe, to be careful. *You can't be sure of this,* warned the voice. *Wait until you get your memory back.* She knew that that voice came from the cautious, timid part of Nina Dennison—the part that had decorated her tasteful but bland apartment and chosen her beige wardrobe and steered clear of emotional entanglements. But there was another part of her, born when she woke up in a hospital bed without a past. The injury that had cut her off from her memories had also cut her off from her fears and inhibitions. There was a part of her now that believed in facing things head-on and in taking chances, a part of her that wasn't afraid to reach out for what she wanted. That part of her was still new and inexperienced. But it was growing stronger all the time.

Nina came to a decision. She would be flying back from Colombia in a few days. As soon as she returned she would call Mike Novalis. That would give her time to decide what she wanted to say. She had no idea how he would respond to her, but at least she would know that she had tried.

Nina's mood brightened. She had a plan. She felt suddenly hopeful and energetic. Her apartment seemed sterile and boring. Outside, the late-afternoon sunlight had faded. Lights had begun twinkling in the autumnal twilight, and the evening air seemed full of promise. Nina decided to go for a drive.

By Sunday afternoon Mike was almost ready to pull the plug on Operation Dennison. It had become well-nigh impossible to justify his stakeout of Nina as anything remotely resembling police work. With no evidence of any crime, he was starting to feel more than a little like a Peeping Tom.

Nina was in her apartment. *I'll hang around until dark,* he decided, *and then I'll go home. And stay there.* Just then Marta's red Jag pulled up, and a few moments later Nina came downstairs carrying a gym bag and climbed into Marta's car.

Oh, what the hell, Mike thought, and after allowing several other cars to come between the Jag and the Grand Am he pulled away from the curb to follow them. But as he was turning the corner a familiar flash of silver in the rearview mirror caught his eye. It was Julien Duchesne's Mercedes, swinging onto Nina's block. Mike grinned. Julien had just missed Nina. Or maybe, he thought suddenly, Julien had waited until she was gone to show up.

Mike made a split-second decision and gave up on the women. He knew where they were going, anyway; he'd tailed them to Marta's gym twice during the week. He drove his car into the first driveway he came to, hoping the occupants of the house weren't home. It would be hard to stay inconspicuous if they came bustling out indignantly to chase him away.

Luck was with him. Nobody rousted him from the driveway, and through the shifting leaves of a ginkgo tree he could see Nina's building. Duchesne's car pulled into Nina's lot and was hidden from his view by the corner of her building.

Mike waited for Duchesne to appear at Nina's front door. Five minutes later he was still waiting. He rummaged in his overcrowded glove compartment and found a pair of sunglasses and an old baseball cap with a green bottle and the words Grab a Heinie stenciled on it. Not much style, but it might keep Duchesne from recognizing him.

He drove slowly past Nina's address, scanning her parking lot. Duchesne's car was there, and behind it Mike could see a bit of the rear bumper of Nina's brown car. Otherwise the lot was empty; Nina's fellow tenants were probably all out enjoying the Indian summer afternoon. Julien Duchesne was nowhere in sight. Mike slowed to a crawl, but then a honk from the irate motorist behind him forced him to speed up; he didn't want to risk attracting Duchesne's attention by provoking another blast of the horn. He circled around as quickly as he could, cursing the one-way streets that made him go two blocks out of his way, and passed Nina's building again. No sign of Duchesne, although his car was still there, blocking the entrance to the parking lot.

On Mike's third circuit of Nina's block, Julien Duchesne popped into view like a jack-in-the-box. It looked as if he'd been kneeling between his car and Nina's. Fixing a tire, maybe. Once again, traffic forced Mike to keep moving, and by the time he had come around again both Julien and his car were gone. *He rang Nina's buzzer, decided she's not home and took off*, Mike reasoned. *Big deal. Still...I guess I'll hang around a little while longer. Maybe he'll come back.*

With apologies to Sig for postponing that long run in the park one more time, Mike found a parking space, tilted his cap to keep the afternoon sun out of his eyes and settled in to wait until Nina came home.

An hour or so later she came home in a cab—for once without either of the Duchesnes shepherding her along. Intrigued, Mike watched her apartment, fighting his desire to ring her doorbell. *You've been through all that*, he told himself sternly. *She doesn't need you complicating her life. And you sure as hell don't need her complicating yours*. So he merely waited and watched, half expecting Julien and Marta Duchesne, Nina's ever-present shadows, to appear any minute.

Instead, just as darkness was falling, Nina came through her front door and ran lightly down the steps. Mike caught his breath; she looked so fresh and lovely. Her step was buoyant, and she was smiling. Mike would have given anything to have her run to him with that smile.

She got into her car and drove off. Mike slipped into traffic and followed, several cars behind hers. She drove around her neighborhood for a few minutes, past a little park, up and down the narrow streets. She even drove past her own house before heading toward the waterfront.

Mike whistled tunelessly and drummed his fingers on his steering wheel. If this had been an ordinary stakeout, he'd be convinced that the subject was trying to see if she were being tailed. Nina's circling and backtracking maneuvers were the classic tactic for flushing a surveillance car into the open. But Nina wasn't a pro. Or was she? Did she have something to hide? Mike was pretty sure that she hadn't spotted him; he'd stayed well back from her car, keeping the Grand Am out of her field of vision as much as possible.

Now she was on Delaware Avenue, heading north, picking up speed as she merged with the heavier traffic. *Where is she going?* At Callowhill Street she steered the car onto a long, curving exit ramp that would take her right into the heart of the deserted warehouse district. In fact, Mike realized, she was headed for the very same part of town where the shooting had occurred. *What the hell is she doing?* He had a bad feeling that Nina was headed into trouble. Maybe she was going to pick up a drug drop; maybe her errand had something to do with the FBI's smuggling case. Whatever it was, Mike didn't want Nina mixed up in it. The last time she was here, she'd nearly been killed—

Nina's BMW had pulled ahead of him and was far down the ramp, approaching the turn onto Callowhill. He stepped on the gas.

Nina hadn't really had a destination in mind. At first she'd thought about driving past the art museum and along East River Drive. But she'd turned around after a block or so, realizing that the scenic drive wouldn't be very scenic this late in the day. She'd almost gone home, but at the last minute she'd driven to the waterfront instead. She'd cruised past the place where she'd parked with Mike on that first day. She could so easily imagine him sitting there next to her, solid and reassuring—

"Plans are made to be changed, right?" Nina said aloud. She gunned the car and pulled onto Delaware Avenue, headed north toward the factory district.

It wasn't until she was headed down the exit ramp that Nina realized that something was wrong. She had her foot on the brake, but the car wasn't slowing. Frantically she pumped the brake, but the heavy sports car didn't slow down. Instead, thanks to the steep incline of the ramp, it was picking up speed. She held down the horn, but she was already too close to the intersection for the traffic there to get out of her way. So Nina did the only thing she could think of. She swerved toward the grass verge of the ramp and yanked on her emergency brake.

The car bumped over the edge of the roadway and then skidded wildly on the steep, slippery grass slope of the verge. She was sliding downhill now, almost sideways, praying that the car would come to a stop before it reached the row of trees at the bottom of the hill. Suddenly a tree trunk loomed up right in front of her, pale and ghostly in the jouncing beams of her headlights. Nina jerked on the wheel, but the car crashed into the tree with the grinding scream of tearing metal. Nina was jolted forward; she slumped over the wheel and was not even aware that the car had finally come to a halt.

Chapter 8

Mike saw the sports car's brake lights go on and knew right away that something was wrong; Nina's car was picking up speed as it bore down on the crowded Callowhill Street intersection. He gunned his own engine. The foot of the ramp was blocked with cars stalled in slow traffic. *Turn, baby,* Mike prayed, *don't run the intersection.* As soon as her car left the ramp he slammed on his own brakes. He was out of his car before it had stopped moving, running as fast as he could in the wake of Nina's runaway car. It careened down the slope, leaving a swath of chewed-up turf behind it.

He didn't just hear the crash when Nina's car hit the tree; he felt the impact through the soles of his feet. A few seconds later he was at her door. She was bent over the steering wheel—damn it, why hadn't her air bag inflated? But she was moving, shaking her head groggily. Mike dared to hope that she was all right. Then he smelled something that sent fear racing along his nerves: the sharp tang of gasoline and the burn of hot metal.

He tugged at her door handle; it wouldn't open. Of course not. Nina was a careful driver who always locked all the doors in the car. In a frenzy he pounded on the window, shouting, "Nina! Open up! Open your door!"

She gazed at him blankly. Clearly she was still stunned from the crash. With no time to waste, Mike drew his gun, stepped back and fired a round through Nina's left rear window. There was no danger that he might hit her, but he knew that the shot would be as concussive as a blow at such close range. The window shattered into a million rounded pellets, and Mike reached in, stretched his arm past Nina and flipped the door-lock switch to the open position. He opened her door from outside, yanked her out—praying that he wasn't hurting her by moving her so roughly—and wrapped one arm around her, tucking her head into his shoulder. "Now run, damn it!" he yelled, and pulled her with him as fast as he could move, straight away from the car.

They'd covered about thirty yards when the car blew. There was a great whomping roar behind them, and a hot blast wave blew them off their feet. Mike rolled on top of Nina and covered her head with his chest and arms. After a few excruciating seconds the worst of the heat had passed; Mike pulled Nina to her feet and dragged her along for another couple dozen yards. As soon as he felt he could breathe without scorching his lungs, he let her collapse to the ground and sank down beside her. Without stopping to think about it he took her in his arms and held her close.

"Nina," he murmured into her hair, "talk to me, honey. Tell me you're all right. Please be all right."

She stirred in his arms and then turned her smudged, wide-eyed face up to his. "Mike?" she said incredulously. "Is it really you?"

She touched him as though she thought she were dreaming, and then her arms twined around his neck and all he could think of was that she was still alive and she was

holding him. He kissed her. It was a hard, exultant kiss—
a survivors' kiss, snatched like a trophy out of the hand of
death. He felt her yield to him, but when her lips parted
under his he forced himself to break away. If the kiss had
gone on any longer, he'd have been making love to her
right here on Callowhill Street, under the eyes of the excited crowd that had gathered to gape at the wreck.

Nina was looking at him, and he saw the confusion clear
from her eyes.

"Are you hurt?" he demanded.

"I—I don't think so."

He moved her arms and legs and looked her over for
contusions. Remarkably, she seemed to have come through
the accident unscathed. Except maybe for concussion.

"Did you lose consciousness?"

"No, I remember everything. I think I just got shaken
up." She climbed unsteadily to her feet. "Oh, my God,
look!"

Her car was blazing like a Yule log.

"What happened?" Nina asked.

"I don't know. It looked to me like your brakes failed."
Mike heard sirens. "The cops are on the way. They'll do
some tests on the car, see if they can find out what went
wrong."

"I could have been killed. You got me out of the car—I
remember that now." Then she looked around, puzzled,
as if the setting and the sequence of events were only just
now falling into place. "But what were you doing here?"

"I was following you," Mike told her.

"Following *me?* But why?"

Mike had tried for a week to answer that question, and
he hadn't come up with the right answer yet. *Because I
think I might be in love with you and I'm worried about
you and jealous as hell? Because I'm afraid you're up to
something and I want to know what?* So instead of answering her question he countered with one of his own.

Police cars and an ambulance were screeching to a stop, and he figured he had about thirty seconds or so to interrogate her. Then he'd better fade into the background and let the officers on duty take over.

"Nina, tell me something. What were you doing here? Where were you going?"

Her face flushed and she looked away from his gaze. He gripped her arms and shook her gently. "Look at me. Damn it, this is important! Right now you're one block from where you were shot. I need to know why you came back here."

She looked at him then, outraged and accusing. "You think this had something to do with the shooting, don't you? You still think I'm up to something illegal, and you were hoping to catch me in the act." She didn't shout. She didn't have to; her voice was low and tight with fury. "Well, Novalis, you can go to hell. I don't have to answer your questions. Just leave me alone."

By now the paramedics and police were swarming over the scene, and Nina was swallowed up in the bustle. With a final scornful look over her shoulder at Mike, she submitted to being looked over by a medical technician.

Mike walked over to where the combined police-fire unit was hosing the bonfire that was Nina's car with foam.

"You a witness?" asked one of the officers.

"Yeah," said Mike, and showed the guy his badge.

"What d'you figure happened, Lieutenant? Think she just lost control?"

"No, I saw her brake lights go on. I think the brakes failed. You're towing this wreck to the police garage, right?"

"Sure. Standard procedure in a total flameout like this. One of our mechanics'll look it over, make a report and then release it to her insurance company."

"Do me a favor. Keep my name off your report, will you? I'm here strictly unofficially."

The cop gave Mike a quizzical look, but like all good city cops he knew when to keep his mouth shut. "Sure thing. Never saw you." He closed his notebook.

"Thanks." Mike hung around for a little longer on the fringes of the crowd. He saw that Nina was engaged in a spirited argument with the medical technician, and a moment later he drew one of the paramedics out of the crowd, flashed his badge and said, "What's up with the victim?"

The young man shrugged. "We keep telling her that she has to go to the hospital, and she keeps saying that she's fine. She knows her rights, and we can't make her go. Says she just wants to go home."

"You think she's really all right?"

The paramedic grinned. "Yeah, she's okay. She's one lucky lady."

"And pretty stubborn, too. Take my advice—just give up and let her go home."

"I guess we will."

Mike nodded and melted into the night. He'd have liked to take Nina home himself, but he figured that right now she was too mad at him to get into his car. At least he knew that she hadn't been hurt in the crash, and that nothing could happen to her now in the middle of a crowd of cops. Besides, he had a job to do.

It wasn't easy tracking down an off-duty mechanic on Sunday night, but finally Mike traced Gina Donnelly to her sister's house in New Jersey. Gina was a damned good mechanic who worked full-time in the police garage. She was also one of the few friends Mike still had around the force; she had grown up in Jack Renzo's old neighborhood and gone to school with his sisters, and unlike some of Jack's buddies, she had never blamed him for what had happened to Jack.

"This better be good, Novalis," she said when she finally came to the phone. "You're interrupting my niece's confirmation party."

"I'm sorry," he said, "and apologize to your niece for me, too. But it's important, Gina. I need a favor."

"Don't tell me that rusted-out piece of junk you drive finally broke down on you? Nah, you wouldn't call me on a Sunday night about that. What's up?"

"I want you to get to work early tomorrow. Real early."

Gina groaned.

"There'll be a burned-out car in the garage—what's left of a late-model brown BMW. The accident happened about an hour ago. The driver lost control and hit a tree. She claims she hit the brakes but nothing happened."

"So? What do you want from me?"

"I need your opinion about what might have caused the accident. Did the brakes fail? If so, why? And her air bag didn't inflate. Why?"

"You don't want much, do you?" Gina asked dryly.

"There's one other thing. This isn't my case. So get in early and check the car out, and let me know what you find out, but keep it quiet. I'll call you at the garage at seven."

"What?"

"I wouldn't ask if it weren't important, Gina, you know that."

"Yeah, all right. You'll tell me what this is all about sometime?"

"Sure." *If I ever figure it out.*

"Okay. Seven." Before he could thank her, she hung up.

Mike's phone rang at 6:50 the next morning.

He picked it up and asked, "That you, Gina?"

"Yeah. I did what you asked and gave that wreck a going-over. What's left of it, that is."

"What've you got for me?"

"You know, Mike, after a car's been flamed, there's not a lot of hard evidence left. I can tell you this much—the accident was definitely caused by brake failure."

"And what caused the brake failure?"

"I know what you're getting at, but I can't help you. The brake fluid lines *could* have been cut. Or maybe not. At this point there's no way to tell. Sometimes brakes do just go out."

"Yeah. And sometimes pigs do fly. What about the air bag?"

"Same story. Could have been tampered with, could have been a mechanical failure."

"That and the brakes together? That's a hell of a coincidence. If you had to call it—"

"Off the record," Gina said, "I'd say someone tinkered with the car to cause the accident. But there's absolutely no way to prove it."

"I don't need proof. I know who did it." Mike was startled by the quiet menace in his voice.

"One more thing," Gina said quickly. "There's a bullet embedded in the back seat—"

"Oh," said Mike, "that was me."

"I don't even want to know," said Gina, and hung up.

Mike reached Julien Duchesne's apartment building ten minutes later. He figured Duchesne wouldn't have left for work yet, and he was right. Duchesne, clad in a mulberry-colored silk dressing gown, opened the door a few inches, leaving the chain secured.

Mike showed his badge and said, "I'd like a few words with you."

"In reference to—?"

In reference to my kicking your teeth in, you slimy bastard. "In reference to Nina Dennison."

Julien's brows rose. "My dear Officer, er, Novalis, I don't see what you and I have to say about Miss Dennison. Is this an official inquiry?"

"I'm concerned about her safety," Mike said. "As her fiancé, I assume you're concerned, too."

Something flickered in Julien's eyes then; it was a look almost of triumph, as if Julien knew something that Mike didn't. But when he spoke his tone was polite and exaggeratedly patient. "Is there some reason I should be concerned?"

"I assume you know that Miss Dennison was in an automobile accident last night."

Duchesne gasped. "Is she . . . is she all right? What happened?"

"You didn't know?"

"No. I spent the evening here alone. I had a headache and took my telephone off the hook. Tell me, what happened to Nina?"

"Nothing happened. She wasn't hurt." Duchesne grinned nervously; Mike supposed that the grin might have been one of relief, but he didn't think that it was.

"Thank God," said Duchesne fervently. "If you'll excuse me, I must go to her."

"Just a minute," Mike said, and he shoved his foot into the door so that Duchesne couldn't close it. "Don't you want to know how the accident happened?"

"Whatever I need to know I'll hear from Nina," Duchesne said coldly. "Now please remove your foot."

"I'll tell you how the accident happened," Mike went on as if Duchesne hadn't spoken. "It happened because some scumbag sliced the brake fluid line on her car. And just for insurance he jimmied her air bag. Now, Duchesne, do you want to tell me what you were doing to Nina Dennison's car at three o'clock yesterday afternoon?"

Julien stared at Mike, and the blood drained from his face. "Are you accusing me— You're crazy! I don't have to talk to you."

"I want some answers, Duchesne. Why'd you rig Nina's car? Was it you who shot her?"

"You're insane," Duchesne said, "and I'm not listening to another word unless you have a warrant."

"I don't need a warrant to tell you this, Duchesne. If anything happens to Nina Dennison, *anything*, I'll be back. And your door won't be the only thing I kick in." Mike gave Duchesne's door a single powerful kick. The chain broke and the door flew wide open.

Julien sprang back. "Get out! Get out of here right now!"

"Don't forget what I said," Mike told him, and left.

"I'll have you kicked off the force for this!" Julien screamed after him before slamming the door and locking it.

Just as he expected, Mike didn't have to wait long. The summons to Hecht's office came before ten o'clock.

Entering the chief's office, Mike had a feeling of déjà vu so strong that he almost laughed. Hecht was there, and so was Irons, dressed in the same gray suit—or one just like it. Hecht was frowning and chewing the soggy end of an unlit cigar. Mike was impressed; Irons must have ordered Hecht not to light up, and Mike knew that Hecht wouldn't have enjoyed taking orders in his own office.

"Novalis, what in God's name do you think—" began Hecht, but Irons held up a hand.

"I'll handle this," he said in his precise, clipped voice.

Irons looked to Mike to be more curious than angry. "Detective Novalis, I'd like you to explain to me just what took place at Julien Duchesne's apartment this morning."

Mike told the truth: He had gone to Duchesne's apartment to shake the man up and, he hoped, scare him away from making any further attempts on Nina Dennison's life. He explained that he'd seen Julien near Nina's car and that he'd been following her when her brakes failed.

"Are you aware, Detective Novalis, that the police mechanics found no evidence that Miss Dennison's car was sabotaged?"

Mike wasn't about to drag Gina Donnelly down with him. All he said was, "It doesn't surprise me. That kind of sabotage is almost impossible to prove, if it's done right."

"And you believe that Julien Duchesne was responsible."

"Yes."

"Then it may interest you to know, Detective Novalis, that Julien Duchesne is working with me."

"He's FBI?" Mike said disbelievingly.

"No, he's a civilian. But he's cooperating with our investigation of Zakroff and Duchesne. He's our man on the inside. This is completely confidential information, Novalis, and I wouldn't be telling you anything if I weren't afraid that you might somehow manage to screw things up worse than you already have."

"You checked Duchesne out?"

"Of course. His record's completely clean. We know him inside and out. He's got a personal relationship with the Dennison woman, but I've got no reason to think he rigged her car to try to kill her. He also told me that you accused him of being the shooter in the attack on Dennison." Irons's voice grew acid sharp. "I told you that was just a drive-by, Novalis. When are you going to get it through your head that I know what I'm talking about?"

"Duchesne's alibi checked out for the time of the shooting?" Mike persisted.

Irons sighed. "Yeah, it checked out. I've got forty witnesses who say he was in a nightclub in Geneva, Switzerland, when Dennison was popped. Do you want to see their sworn statements?"

Mike shook his head. Irons was no fool; he wouldn't have discussed the alibi if it weren't tight.

"Good," said Irons. "Look, Novalis, I'm not out to yank your chain on this. Maybe you had something going with the Dennison woman, I don't know. It wouldn't be the first time, would it?"

Mike stared back at him, giving no answer.

"You say you've been watching Dennison for a week. Let me remind you—" here Irons glanced at Hecht, who nodded "—that your superior officer gave you a specific order to stay away from her. I don't know how he intends to discipline you, and I don't care. But I'm warning you, you're starting to look like a psycho. Maybe you've got it in for Julien Duchesne because he's putting it to the Dennison woman."

Mike hated sitting there like a kid in the principal's office, listening to this pompous jerk pick him apart. He could feel himself boiling just beneath the surface. *Stay cool,* he ordered himself. *You've heard worse.* And he had. Some of the sessions he'd had to sit through after Jack Renzo's death would have tested the patience of a saint. God knew they'd almost broken his.

"So let me make this real simple, Novalis," Irons said, his face hard. "From now on, Julien Duchesne is off-limits. Nina Dennison is off-limits. Everyone and everything connected with Zakroff and Duchesne is off-limits. One slip and I'll have you up on charges. Do I make myself clear?"

"Yeah, you're real clear." Mike stood and leaned forward, looking down at Irons. The man's hair was getting pretty thin on top, Mike noticed absently. In fact, he had a regular bald spot going on the crown.

"Just tell me this," Mike said. "Are you and your team of hotshot feds going to do anything at all to protect Nina Dennison?"

Irons threw his hands in the air and turned to Hecht. "How do you get through to him?"

"Give it a rest, Novalis," Hecht snapped.

Mike addressed his boss. "Come on, Morris, you can't tell me there isn't something hinky about this woman almost getting killed twice in two weeks?"

It was Irons who answered. "Coincidence," he said. "Unfortunate, but things happen."

That pushed Mike over the edge. He seized Irons by the lapels and glared down at the smaller man. "Coincidence, you bureaucratic son of a bitch? Are you gonna say it's just coincidence when the next accident happens—"

"Novalis!" Hecht roared.

Irons shook himself free of Mike's grip. "That's it, Novalis. I've tried to give you a break because of your record, but you've crossed the line. Hecht, are you going to deal with this—" he straightened his jacket "—or am I?"

"You're suspended, Novalis, as of right now," said Hecht. He held out one meaty hand.

A long minute passed. Then Mike unholstered his gun and took his badge out of his pocket. He laid them both in Hecht's hand.

"Damn it, Novalis, you know I have to do this."

Mike just nodded. "And I had to do what I did."

Hecht shook his head. "You're a good cop, Novalis, but you've gone off the rails on this one. Now I'm out one man, and I'm already shorthanded. Well, you know the drill. Go home, get some rest. There'll be a disciplinary hearing—I'll be in touch."

Mike turned to leave.

"One more thing, Novalis." It was Irons. "I've spent too much time setting up this investigation to watch it go down the tubes now. Stay out of our way."

"Listen to the man, Mike," Hecht urged. "Or it'll be worse than suspension. You know what it's like when the feds get involved." The glance he shot at Irons wasn't friendly. "I won't be able to bail you out."

"I understand," Mike said tonelessly. Then he walked out of his boss's office, dumped his current case files on Detective Sarris's desk and went home.

Chapter 9

Mike realized that he hadn't eaten since the previous afternoon. He stopped on the way home for a bag of fast-food cheeseburgers and ate two of them in the car, tossing the crumpled wrappers into the back seat. The third burger was for Sig.

"Here you go, buddy," he told the grinning dog, who wolfed down the cheeseburger in a single chomp and then commenced leaping madly about the loft, clearly delighted to see his master home in the middle of the day. "Get used to it, boy. You're gonna be seeing a lot of me for a while."

Mike took Sig for a walk. Then he did his laundry. Then, just for the heck of it, he took Sig for another walk. All the while he chewed on the puzzle of Nina Dennison and Julien Duchesne.

He still wasn't sure about Nina. Maybe she *was* mixed up in the smuggling racket. Or maybe Irons was right, and she was a completely innocent, phenomenally unlucky bystander. But this scenario bothered him—two near-fatal accidents in two weeks just didn't make sense. He couldn't shake the feeling that someone was out to get Nina. Would the unknown attacker be luckier the third time?

And what was the real deal with Duchesne? It stuck in Mike's craw that Duchesne was in tight with Irons and the feds; Mike was positive that Duchesne's presence near Nina's car had been no coincidence. But he had no proof, and Duchesne looked to be untouchable. He wondered what Duchesne had done to earn Irons's confidence. Probably volunteered to spy, or set someone up. Irons could talk all he wanted about how Duchesne was on the side of the angels—Mike didn't trust him. And it wasn't just jealousy, although Mike's innate fairness forced him to admit that there'd been a grain of painful truth in what Irons had said.

As Mike paced restlessly around his loft, trying to decide what to do with himself, he noticed that the message light on his answering machine was blinking. He hadn't seen it earlier because it was half-hidden by a sprawling Boston fern.

He stared at the light for a moment without moving. There was no reason in the world to believe that Nina had called him. In fact, there was every reason to believe that he was the last person she'd want to talk to right now. He hadn't forgotten the look on her face last night when she'd discovered that he'd been following her. She'd accused him of being suspicious of her, of thinking that she had lied to him all along. That look had held all the hostility of their first encounter in the hospital, and something else as well: pain. As though he'd betrayed her. It had cut him like a knife. But what really hurt was the knowledge that she'd been right. He *had* been suspicious of her. Even after he'd gotten to know her, even after he'd spent the night with her—even after he'd fallen in love with her, damn it!—he'd been unable to take her word. He'd wanted to believe her, he really had, but he just hadn't been able to forget the hard lesson Karen had taught him. Nina had deserved better.

He moved slowly toward the phone, hoping against hope that he was going to get another chance. He could almost hear Nina's voice. So he wasn't completely surprised when it came floating up out of the machine.

"Hello, Mike, this is Nina," ran the message. "I'm sorry you're not at home, because I've realized that in all the confusion last night, I never did thank you for saving my life. So, thank you." There was a pause; the tape crackled and hissed. "I'd really like to talk to you. I'm leaving for a business trip—I'm going to a gem auction in Colombia with Julien and Marta. I'll be back in a couple of days. If you'd like to get together, call my home machine and leave a message. If not, no problem. I'll understand. Anyway...thanks again."

Mike's heart was pounding. The fact that Nina wanted to see him again was almost overshadowed by his sudden, sharp anxiety. She was going to Colombia with Julien Duchesne? Forget jealousy—this trip was just plain crazy! He remembered Nina's description of the wild and woolly gem auctions and the even wilder emerald mines. Anything could happen to her down there. An accident would be laughably easy to arrange.

He dialed her home number. Her machine answered. Mike almost hung up, but then he decided to wait—she could be screening her calls while she packed for her trip. "Hi, this is Nina," her machine said. "Please leave a message and I'll call you back." There was a single short beep before the tone; Mike knew that it meant there was already one message on the machine. After the tone he said urgently, "Nina, if you're there, pick up! This is Mike."

There was no answer. Mike punched in Nina's remote call-in code; he'd seen it in her address book when he searched her belongings after she was shot. He didn't feel particularly virtuous about listening to a message that someone had left for her, but he was beyond worrying about details like invasion of privacy. The tap had been taken off Nina's line so he couldn't pick up her messages the usual way. And hopefully, nobody else could. He figured he needed all the information he could get. Listening to her machine could be a matter of life or death. Nina's life or death.

The message on her tape played back: ''Hi, sis, this is Charley. Listen, I got this package that you sent. What am I supposed to do with it?''

That was all. Charley was Nina's brother in Chicago, Mike recalled. So she had sent him something. Maybe the package contained emeralds—Nina's share of the smuggled stones. Maybe it held some kind of evidence—whatever the searcher had been looking for in Nina's apartment. Or maybe the package was just someone's birthday present, in which case Mike knew he was going to end up looking like an idiot. But he didn't care.

Quickly he dialed Nina's office number and got Debbie, Nina's secretary, who informed him that Nina had already left for the day. ''She won't be back for several days,'' Debbie said. ''Can I take a message?''

''Debbie, this is Detective Novalis. I was in the office a week or so ago. Remember me?''

''Sure do.''

''I need a favor. Can you tell me what flight Miss Dennison is booked on to Colombia?'' Mike was betting on the fact that most law-abiding citizens never questioned a request or an order from a law-enforcement officer. He was in luck—Debbie chirped out the information without hesitation and didn't even ask why he needed to know. She knew him as a policeman; it would never have occurred to her that he'd been suspended from the force just two hours earlier.

''Flight 555 through Miami,'' he repeated. ''Thanks, Debbie.''

He checked his watch: the flight was scheduled to leave Philadelphia International in less than half an hour. There was no time to try to get a message to Nina at the airport. Besides, what would he say? He ran down the rickety warehouse stairs—the elevator was too slow—and jumped into his car.

Mike had a couple of near misses on his way to the airport, but luckily he still had his portable flasher. He clapped it to the roof of his car and drove like hell, making liberal use of his horn. Still, it took him twenty minutes to get to the airport. He double-parked in front of the TWA terminal, grateful for the police plates that he'd been using ever since he came off undercover duty. The airport cops might grumble about having to direct traffic around his car, but at least they wouldn't tow it.

"Flight 555, quick, which gate," he snapped to one of the curbside baggage handlers.

Surprised, the man blurted out, "B 13." As Mike ran off, he heard the handler mutter, "Swell manners."

Mike tore through the terminal, putting on an extra turn of speed when he heard the final boarding call for flight 555. He reached the gate just as the technicians were preparing to disengage the jetway.

"Hold it!" he called out.

The ticket agent said, "Sorry, sir, this flight is ready to depart."

Mike had given some thought to what he would use to impress people now that he no longer had a badge. He pulled out his wallet and flashed his police union card. With an ID photo and a fancy seal, it looked fairly official, unless you scrutinized it closely. Or unless you stopped to remember that a police officer was supposed to have a shiny gold badge. He was hoping that he could keep the ticket agent so off-balance that he would do neither.

"Philadelphia police," he said in a low voice. "I need your help. Can you stop this plane from taking off?"

The agent waved to the technician. "Wait a second, Carl." Then he asked Mike, "What's going on?"

"I've got a delicate situation here, but I'm sure you've had plenty of experience with this kind of thing." Mike had learned that appeals to people's vanity rarely failed to enlist their cooperation.

"There's no danger, none at all to you or to your plane or passengers," Mike hastened to assure the agent, noting that he had turned rather pale. "But there's a passenger on that plane who can't be allowed to leave. I want to get her off the plane without any fuss."

The agent asked for the passenger's name and used his computer to verify that Nina had checked aboard. "She's one of our first-class passengers, Officer," he said, sounding shocked.

"Yeah. Now I can't just march onto the plane and get her, because she's traveling with someone, and I don't want to tip him off. So how do we get her off the plane?"

The agent beckoned to one of the flight attendants who had been standing near the jetway staring curiously at Mike. "This is Janet, our first-class cabin attendant," he said. "Janet, the police need our help."

Mike gave her his most winning smile. "Okay, Janet," he told her, "here's what I want you to do...."

Nina had thought about canceling her trip and letting Julien handle the auction on his own. She'd been brought home in a police cruiser Sunday night—after resisting all efforts to get her to the hospital. She'd had enough of hospitals lately, and she knew that she was all right. "I'm just shaken up a little," she had insisted, and finally the paramedics had packed up their ambulance and driven off.

She *was* shaken, literally: still shivering with reaction long after the crash. But her thoughts kept turning to what had happened right afterward, when Mike had appeared as if by magic outside her car and pulled her to safety.

She'd been dazed, in shock, but his kiss had brought her to life.... Later, the memory of that searing kiss had made her burn—with rekindled desire, she couldn't deny that. But also with indignation. What did Mike think he was up to, following her around as though she were a criminal? In his eyes, it seemed, she was.

In the end, Nina's anger at Mike and his dogged, suspicious pursuit had helped her get over the aftereffects of the accident. It had warmed her, driving out the chill of panic and shock. She stopped shaking and was even able to go through her desk and locate her auto insurance policy and a photocopy of the car's registration. By the time she went to bed after a long, hot soak in the tub, she felt that she was almost back to normal. *Or as normal as it gets for a psychic amnesiac,* she thought.

She'd woken the next morning with her mind made up about two things.

First, she'd go through with the trip to Colombia—she didn't want to let Armand down, and anyway there was nothing for her to do as far as the accident to her car was concerned: she'd already filled out the police report, and the insurance company would take care of everything else. Besides, she'd be back in a couple of days, and she desperately needed a change of scene.

Second, she would call Mike Novalis. If nothing else, she owed him her thanks for saving her life last night. Maybe he'd turned up at the accident site for the worst possible reasons, but the fact remained that he'd gotten her out of her car when she was too dazed to do anything. If he hadn't done so, she'd have been killed when the BMW blew up.

But there was more to it than that. She remembered her earlier decision: to talk to Mike after she returned from Colombia. Now, thinking of the kiss and her reaction to it, she was more certain than ever that there was unfinished business between the two of them. And it wasn't just the passionate kiss that had convinced her of that—it was the way he had held her, murmuring to her and touching her hair with his lips, as if nothing in the world mattered to him but her. So she'd make one more try to break through his suspicion and resistance. It would be worth the effort if only she could feel his arms around her like that again.

She'd gone to the office, and after a briefing with Armand and a call to her insurance agent she had sat at her desk, staring at the telephone. She really should tell Mike that she was grateful for what he had done...and at the same time she could tell him that she wanted to talk to him. Why wait until she got back? She reached for the phone and dialed his home number, figuring that he was unlikely to be home in the middle of a Monday morning. This way she could say what she wanted to say without putting him on the spot; he'd have time to decide how he wanted to respond, and if he didn't want to see her...well, he didn't have to call back. It was his choice. Nina realized that her strategy wasn't designed to make it easy for Mike alone. By talking to his machine instead of to him, she was also protecting herself from a direct rejection. Of course, the downside was that now she would have to wait to find out how he was going to respond.

She left her message and hung up, and almost at once she began replaying what she had said. Had she stammered? Had she sounded whiny? Maybe she shouldn't have left a message at all—

Cut it out! she ordered herself. *What's done is done. There's nothing so irrevocable as a message left on someone's answering machine. You did what you wanted to do, didn't you? You can live with it.*

Nina cleaned off her desk, took Debbie to an early lunch and then said goodbye to Armand. She walked briskly back to her apartment, picked up her suitcase and took a cab to the airport to meet Julien and Marta. The Duchesnes were horrified to hear about the accident; Marta threw her arms around Nina and cried, "Thank God you weren't hurt!" and Julien promised her that Z and D would provide a rental until she could get around to replacing her car. Nina had been a little concerned about how she and Julien would get along; it was, after all, their first meeting since she broke the engagement. Her fears proved to have been groundless. He couldn't have been friendlier or more sympathetic. And now here she sat, comfortably ensconced in first class, with Marta next to her and Julien across the aisle, waiting for the last few passengers to trickle aboard so that the plane could take off.

A flight attendant appeared at Nina's side. "Miss Dennison?"

"Yes." Nina looked up, curious.

"Can I see your seat assignment card, please?"

Nina fished the cardboard stub out of her purse and handed it to the woman, who examined it with a puzzled frown. "There's nothing wrong with this ticket," she said.

"Is there a problem?" Julien asked, leaning across the aisle.

"Just checking something, sir," the attendant told him with a brisk professional smile. She turned back to Nina and spoke in the low, carefully modulated voice that people who work with the public use to deflect attention from potential scenes. "I don't know how this happened, but we have a gentleman with the same seat assignment as yours," she explained quickly. "His ticket doesn't look quite right, but frankly, he's causing a bit of a scene in the gate area. We'd put him in another seat, but as you can see, our flight is full today. This gentleman may be holding an illegal ticket, but before we can notify airport security, we need to check your seat card against his to show that yours was issued first and has the proper authorization codes."

Nina couldn't follow the attendant's bureaucratic explanation. All she knew was that the woman needed her cardboard stub. "Go ahead, take it," she said.

"Oh, no." The attendant looked shocked. "You must *never* relinquish your seat card, not even to a flight attendant. Keep it with you at all times. If you'd just step out to the gate area, we'll get this settled in a second and get you on your way."

"Okay." Nina got to her feet.

"This is ridiculous!" Julien exclaimed.

"It's just routine, sir," the attendant said soothingly. "We'll be under way in a moment. In the meantime, would you like another glass of champagne?"

Nina shrugged apologetically at her traveling companions, and the attendant ushered her down the aisle and out of the plane. As she stepped out of the far end of the jetway, someone walked up and took her arm, and she jumped a little in alarm.

"Mike!" she said. "What are you doing here?"

Mike wasn't sure that he had pulled it off until he saw the flight attendant coming out of the jetway. With her was Nina, her long green raincoat swinging around her ankles. Mike gave a hasty glance down the jetway. No one was following the two women—yet.

He took Nina's arm, and when she stared at him in surprise all he said was, "I'll explain later." To Janet he said, "Good work. Thanks."

The ticket agent stepped forward anxiously as Mike began hustling Nina out of the gate area. "Is everything all right?" he asked over Nina's increasingly loud protests.

"Just fine." Mike tugged a little harder at Nina. He gave the man a broad grin and said, raising his voice a bit. "I'll get out of your way now. And remember, I'm counting on you to keep *anyone* from leaving that plane."

"How am I supposed to do that? Officer? Officer?"

Mike ignored the agent's worried questions and strong-armed Nina into the corridor.

"What are you *doing?*" she was sputtering indignantly.

"We've got to get out of here" was all he said. "Hurry up."

Instead she dug in her heels. "But I'll miss my plane— I'm going to Colombia."

He took her by the shoulders. "Oh, no, you're not. You're coming with me. Now get moving."

She glared at him. "I may have lost my memory, but I haven't lost my mind," she said. "I don't know what this caveman act is all about, but believe me, we can talk when I get back—"

"I'm not putting a move on you, for God's sake," he yelled. "I'm trying to save your life." Dimly he was aware that passengers had stopped to stare at them.

"But I don't understand— I've got to explain to Julien—"

"Julien's the one who's trying to kill you. Now run!" He took her by the wrist and pulled her after him. And she ran. She kept gasping out questions and protests, but she ran.

He got her all the way to the front of the terminal, but she backed off when he tried to put her in his car.

"Look, Mike," she panted, "you've got to tell me what's going on. I can't just run off with you. Where are the other cops? What's this about Julien? And let go of me, you're going to break my arm."

"Just get in the car," he said urgently. "I'll explain after we get out of here."

"Explain now," she challenged.

"There's no time." He let go of her arm, and she rubbed her wrist but did not run away. "Do you trust me?" he asked her.

She looked at him. "Yes."

"Then get in." He climbed into the driver's seat and an instant later he heard her door slam. He gunned the engine and roared out of there.

Chapter 10

"Buckle up," Mike growled as he took a corner on two wheels at forty-five miles an hour, and Nina obeyed.

"I've already been in one car crash this week," she observed mildly. "Let's not try for two."

He took his eyes off the road for a split second, just long enough to grin at her, and she felt as if her heart would burst. He looked wild, dangerous and exactly right.

"Do you mind telling me where we're going?"

"We're getting out of this airport—" Mike cursed under his breath as the driver of a white sedan, obviously confused by the maze of ramps and bridges leading out of the airport, abruptly changed lanes in front of him "—and then we're gonna find a phone."

"To call help?" Nina prompted.

"Not exactly." Mike bypassed the highway turnoffs and instead took a sharp right under a bridge and over a railroad crossing, heading into South Philly's maze of narrow streets. He kept one eye on the rearview mirror. So far there was no sign of pursuit, but he knew that the time he'd bought by yanking Nina from the flight had been only a matter of minutes. Once she failed to return to her seat, it wouldn't take Julien Duchesne long to figure out that something was up. He'd undoubtedly come storming out of the plane, demanding an explanation. Mike had prepared the ticket agent and the flight attendant with a cover story, hoping to keep Duchesne from figuring out that he had engineered Nina's disappearance. He was pretty sure he could count on Janet to stick with the story, but once Julien got arrogant and started to throw his weight around, the nervous ticket agent might very well crumple.

Mike stole a quick glance at his wristwatch. Eight minutes had passed since Janet brought Nina off the plane. Duchesne would be raising hell soon—if he hadn't started already. He checked the mirror again. Nothing.

"What are you looking for? Do you think someone is following us?" Nina was twisting in her seat, craning to look out the back window.

"Not yet. But maybe soon."

"Mike, please, tell me what's going on."

He heard the fear in her voice and gave her a reassuring smile. "I meant what I said back there. I think your life's in danger. I think if you'd gone to Colombia with your fiancé Duchesne you never would have come back."

"Julien's not my fiancé," she said absently, then asked, "Why would he try to kill me?"

"He's not? Since when?"

"Since Saturday night. I broke it off." She gasped, horrified. "That's not what makes you think he's trying to kill me, is it?"

"I don't know why he's after you. I'm just glad you dumped the scum." Quickly Mike detailed the case against Julien: the fact that he had seen Julien near Nina's car, and Gina Donnelly's hunch that Nina's brakes and air bag had been tampered with. "And, yes, I was staking out your apartment," he told her before she could ask how he'd happened to see Julien there. "I know you're not going to like this, but I've been following you for a week. I—I don't want anything to happen to you."

"My God, you're serious," Nina exclaimed. "Are the police going to arrest Julien?"

Mike had been waiting for this. He hated to drop the bomb on Nina, but he wouldn't allow himself to deceive her. "The police aren't in on this, Nina. Just me."

She looked at him, puzzled, and he spelled it out. "Right now I'm not even officially on the police force. I was suspended this morning."

Her eyes widened. "Why?"

"Because I threatened to pound the snot out of Julien Duchesne if anything happened to you. Oh, and I also manhandled a senior FBI agent."

"You did what?" Nina's head was spinning. She'd been off-balance and out of breath ever since their mad dash through the airport. Now she wondered if she was hearing things.

"There's a lot you don't know about what's been going on, Nina," he said. "I don't know much of it myself." Mike knew that if he told Nina about the FBI's top-secret smuggling case he could kiss his future in law enforcement goodbye. As it was, he'd be bloody lucky not to wind up in jail for interfering with a federal investigation. It was a risk he was ready to take—he'd crossed the line when he asked Debbie for Nina's flight number. So he proceeded to fill her in on the little he knew about the FBI investigation: that it involved international gem smuggling with suspected links to the Colombian cocaine cartels, that Z and D was one of the import firms under investigation, and that Julien Duchesne was working with the feds. "Duchesne's protected," Mike wound up bitterly. "He's in so tight with the feds that they won't listen to anything against him. And I've got to admit I don't have any hard evidence."

Nina was still trying to adjust to the fact that the suave, polite man with whom she'd lunched and dined for the past week had tried to kill her. It wasn't easy. Despite all the shocks she'd suffered since waking up with amnesia, she still expected the world to be a fairly logical, orderly place. But she believed Mike. More than that, she trusted him. If he said she was in danger, she had to take his word for it—and she had to let him help her.

"Okay, so going to the police is out," she said gamely. "What do we do?"

"I'm afraid it's even worse than that," he told her grimly. "As of now, we're fugitives."

"What?"

"After I blew my top at the federal agent and was suspended, I was ordered to stay away from you. Duchesne's going to get on the phone to his FBI buddy—in fact, he's probably already done it—and they're going to put out a 'stop and detain' order on me for messing up their investigation." He cut her a sidelong glance. "I'm afraid I've dragged you into a mess."

"It sounds like you dragged me out of a worse one," Nina said, and impulsively reached out and clasped his shoulder. "Don't worry, I'm okay. I know you'll figure something out."

"There's another thing...ah, just what I'm looking for." Mike pulled into a small, dingy shopping center: a convenience store, a dry cleaner, a copy shop and a singularly uninviting Chinese restaurant.

"I hope we didn't come here for dinner," Nina murmured.

Mike brought the car to a halt next to a phone booth. "Nope. I want you to make a call."

He told her about the message on her answering machine, bracing himself for a blast of outrage. But she said nothing about the fact that he'd tapped into her messages; she just looked thoughtful.

"So you think this package I sent to my brother, whatever it is, is important?"

Mike nodded. "Just a hunch. But I want you to call him and have him open it and tell you what's in it. Don't worry, I've got his number."

Nina went to the phone. Her brother answered on the third ring. "I can't explain now, Charley," she said hurriedly. "Just do me a favor. Open that package I sent you, right now. Tell me what's in it."

She could tell that he was bursting with curiosity, but he did it. She heard the rustle of paper as he ripped off the wrapping. Then there was a long silence.

"Charley? Charley, are you there?"

"Yeah, I'm here." His voice sounded odd and strained. "Nina, what's going on?"

"Just tell me, Charley, please," she begged.

"All right. It's a green gem, a big one, in a plastic bag. I think it's an emerald. Nina, are you in some kind of trouble?"

"I don't know," she whispered, stricken, and relayed the news to Mike.

Nina went numb for the next few minutes, listening to Mike with one ear and Charley with the other. Charley told her that there were some papers in the package, too, on Z and D letterhead; on Mike's instructions, she asked Charley to fax the papers to her at the nearby copy shop—a sign in its window said Fax Send And Receive, $1 Page. Nina gave Charley the number. She then asked him to describe the stone in detail. "Good thinking," said Mike.

"Big. Green. What else can I say?" complained Charley. "Nina, come on, what's this all about?"

"What shape is it?" she asked him. "How big across? How many facets does it have? Count carefully." When she was convinced that she had as clear a picture of the emerald as she was going to get, she said, "Fax me those papers right away, Charley. It's important. Then just hang on to them and the stone. And whatever you do, don't tell *anyone* I called you. Please.''

"I'm worried, Nina. I'm your brother and I love you. Tell me what's going on.''

"I love you, too, Charley," Nina said, voice breaking. "I'll call you as soon as I can.'' She hung up.

Then she was in Mike's arms. She didn't know how she had ended up there; she had simply turned to him as if it were the most natural thing in the world, and as soon as they touched she started crying as though her heart would break. He held her and let her cry, patting her hair and murmuring to her as one would soothe a sobbing child. He knew that it wasn't just the wrenching conversation with her brother that had broken her down—her tears were the culmination of nearly two weeks of stress and fear, topped off by the realization that she was a murder target in the company of a renegade cop. The final straw was learning that she'd mailed a valuable gem to her brother, and now she didn't know why she'd done it. But she knew it looked suspicious as all get-out. No wonder she was crying.

Suddenly Mike realized what he'd been thinking: She didn't know why she'd done it. He couldn't have been thinking that if he still suspected Nina of faking the amnesia. Somewhere along the way, without quite being aware of it, he had crossed another line—the line separating doubt from belief. He trusted her now. Sometime he'd have to tell her about it. But right now, his top priority was getting her out of the mess she was in. His arms tightened around her briefly, and then he let her go.

Her face was wet with tears, her eyes were red and her nose was swollen. Mike thought she was gorgeous.

"Do you have any tissues?'' she asked. "I left my purse on the plane.''

"There's something in the car.'' He burrowed in the glove compartment and offered her a crumpled napkin. She took it with a jaundiced look and blew her nose.

"Come on," he said, "let's go pick up our fax." He held out his hand.

Nina was about to take it when she stumbled; her eyes were blinded by a flash of white light. She knew at once what was happening. After a week of dormancy, she was finally having another of her visions.

Like all the others, it lasted only a couple of seconds. But unlike the rest, this vision left her feeling sick and terrified.

Mike was holding her arm; his blue eyes dark with concern. "What's the matter? Another memory flashback?"

She stared back, unable to speak. *You have to tell him,* she thought. *He's not going to believe you, but you've got to try. You've got to make him believe!*

"They're not memories, Mike." She spoke through dry lips. "I figured it out. I know it sounds crazy, but when I see those flashes of light, I'm seeing . . . visions of the future."

"Nina, for God's sake, have you gone nuts? We're in enough trouble as it is, honey. Please, don't start jerking me around with some wild story!"

She grabbed his arm and pulled him around to face her. "I'm not jerking you around. I've listened to you, and I've believed you, and now, damn it, you'll listen to me." His jaw tightened with impatience, but he listened while she tried to explain about the visions she'd had, and how several of them had come true. She even told him about the vision she'd had of him—the vision that was later fulfilled in every detail when she visited his loft. She could see that she wasn't getting through. His expression remained incredulous.

"I can't buy it, Nina," he said after she finally stammered to a halt. "It's just too far-out. But we can worry about that later, it's not important." He started for the copy shop.

"No," she said, "we have to worry about it now."

Slowly he turned back to her.

"You haven't asked me about the vision I just had," she said bleakly. "You were in it." She ran to him. "Mike, I'm frightened. I saw you and another man. You were fighting, rolling around on a wooden floor. He was snarling. He looked desperate. And, Mike—he had a gun."

He took her hands and enclosed them gently in his. The fear in her face was inexpressibly touching; he wanted only to drive that fear away. So he said softly, "Sweetheart, don't you see that doesn't mean anything? You know I'm a cop. I've told you that I used to work undercover vice. It's a dangerous job, and maybe you've been thinking about me, worrying about me. But it's okay, I promise you. I've survived every fight I've ever been in." He smiled, trying to lighten the mood.

Nina remained somber. Her face was drawn, and her eyes were shadowed green pools. "Did you ever fight with a short man, muscular, with olive skin and heavy eyebrows and short black hair? And a bald spot on the top?"

"Not that I remember," joked Mike—and then he was brought up with a jolt. He *did* know somebody who fit that description. "Did you say he was bald on top?" Mike asked carefully. He drew a little circle above the crown of his own head. "Right about there?"

Nina nodded.

"I'll be damned," Mike said half under his breath. "Irons." As far as he knew, Nina and Irons had never met. So how come she had just given a description of him that was good enough to have come off one of the FBI's own reports? Either Nina was lying for some reason, trying to turn him against Irons, or she was telling the truth about this psychic business. And if she was telling the truth, that meant that Irons was really going to try to kill him.

"Do you know who it is?" Nina was asking. She slipped her hand into his. It was cold, and he tucked it into the pocket of his jacket. She smiled tentatively. "So you believe me?"

"That's asking a lot.... The guy you described sounds like David Irons, the FBI special agent who's heading the investigation I told you about." Mike grinned a hard, wolflike grin. "He doesn't like me much, but I didn't think he'd go as far as shooting me."

"There's more. Remember that first vision I had? The one of two men in a little room somewhere? One of the men turned out to be Julien. The other was the same man I just saw—this man Irons."

"That would make sense," Mike said, "since Irons and Julien are working together—"

He stopped short as the implication sank home. Could *Irons* be dirty? Mike had been assuming that Julien was scamming the feds, pretending to work with them while running some operation of his own on the side—some operation that necessitated the attempt on Nina's life. But what if Irons and Duchesne were in it together? Maybe Irons was behind the attacks on Nina. Why? And could Mike really take Nina's word for anything—the word of a self-confessed psychic amnesiac who, judging from the package she had mailed to her brother, might also have something to hide?

The whole situation was crazy, and it kept getting crazier. Not only that, but Mike was getting anxious. Time was passing, and for all he knew Hecht could be putting out an APB on him this very minute.

"I need to think all this over," he said abruptly. "Let's get that fax and get moving."

Nina studied the fax while Mike drove west through the Philadelphia suburbs. The fax consisted of three pages of gem valuations on Zakroff and Duchesne letterhead. Nina's signature was on all of them. She scanned them quickly. Each of the fifteen gems described was an emer-

ald. Not one of the descriptions fit the large stone she had
sent to Charley. Each sheet, she noticed, bore the same
date; it was a date in June, corresponding to the last quarterly gem auction in Colombia.

"I think," she suggested to Mike, "these must be the
stones I bought for Z and D the last time Julien and I went
to Colombia. But the emerald I mailed to Charley isn't
described here."

Silence hung heavy, threatening to overwhelm the fragile truce that had sprung up between them, a connection
compounded of growing trust and kindling desire. Mike
reached for her hand and squeezed it.

"We'll get through this, I swear it," he said simply.

And, feeling the comforting pressure of his strong hand,
Nina allowed herself to believe him.

They talked about the package she had sent to Charley
and what it might mean. Nina was appalled by some of
Mike's suggestions, but she saw that he wasn't accusing her
of anything. He was simply exploring the possibilities. The
emerald was clearly valuable. Nina might simply have stolen it—but then why would she have sent it to Charley, and
why would she have included a wad of paperwork?

Nina suggested that she might have sent the emerald to
Chicago for safekeeping, as a way of getting it out of the
way in case someone came looking for it. That made sense
to Mike; after all, someone *had* searched Nina's apartment. In that case, was the emerald her share of the loot
from a smuggling operation? Or was it her insurance
against a double-cross, something she could use to black-
mail her partners in crime if they tried to cut her out?

"There's another possibility," he said. "Maybe you're
completely innocent, and you just stumbled across something underhanded at Z and D. The emerald and the papers could be evidence that you discovered. If you were
suspicious about something, you might have sent them to

your brother to hold for you until you found out what was going on.''

''I like that idea,'' Nina said, brightening. ''But I can't imagine Armand as a crook.''

''Maybe he's not, any more than you are.'' Mike didn't add that there was no proof that Nina was in the clear. *Something* was going on at Z and D, the federal investigation was proof of that. At this point, though, it was just his intuition telling him that Nina Dennison was arrow straight and squeaky clean. And that, he acknowledged, could be wishful thinking. He wanted her to be clean. Face it—he just plain wanted her.

A curious peacefulness settled over them, as though they'd lived through a storm and were now simply glad to be alive and together. Mike glanced at Nina. There she sat in the same clothes she'd been wearing in the hospital: jeans and a black turtleneck. Her hair was mussed and her face was shiny. Any other woman, Mike thought admiringly, would have been bemoaning the loss of her luggage and her handbag. But Nina was quiet, gazing out the window as the car glided along a secondary highway headed northwest.

''There's something I've got to ask you,'' he said. ''It's been bugging me all day. Where *were* you going last night when you had the accident?''

She smiled, and for the first time he noticed the way her mouth curled up on one side when she was being mischievous. ''Figure it out,'' she said.

''There's nothing down there but—'' Then it hit him, right between the eyes, and he couldn't keep from laughing at his own foolish blindness.

''You were coming to see *me*.''

''Yep.''

''And I shot my mouth off at you after the crash. God, Nina, I'm sorry.''

"Don't be. I've said some mean things to you since this whole business started."

"But that's over now."

"Yes," Nina said, and a shiver ran through her, as if he'd touched her in some tender place. "That's over now."

A few moments later Nina said, "By the way, where the heck are we going?"

"I've got a place in mind where we can lie low. It's a cabin up in the Poconos where I go fishing sometimes. We can spend the night there while we figure out what to do." He swallowed. The idea of spending the night alone with Nina in a cabin in the woods was starting to look a little too good to him. He'd thought of the cabin because he knew they needed to get off the road. As a senior FBI agent, Irons had the power to command every law-enforcement officer for miles around. The whole area was probably being combed for Mike and Nina right now; he'd be lucky to stay one step ahead of the dragnet.

"What about Sig?" Nina asked suddenly, and Mike's heart warmed. She was on the run from an international smuggling ring and from the law, and she was worried about his dog.

"Don't worry about that big boy," he told her. "I've got a neighbor, an artist who uses the next loft as a studio. He comes over every day and takes Sig for a walk. He'll look after the mutt."

Nina shifted to a more comfortable position and drew her coat closely around her. The past hour had been one long roller-coaster ride: everything that had happened since Mike's dramatic appearance at the airport had kept her emotions keyed up to fever pitch. Now she felt drained, and as confused as she'd ever been. *That's not saying much. Your whole memory is only about a week and a half long.*

"Mike," she asked in a tired voice, "do you really think Julien would have killed me? I mean, he *was* my fiancé."

''Maybe he wasn't.'' Mike had been thinking hard, and now he laid out his ideas for Nina. If her guess—Mike couldn't bring himself to call it a vision—was right, and Irons *was* bent, that only strengthened the case against Duchesne. Mike knew that Irons and Duchesne were pretty close. Irons had said that they were working together on the side of the good guys, but they could just as easily be partners on the other side.

It wasn't too hard for Mike to see Irons in the role of villain. He wouldn't be the first overworked, underpaid lawman to be tempted off the straight and narrow path by the lure of enormous payoffs. As a Bureau insider, Irons would know a lot about the drug underground. He might even have brought Duchesne and the Colombians together in the first place. Z and D would have provided a nice little cover for someone who wanted to launder Colombian drug money by converting it into gems and smuggling them into the States. A courier for a respected firm like Z and D could travel to Colombia frequently, each time bringing in a legitimate cargo of emeralds purchased at auction—and also an illegal stash of undeclared stones. The courier could be paid off with a cut of each shipment.

Mike knew that the FBI investigation had started with Interpol and the DEA trying to track down a money trail that originated in Colombia. Once that trail led to emeralds and gem importers, Irons could have used his position at the FBI to get himself put in charge of the case. That way he could make sure that the investigators didn't find out what was really going on.

As for Nina, perhaps she had accidentally come across something that made her suspicious. Before she could act on it, Irons or Duchesne, or someone working for them, had tried to kill her by shooting her. When that failed and they learned of her amnesia, Duchesne pretended to be her fiancé in order to get close to her and find out what she knew. The rigged car crash was the second attempt to wipe her out, and the second failure. The trip to Colombia offered the perfect opportunity for a third try.

"So we weren't really engaged," Nina mused.

"I don't think so. None of your friends, not even people outside Z and D, knew anything about you dating him. You didn't have his number written down anywhere, you didn't have a trace of him in your apartment.... I think he lied about being engaged to you, either to test your amnesia or to put himself into a position to take you out. And I don't mean on a date."

"It fits," said Nina, thinking of the discrepancies she'd noticed: Armand's surprise at Julien's announcement of their engagement, the absence of references to Julien in her diary. "I hope it's true. I didn't really like him, you know, even before I knew he was trying to kill me."

Mike didn't mention it, but he knew that any cop would spot another possibility. Nina might have been working with Irons and Duchesne. The shooting could have been a falling-out among thieves. Even if she had told him nothing but the truth about her amnesia, she could still have been in on the smuggling. But he couldn't let himself believe it. He'd thrown his career away for this woman, and he'd do it again in a minute; he had to have faith that she was worth it.

Darkness was falling as they turned off the two-lane highway and passed through a small town. Mike stopped at the local supermarket, saying, "We'd better pick up something to eat. There won't be anything at the cabin."

"Good idea. I'm getting hungry. And," Nina added, spotting a drugstore next to the supermarket, "I can pick up a toothbrush and a comb and a few other things. I feel pretty grubby."

Mike gave her the once-over and couldn't agree. If he looked as good to her as she looked to him, they'd have a hard time keeping their hands off each other tonight.

He handed her some bills. "I'll get the groceries, you get what you need. And pick up a toothbrush for me while you're at it."

Shopping didn't take long. They met at the car in less than fifteen minutes, stowed their bags and got back on the road. "Not too much longer now," Mike told her as the lights of town dropped out of sight behind them. He turned onto a narrow dirt road that wound up and up. Hills rose steep and dark all around; every summit and ridgeline bristled with the pointed silhouettes of pines and firs, black against a sky that still held the last of the pale evening light.

Soon they came to a wide lake. Only a handful of lights glimmered around its shoreline. The car bounced along a rutted track for a quarter mile or so, and then Mike turned up a narrow driveway, little more than a clearing in the trees. There stood a small wooden cabin, shuttered and dark.

"This is going to be a bit on the primitive side," Mike warned. "Nobody's been here for a month or so."

He unlocked the cabin and quickly lit a fire in the wood-burning stove. "There's electric light and running water, but no heat," he explained. "This'll warm the place up in a few minutes."

Nina looked around. The cabin was as rustic on the inside as on the outside: The walls were of rough, uninsulated timber, and above she could see through the rafters all the way to the roof. The floor, too, was of wood, but the oak planks had been smoothed by long use, and a couple of rag rugs added spots of warmth and color. There was a much-chewed Frisbee on one of the rugs, and Nina smiled; no need to ask whose toy that was.

The kitchen was simple—a small refrigerator, a two-burner stove and a sink along one wall. A cubicle in the corner held a toilet and a shower stall. The rest of the furnishings consisted of a table and chairs, a shelf of paperbacks and a bed piled with blankets. Only one bed. Nina couldn't help noticing that it was large and looked warm.

Mike came in with the bags from the supermarket and the drugstore. He set them on the table and started taking items out of his bag one by one, displaying his purchases for Nina's approval. He'd bought bread, cheese, sliced turkey, some apples, orange juice, a package of vanilla wafers and a bottle of wine. "I thought you might need a drink," he said, setting the wine in the little refrigerator to chill. "I know I could use one."

Then he dumped the contents of Nina's bag onto the table, and her face flamed scarlet. There in a little pile were two toothbrushes, a tube of toothpaste, a small bottle of shampoo, a plastic comb, a bar of soap, a stick of deodorant and a tube of lip balm. And, unmistakable in their black-and-silver foil wrappers, a dozen condoms.

Neither of them spoke. Their eyes were riveted on the tabletop. Nina was mortified; she hadn't intended to appear so...so calculating. So eager. She'd only thought that they should be prepared, just on the chance—

Mike broke the awkward silence. "Nina, I'm flattered," he said, voice brimming with amusement. "You must think I have some stamina. Or maybe you thought we'd be spending a couple of months here?"

She jammed her fists into her coat pockets and turned her back. "Just forget about it," she muttered furiously. She felt warm with embarrassment.

"No, I'm not going to forget about it," he said, and the tone of his voice had changed. It was thick, husky, charged with promise. "Nina, look at this."

She couldn't help it; she had to turn around. Mike picked up the supermarket bag and upended it over the table. Out fell a box of condoms. Nina stared at it, then burst into laughter.

"And you had the nerve to tease me," she said. "Just for that, I ought to go stay in a motel."

"But you're not gonna, are you?" Mike came toward her. His eyes were so bright and so blue that Nina wanted to dive into them.

"No," she said. "I'm not gonna."

Chapter 11

At first their kiss was fierce, as each rushed to satisfy a hunger that had been too long denied. Their mouths worked desperately against each other; their hands grasped and clutched. But after a moment they grew tender, almost tentative, as they realized that there was time for them to explore each other. The kiss became a silent, sweet communion; each felt with breathless, half-fearful certainty that although they had been lovers before, now they were on the verge of entering new and uncharted territory.

Nina rested her head on Mike's shoulder and wrapped her arms around him. He was as solid as a tree, as warm as a fire on a cold night. She felt utterly safe and secure, snuggled against him with his strong hands cradling her, and she gave a blissful sigh of relief. Her tranquil mood didn't last, however, for the fever of desire was burning too strongly in her. She raised her mouth to his again and pressed herself to him, feeling his hard arousal through both their jeans. She moved her hips against him and he bit back a groan.

"I've been ready for you for the past two hours," he said into her hair.

She drew back and looked up at him, unafraid to match his passion with her own. "I've been ready for you for the past week."

When he started to remove her sweater she put his hands aside. "No," she whispered. "Let me. Please."

She guided him to the bed and undressed him. Her fingers fumbled at times with shoelaces and zippers, but neither of them noticed. Mike forced himself to remain still, banking the flames of his own need. He was aching to take her quickly, but instead he let her set the pace; he sensed that if he gave her the freedom to do all that she wanted, both of them might reach realms of pleasure that he had never imagined.

For Nina, the world outside had ceased to be. Even the tumult of her own passion was hushed for the moment. It was with a sense almost of reverence that she freed Mike's body of the last of its encumbrances. She looked at him, shaken by his beauty: the lean, hawklike face, the dark swooping brows and the eyes that beckoned her now like blue beacons; the curves and hollows of his muscled arms and legs; the wide chest that tapered to his flat stomach; his proud maleness rising from a nest of black hair. Her hands roamed over his body, gently, hardly daring to touch him, remembering and relearning the feel of him. She touched his flat nipples and watched them harden. Suddenly she needed to do more; she had to feel more of the heady delight that filled her when she saw how he responded to her. She leaned forward, her hair tickling his chest, and licked his nipples, teasing them with the tip of her tongue. He stirred restlessly. His hands came up as if to hold her, but she pinned his wrists to the bed.

Slowly, as if pulled by the very force of his desire, she moved her mouth down his chest and across his belly, licking, kissing, teasing. He held his breath, commanding his quivering flesh to stillness, and then, ever so softly, she lowered her lips and kissed the head of his manhood, wrapping her hands around the thick shaft. His breath erupted in a gasp of delight. Her touch was shy, almost uncertain, but nothing had ever brought him so close to losing control.

Something inside Nina began to throb in answer to Mike's ragged breath, his gasps and moans. Reveling in her power to arouse him, she trailed kisses along the length of his sex. Her nostrils filled with the male smell of him, the primal scent of sexual heat, and she marveled at the velvety softness of the tender skin that sheathed his hardness.

He was panting her name, begging her to stop, begging her never to stop. And then she took him into her mouth, and he nearly exploded.

Warmth spiraled within Nina as she moved her mouth on Mike. She had no need to ask or learn; she knew what to do, for she knew exactly how it would feel if Mike were sucking her breast. His mouth would be hot and wet, tight and yet gentle as his lips and tongue stroked her to new heights, and so she loved Mike with her own mouth in just that way. The warmth between her legs was spreading, setting her afire. Dimly she was aware that her hips were rocking, that she was pulsing with a need that came closer and closer to consuming her—

"Nina," Mike spoke through gritted teeth. "Sweetheart, I can't take any more." Gently he pulled her head away from him. He was trembling; another moment and he'd have been over the edge.

Dazed, almost drunk on her own passion and the taste and feel of his, Nina stood on shaky legs. "Stay there," she ordered him.

Quickly she stripped, resenting every second that she had to be away from him. Then, naked and unashamed, she took something from the table. She returned to the bed and unwrapped the condom. Mike had to guide her hands as she put it on him. He waited, erect and ready, and for the first time Nina guessed at the effort it had cost him not to touch her, not to take her as swiftly as his desire demanded.

"How do you want me, Nina?" he asked.

Every way. Forever, her heart answered. She climbed onto the bed and straddled him, lowering herself toward his thrusting sex. She shuddered all over when she touched him; he felt her body shake and saw her nipples grow even tighter and harder. She paused there, feeling him heavy and firm at the very entrance to her womanhood. Her head was thrown back, and her eyes were closed in an anticipation so intense that it was almost painful. Still Mike refused to let himself move.

"Pleasure yourself on me," he told her, and with a long moan she slid down onto him.

The tight heat of her squeezed him, and he knew he wouldn't last long. The condom was a blessing; without it he'd have climaxed as soon as she took him inside her. As it was, with any luck he could hold off long enough to give her what she needed.

She rode him with abandon, rubbing herself against his hardness. Her breasts bounced and swayed. Her eyes were unseeing; she was lost within herself, absorbed by the sensations that flooded her. Mike felt her sex grip him and hold him tightly, clenching in spasms of pleasure as she galloped toward her climax, and he cried out, "Now, Nina." Her taut expression softened and she gave an exclamation of delighted surprise, and he felt her tighten and tremble all along the length of him. And then, knowing that she had found release, he let himself go at last, exploding upward into her as she collapsed into his arms.

Afterward he rolled them both onto their sides so that they faced each other. They lay like that without speaking, their mouths close together, lips meeting for occasional gentle kisses, while their heartbeats slowed. Nina felt a profound peace. She knew now that her amnesia was no barrier to loving Mike. Her past was still a mystery to her, but she knew that she could never have experienced this much passion, this much intimacy, with any other man. It would have changed her, left some mark on her life. As she now felt transformed by being with Mike. She had shown him all that she was, revealing every desire, sharing every secret, and he had trusted her. He had let her have her way. His trust had been the greatest gift he could have given her. By letting her choose, he had made her want to give him even more of herself. As she gazed into his eyes, she prayed that he would give her more of himself.

Mike hadn't touched Nina all through the lovemaking, but now his hands couldn't get enough of her. He wanted to know every inch of her, to bond every part of her to him with his touch. He stroked her face, her back, the curve of her hip. He traced the long line of her thigh and explored her buttocks, cupping their roundness, teasing the small of her back where the cleft began. And then, when he ran his thumb up her rib cage, she moved a little and arched her back. Her breasts offered themselves to his questing hand.

He cupped one of them; it was tight and full in his hand. As he watched, the soft pale nipple tightened and darkened, stiffening as though begging for his touch. He flicked the sensitive peak with his fingertip, and the rhythm of Nina's breathing changed ever so slightly. She rubbed her breast against his hand, asking for more. He stroked and squeezed and pinched, and she responded eagerly.

He wouldn't have believed that anything could rouse him so soon after that last shattering climax, but to his amazement he realized that already he was getting hard again. Nina's innocent eagerness inflamed him; he needed to pleasure her in all the ways she'd pleasured him.

"Ready for more?" he whispered. "Because I am." He lowered his head, captured the tip of a breast in his mouth and suckled. Again that delicious warmth suffused them both, and Nina melted into him, molding her yielding body to his hard contours.

Mike's hand skimmed over her belly. His fingers probed the triangle of curls that covered her femininity, and then they found the silky-soft, slippery core of her. He kept suckling her swollen nipple, sending jolts of sensation through her, while he teased and stroked her tender woman's flesh. She rose eagerly to meet his hand, lifted by the tide of pure need that was rising again in her veins. It was a raging torrent that would not be denied, a flood that threatened to carry her far out to sea. And she cast herself into it. She would hold nothing back from Mike.

He raised his head from her breast. "You're so warm and wet, Nina," he said.

She replied in a slow, passion-drugged voice, "It's you. You make me that way. Every time you touch me, I feel it here." She grazed her nipples. "And here." She put her hand on his, pressing it more deeply into the dampness between her legs.

Mike said, "I want to taste you now." He parted her thighs so that her inmost secret place lay open to him, waiting for him to ease her frantic yearning. Then he lay between her legs and drank deep of her musky sweetness.

Nina cried out incoherently, overwhelmed with pleasure. The shocking, exquisite pressure of his lips and tongue, moving as if he knew exactly how she wanted to be touched, brought her so close to fulfillment that she squirmed, barely able to control herself. Her head rolled on the pillow; she called out his name again and again.

Mike had never known so responsive a partner, never been with a woman who gave him so much, so freely. The taste of her, and the shivering thrill of her response, goaded him to renewed desire. He knew that he had to lose himself inside her again.

He rose swiftly and put on another condom. Before coming back to bed he doused the lights, leaving only the red-gold glow from the grate of the stove to illuminate the cabin.

He knelt between her legs and placed himself against her. But instead of entering her at once, he hesitated, looking down at Nina. Her eyes were smoky and heavy-lidded, and her lips were parted, slightly swollen from his kissing. The silky flesh of her breasts and thighs gleamed wetly where he'd kissed her. She was beautiful, seductive; his manhood throbbed painfully at the sight of her. He desperately hoped that her carnality was pure, untainted by artifice or deceit. If only he could be sure that she wanted him as he wanted her—with an unquestioning need for the one person who could awaken the deepest passions of the heart and the flesh. And satisfy them.

Nina moved her hips, rubbing her waiting womanhood against his shaft, urging him to claim her. She touched her breasts gently, almost wonderingly, as though she were remembering his mouth on them, and then she reached up and tangled her hands in his hair to pull him into her.

"Look at me," Mike said, his gaze fixed on hers, so she did not close her eyes at the instant of his entry. They looked into each other's souls as their bodies joined. Mike buried himself in her to the hilt, and then he was lost. He had meant to make it long and slow for her, but instead it was urgent and rough. He rushed headlong to a climax that he couldn't even begin to control, a rush of release that swept up from the soles of his feet to the top of his head and poured out of him in a savage convulsion that shook him to the center of his being.

They fell asleep not long afterward, nestled together like spoons. Mike lay curved protectively around Nina's back, one arm holding her close, his hand resting on her breast. Late that night she woke and felt him aroused again, rigid against her buttocks. Feeling the answering tremor of hunger she rolled to face him. Too tired or too languid to fetch a condom from the table, they touched each other gently, lingeringly, until they brought each other to completion. He kissed her tenderly and wrapped his arms around her. With a whispered, "Go back to sleep, sweetheart," he then buried his face in her hair. Beneath the mingled odors of lovemaking, wool blankets and wood smoke, he noticed, her hair still smelled faintly fragrant. He thought that maybe the fragrance was sandalwood.

Mike didn't fall asleep right away, and he knew that Nina was awake, too. Words hung unspoken in the air: three little words that Mike had come close to saying more than once that night. Each time something had held him back. *You have no right,* he'd said to himself. *You're on the run, you've got nothing—less than nothing—to offer her. She's scared and alone, she's clinging to you. It wouldn't be fair to pressure her now. Wait until this mess is over. Then you can tell her.* Of course, his reasoning begged the question of how and when their current mess would be resolved. And there was one other thing that Mike couldn't put out of his mind. Was he really trying to be fair to Nina by staying silent? Or was he still haunted by doubt and mistrust—by the ghost of Karen?

Nina, too, wrestled with demons as she lay in Mike's embrace. She had no idea at all what would happen to them on the morrow, or what would be the outcome of the bizarre situation in which she'd found herself. And what of Mike? She didn't believe that two people could share what they had shared unless the feelings between them were as deep as the sea and as true as the North Star. Mike loved her, of that she was convinced, but she needed to hear it from him. What good was love if it remained unacknowledged? Would he ever be able to put his feelings into words?

When she finally fell asleep, Nina slept soundly. It was long after dawn when she woke, and the cabin was chilly;

the wood fire in the stove had long since burned out. Mike was up and dressed, rubbing at his damp hair with a towel. She stretched and emitted a creaky moan, and he grinned at her.

"You'll feel better after a shower," he advised. "And some food. We forgot all about eating last night."

The table was set and Mike had made breakfast. Admittedly, it was a rather odd breakfast. The orange juice was normal enough, but Nina wasn't used to eating turkey-and-cheese sandwiches and vanilla wafers first thing in the morning. Nonetheless, she licked her lips. "It looks delicious."

He laughed. "You're so hungry right now that possum burgers would look good."

She looked up sharply. "You have some?" Wrapping a blanket around herself in lieu of a bathrobe, she padded to the table and began demolishing her share of the food.

"Look, Nina, I've been thinking," Mike said. "We need help. We can't just leave here—Irons will have us picked up as soon as we show our faces, and if he's as bent as I think he is, God knows what'll happen. He could get us both put away on falsified evidence. Or worse."

"Can't we just stay here?" Nina ventured.

"Not for much longer. A few people know about this place. It used to belong to my partner—Jack Renzo, the guy I told you about." Nina glanced at Mike's face, but it held only a gentle sadness, not the wrenching misery she'd seen there when last he spoke of Jack Renzo. She thought that perhaps his deeply buried hurt had begun to heal, and she was glad.

"He left it to me in his will," Mike went on. "We used to come up here together to fish and talk about what hotshots we were." His face and voice were remote and wistful, as if he were looking at something long ago and far away. Then his expression cleared and he returned to the present. His eyes were laser bright and sharp this morning. Everything about him radiated energy; he was like an athlete who had geared himself up to face a daunting challenge.

"The point is, I could be tracked up here. We have to get on the road as soon as we can. But we're not Bonnie and Clyde. We're going to turn ourselves in to the authorities—but we have to do it in the right way, so that maybe we have a chance of being listened to. Although," he added with more than a trace of grimness, "I don't know how we're gonna convince anyone that Irons and Duchesne are the bad guys. All we've got is my hunch. And your psychic visions."

"They're real," Nina insisted.

"Yeah, maybe." Mike didn't sound convinced. He wasn't relishing the prospect of trying to persuade Morris Hecht that Nina had had a vision of the future in which a senior FBI agent had tried to kill him. Hell, Hecht would probably be ready to kill him himself. But it had to be done.

"I'm going to drive down the road to town and try to call Morris Hecht," he explained. "He's the chief of my detective division, and he's known me for a long time. He's not too pleased with me right now, but maybe I can make him listen to what we have to say. If I can just get him to raise the question of Irons's guilt, or Duchesne's, the feds will send some other officers in to clear it up, and we should be safe."

"Unless they discover that I'm part of the smuggling ring," said Nina, not angrily or defensively but forthrightly, meeting Mike's gaze.

"We have to take that chance," he said. "But I don't think it's true."

Nina's heart flooded with gratitude. "Thank you," she said, soft voiced.

Mike shrugged into his leather jacket. "I'll be back soon," he said. "But, Nina...if something happens to me, you try to get in touch with Hecht. And make Armand Zakroff get you a damned good lawyer.''

She ran to him and put her hands on his chest, feeling the strong and steady beat of his heart. ''Nothing's going to happen to you,'' she said fiercely.

He lightly kissed a cookie crumb away from the corner of her mouth. ''Get cleaned up and ready to roll.''

She nodded, and he slipped out of the cabin into the cool mountain morning.

Nina stowed the remains of their meal in a trash bag and brushed her teeth at the sink. Then, shivering a little, she dropped her blanket and stepped into the shower.

Mike had been right, she decided in the blessed, steamy heat of the water. Showered and with her hair washed and combed, she would feel a little better able to face the day. She had just turned off the hot water—reluctantly—when she heard Mike coming up the path. She grabbed a towel and headed for the door to greet him.

The door burst inward with a rending crash, and a dapper, dark-haired man in a gray overcoat strode into the room. He was carrying a large gun. Nina recognized him at once.

''Irons.''

He raised his brows and smiled thinly. ''I see you know who I am. Sorry about kicking in the door. Apparently—'' and his eyes roved over her wet body, barely covered with the towel ''—you weren't expecting me.''

''Where's Mike?'' Nina tried to sound brave, but she heard the quaver in her voice. She was afraid for herself, and she was right to be. The hard glitter in Irons's eyes left her in no doubt about that. But she was even more afraid for Mike. ''What have you done with him?''

''Don't ask questions,'' Irons ordered, brandishing the gun. ''Don't say another word unless I tell you to talk.''

She opened her mouth to protest—and then closed it again. Irons was watching her like a basilisk. ''That's right," he said malevolently. "Do what I say. Believe me, nothing would please me more than having a reason to beat the crap out of you. You have no idea how much you've cost me. Now get dressed. Hurry."

Biting her lips to keep them from trembling, Nina turned her back on him and pulled on her clothes as fast as she could, shaking with rage and terror and shame. The only thing that kept her from breaking down was the thought that Irons was probably not at all interested in her nakedness; he had other things on his mind. That, and the hope that Mike was still alive and was calling for help.

Keeping the gun aimed at Nina, Irons took a quick look around the cabin. "You may be wondering why I haven't shot you already," he said conversationally. "Don't get your hopes up. I am going to kill you. But not here—bodies have the damnedest way of turning up, even if you bury them in the middle of the woods. And not with a gun that could be traced to me. So we're going to take a little ride. You're going to walk down the path and get into the back seat of my car. Don't even think of trying anything. I said I wouldn't shoot you. But I can hurt you so much that you'll pray for a bullet." The purr in his voice froze Nina's blood.

They walked down the path, golden leaves crackling underfoot. Nina stumbled once and heard a warning snarl from Irons, who was walking behind her. When they reached the car he said, standing well back from her, "Open the back door. Get in."

She followed his orders.

"You'll find a pair of handcuffs on the seat," he continued. "Fasten one of the cuffs around the handgrip on the back of the front passenger seat. That's right, now pull it so I can see that it's fastened properly. Okay. Now fasten the other cuff around your wrist. Left or right, it's your choice." He smiled.

Nina handcuffed herself and demonstrated that the cuff was snug.

"Good girl. Now lie down on the seat." Nina did so, and Irons slid into the driver's seat and started the car. He turned and looked down at her. "You're going to lie there and not make a sound until I tell you otherwise. Got it?" She nodded.

Irons shifted gears and they drove off. Tears trickled down Nina's cheeks and she struggled not to sob. She was pretty sure that Irons would classify crying as making a sound, and she didn't want to know what he would do if she disobeyed him.

A long time passed—an hour or so, Nina guessed. Her right arm, held at an unnatural angle by the handcuffs that shackled her to the car, was beginning to ache. She focused fiercely on the physical pain, trying to blot out the fear that was lapping at her like a black sea. *What would Mike do?* Quelling the tears that threatened to flow again each time she thought about Mike, she told herself that he would stay alert and pay attention to what was happening. He'd want to gather as much evidence against this bastard as he could . . . just in case he ever had a chance to use it.

They had traveled straight and fast, without any turns, since soon after leaving the lake. *The interstate,* Nina thought. Irons was probably heading back to Philadelphia by the most direct route.

The car slowed. Irons pulled off the main road and eased to a stop. She could see part of the front seat through the gap between the bucket seats, and now she saw that Irons was dialing a cellular phone.

"I've got her," he said. "You know what we have to do now."

Then he said, "No, we'll go in one car. Yours is too conspicuous, he won't recognize this one. Meet me here.

I'm at the rest area near mile marker 90 on the interstate." *I was right. At least I know where we are,* thought Nina. It wasn't much of a triumph, but she clung to it. "Leave this minute—we don't have a lot of time," Irons was saying. "Yes, of course I'll tell her. I'll do it right away. And for God's sake, don't get stopped for speeding," he added disgustedly. "I can't get you off this time."

Irons clicked off the call and then punched in another number. "It's me. No, nothing yet. I've got men checking the highways. You keep an eye on her place in town. I'll get back to you in a couple of hours."

He hung up and turned to Nina. "We're going to take a little rest here. As far as anyone knows, you're asleep. Keep your eyes closed and stay quiet." He took a silk scarf from around his neck and draped it over Nina's arm, hiding her hand and the telltale handcuffs from the casual glances of anyone who passed by. The last thing that Nina saw before she closed her eyes was Irons pouring himself a cup of coffee from a Thermos.

An hour and a half crept by, maybe longer. Time passed with agonizing slowness. Occasionally a car would pull into the rest area, and Nina would hear voices and laughter, or the patter of footsteps passing their car. Each time someone approached she felt a wild stab of hope. Maybe this time help was arriving. Maybe Mike had gotten through to Morris Hecht. Maybe every cop and state police officer in Pennsylvania was looking for Irons right now.

One set of footsteps came closer and closer to the car. It could be Mike, coming like an avenging angel to tear Irons apart....

The footsteps reached the car and the door opened. Nina's eyes flew open. Julien Duchesne was climbing into the front seat. "Hello, darling," he said with a sneer. "Surprised to see me again so soon? That was a cute trick you pulled at the airport," he added viciously. "Who tipped you off? Your cop buddy?"

"Shut up," Irons said dispassionately. "Did you bring it?"

"What do you think?"

Neither man was looking at Nina now. Carefully, trying to move slowly and imperceptibly, she craned her neck and peered into the front seat. She saw that Julien was carrying an attaché case. He opened it and withdrew a metal strongbox. Glancing around to make sure that no one was looking at the car, he lifted the lid of the strongbox and showed its contents to Irons.

Nina got a quick look inside the box. It was full of green fire: a fortune in emeralds. It was the very same box she'd seen during her vision in Armand Zakroff's office. She remembered describing the vision to Mike, and now it had come true. She prayed that she'd have the chance to tell him about it.

Irons saw her looking at the emeralds and drew his gun. Nina cried, "No!" and shrank back, as far from him as the handcuffs would let her go. He reached into the back seat and casually struck her hard across the side of the head with the barrel of the heavy gun. She crumpled onto the floor in a dead faint, dangling from the wrist that was still pinned to the back of Julien's seat.

As he drove back to the cabin, Mike worriedly pondered his next move. He'd been unable to get in touch with Hecht. The station operator had said he was in a meeting. Had her voice been tinged with suspicion when she said, "Who is calling, please? Can I take a message?" Could they be tracing the call? Or was Mike just getting paranoid?

He snarled in frustration. He knew that Nina would be expecting him to come up with some kind of salvation, and he didn't want to watch her face fall when she realized that he had nothing to offer. The best he could think of was to call some trustworthy people he knew on the force and try to arrange a meet—

Mike was out of the car and running as soon as he saw the open door of the cabin. He forgot that he no longer had a gun. He didn't think about the fact that someone could be hiding in the cabin waiting to jump him. All he thought about was Nina. *Oh, God, what's happened to her?*

He knew at once that she'd been bushwhacked. The splintered frame of the kicked-in door told the story. He looked into the cabin, heart pounding wildly, and nearly fainted with relief when he saw that it was deserted. He realized then that he'd been expecting to find her body.

Okay, so somebody snatched her, probably Duchesne or Irons. They've taken her somewhere, maybe to see how much she knew about the smuggling operation. Mike thought of Nina being manhandled, beaten, tortured.... Nightmare images of the hellish things he'd seen during his years as a cop swarmed into his mind. His fists clenched, the veins stood out on his forehead, and in a cold fury he swore a profane oath against David Irons and Julien Duchesne. Then he considered his options.

He was already in deep trouble with the authorities. He knew that it would take time—lots of time—to convince Hecht or anyone else that he had a case against Irons and Duchesne. And time was just what Nina didn't have. He pounded his fists against the wall. *Damn it! Where would they have taken her?* Back to Philadelphia? To some hideout where they could waste her?

Mike hadn't been gone long—not more than half an hour. So they couldn't have much of a start. But the lake was just minutes away from a network of highways; they could be headed in any direction. He didn't have a clue.

Or maybe he did. "You're crazy," he said to himself. But he couldn't just blow off what might be his only lead.

Perhaps, just perhaps, the clue lay in Nina's "visions." Hadn't she said she'd seen him fighting with Irons? Mike gave a harsh chuckle. Let him get his hands on Irons, and she'd see a fight, all right. But the fight hadn't happened yet. If Nina were right about the visions—it was *going* to happen. What else had she said about it? Were there any clues about where this fight was supposed to take place? Her voice echoed in his mind: *"rolling around on a wooden floor."* That wasn't very helpful. There were a lot of wooden floors in the world. Maybe the fight was going to happen right here in the cabin.

What about the other vision in which Irons had appeared, the first vision that Nina had had? Mike strained to remember the details. A blond man and a dark-haired man—Julien Duchesne and David Irons—in a "tiny room." *"And the room looked like it was moving,"* Nina had said. An elevator? Then Mike remembered another of Nina's visions, the one in which she'd seen Julien aboard his sailboat. Of course! The tiny moving room was a boat's cabin, and the wooden floor was the deck. They must have taken Nina to Julien's boat.

Mike was halfway out the door when he realized what he was doing. He was pinning his faith—and maybe Nina's life—on the reality of her psychic visions. He wished that she could know that he was finally taking her at her word. Crazy or not, he had to believe that she really *had* seen glimpses of the future. Because if she hadn't, she might have no future left at all.

Mike hurried back to town, back to the phone booth where he'd tried to call Hecht. He had one card left to play. He called the station house again—and got a different operator this time, to his relief. He asked for Officer Simms. The rookie cop had been on the street the night Nina was picked up after the shooting. He'd seemed smart and sympathetic. It was taking a chance, Mike knew, but it was the only way.

Simms came on the line.

"Don't say anything for a minute, Simms," Mike said quickly. "Just listen. This is Mike Novalis. I need your help. So does Nina Dennison—remember her?"

"Where the hell are you, Lieutenant?" Simms hissed into the phone. "And what did you do? Hecht and everybody else is after your ass."

"Never mind where I am. Are you gonna help me or not?"

"You're suspended, man. And there's a warrant out. I could lose my job right now for not turning you in."

"Yeah, I know. How about it?"

Simms didn't answer for a minute. Mike forced himself to wait while Nina's life hung in the balance.

Then Simms said in a low voice, "What do you want me to do?"

"Julien Duchesne, one of the principals in that Zakroff and Duchesne business, keeps a boat somewhere down on Long Beach Island. The *Diamantina,* it's called. There're a dozen or so marinas there, and I need to know where that boat is. *Fast.* And without anybody finding out about it. Can you make a call to the shore police for me and call me back?"

"Yeah, I guess so," Simms replied guardedly.

"Okay, here's the number. Memorize it, don't write it down. And step on it."

Mike went half-crazy, waiting in that parking lot for Simms to call him back. Every second that passed was carrying Nina farther from him. For the first time, he wished he were a smoker. Anything to give himself something to do. He didn't even want to pace—he was wary of attracting attention to himself. So he sat in his car next to the phone booth and watched the second hand of his watch, trying not to think about what he'd shared with Nina last night. What he might have lost forever.

It was a long, long five minutes before the phone rang.

Simms delivered his information rapidly, in a low voice:
"Duchesne keeps his boat at the Shore Haven Marina, just
north of Harvey Cedars."

"Good job, Simms. Thanks."

"Good luck, man."

Mike hung up and climbed into his car. Fortunately he'd
filled the tank earlier in the morning. It was a long drive to
the New Jersey shore. He didn't dare speed; he might be
pulled over, and he wasn't protected by his police status
now. Every patrol car on the highway was probably looking for him, anyway. He'd be lucky not to get nailed.

His luck held. He pushed it as much as he dared, sailing
a few miles above the limit for most of the trip, and he
didn't get stopped. On the way he alternately cursed Irons
and Duchesne in a low, vicious monotone and prayed that
Nina was still alive.

Mike had asked himself a hundred times if he loved this
woman who had come into his life a scant two weeks ago.
Now he knew beyond doubt that he did. He couldn't bear
the thought of losing her. He'd spent such a long time
feeling dead and cold inside, and she had brought him
back to life. She'd looked at him with her clear-eyed, cou-
rageous gaze, and she'd seen everything good that was left
in him. He had despised himself, but she had shown him
that he was worth loving. Then he reminded himself that
she didn't know everything about him. *I wonder how she'll
look at me when she hears the whole story.* He checked his
watch again and gave the car a little more gas. He was finally ready to tell Nina the truth about himself—if it
wasn't too late.

He found himself talking to her as though she were there
at his side. He said, "There are a lot of things I should
have told you, sweetheart. I just wasn't sure of anything.
I wasn't sure of you—"

His voice broke. He raked a hand through his hair and
shook his head. He wouldn't let himself cry, not until he

knew there was no hope for Nina. *And I'm not giving up hope. No way.*

He cruised through Harvey Cedars and picked up a sign marking the turnoff to the Shore Haven Marina. The marina was quiet. That figured; it was a gray, gloomy Tuesday afternoon in October, and most of the people who kept boats at the Jersey shore were summer weekenders. Mike hung back in the shadow of a big boat lift and scoped the docks while gulls wheeled above, tearing the air with their harsh cries.

There were three long docks lined with boats. Some of the boats were small day cruisers or fishing vessels, but many were large, glossy cabin cruisers. There were even two big boats that, Mike supposed, qualified as yachts; he figured there were a couple of million dollars, easy, tied up in this marina.

Knowing what he did of Julien Duchesne, Mike was sure that the *Diamantina* would be one of the largest, newest and most expensive-looking sailboats in the marina. There were half a dozen likely candidates. From where he stood, Mike could see the names of two of them: the *Kambuja* and the *Someday*. He was going to have to walk out on the docks to check out the others.

He looked around again. The place was quiet; it seemed deserted, although he was sure that there was someone in the marina office. But there was no sign of life on any of the boats in which he was interested.

Slowly, feeling like a tin duck in a shooting gallery, Mike moved out onto the first dock. Two minutes later he had made the *Diamantina*. She was the big boat tied up at the very end of the dock, with a black hull, dark green canvas and a teak deck. *That fits,* thought Mike, remembering Nina's vision. The boat's portholes were shuttered; her hatchway was dogged down.

There was no way to sneak up on a boat, Mike realized. Not unless he had scuba gear, and it was a little late for that. The dock was as barren of cover as a windswept prairie; anybody watching from the *Diamantina* would see him coming. And if they missed that, they'd feel the boat move as soon as he stepped aboard. But there was no help for it. Longing for the reassuring heft of his gun, Mike boarded the *Diamantina*.

The narrow cockpit was empty, its side benches bare of cushions. There was no sound or movement from within the boat. Either those he sought had not yet arrived, or they had been here already and gone. Or they weren't coming to the boat at all, and the trip had been a wild-goose chase, a wrong guess that might have cost him his only chance to save Nina. *I'm not gonna believe that, baby,* he whispered to her in his heart. *You were right about the visions, I know you were. And somehow I'm gonna get to you in time.*

Mike took out his pocketknife, selected the largest blade and inserted it into the jamb of the hatch that led down into the cabin. He twisted it, and the flimsy lock slid open. Mike took a quick look over his shoulder—nothing was stirring down the dock. Apparently no one had paid any attention to the break-in aboard the *Diamantina*. He reflected sardonically that if he lived through the current crisis he could pick up some nice change working as a security consultant to the Shore Haven Marina. He slid the hatch open.

Mike hadn't often known the kind of dread that grips a man's vitals and paralyzes him, filling his mind with thoughts of failure and making him sweat the acid sweat of true fear. He felt it now, and he admitted that he was terrified to walk down that hatchway into the boat. He wasn't afraid that something was going to happen to him. He was afraid that this silent boat might be Nina's tomb. He didn't know what he would do if he found her down there, dead. He only knew that going down those stairs would be the hardest thing he'd ever done.

He descended into the main saloon. The only light came from the hatchway. The room was dark, but Mike could make out wood-paneled walls, a chart table and leather-upholstered seats along the walls. Two doors opened off a passage at the forward end of the saloon—staterooms, Mike supposed. He was about to look around when he felt a gun barrel against the back of his head and a voice said, "Welcome aboard."

Chapter 12

It might have been the agony in Nina's arm that woke her. Her shoulder was on fire and her wrist was numb. She was still hanging from the handcuff in Irons's car. And her head ached abominably where he had pistol-whipped her. She felt dizzy and nauseated, but even in the first confused moment of waking some instinct warned her not to move or make a sound. She didn't want Irons to know that she was awake; he might hurt her again.

The car was still moving. Carefully she sneaked a few quick peeks through barely opened lids. The quality of the light had changed. She was sure that several hours had passed, although the sky had clouded over and she could not catch a glimpse of the sun.

She heard Irons and Julien talking. Gritting her teeth against the pain in her arm, she lay still, pretending that she was still out cold so that they would continue to ignore her.

The two men were in the middle of an argument, apparently going over ground that they had covered before.

"—tell *me* what to do," Irons was saying acrimoniously. "You're the one who screwed things up in the first place. You couldn't leave well enough alone, could you? First you got greedy, and then you got careless, and then you panicked."

"Leave it—I said I was sorry." Julien's voice was sulky. "But I've been thinking it over. There's really no reason to call things off now. Once we get rid of her, we can go on as before. There's no evidence against us. No one can touch us."

"You really are a fool, aren't you?" said Irons. "I told you to put things on hold until the investigation moved away from Z and D, but you didn't listen. Now I'm telling you the whole deal has gone bad. You ought to think about running for cover. And remember that I call the shots."

Julien was silent for a few minutes. Then he said, "Did you call her?"

Irons heaved a sigh of exasperation. "Yes, I called her. Now will you please shut up? We're almost there."

Nina risked another peek out the window, hoping to catch sight of something that would tell her where they were, but all she could see from her vantage point on the floor was a patch of gray sky. As she watched, the first drops of rain hit the window and trickled down the glass like tears.

"Oh, great," Irons muttered. "Now the weather's acting up, too."

Julien gave an amused laugh. "This is nothing. Don't worry."

Nina's head was throbbing. She felt vague and confused; her ears were ringing, as though there were a babble of voices and sounds just out of her hearing. She watched the rain and felt a curious sense of double vision. The rain-streaked window seemed to be blurring and shifting before her eyes. The world had grown dim and foggy. Was the fog outside the car or in her mind? Random thoughts and memories of the past few days drifted through Nina's mind. She heard Marta's voice: *"Don't forget to take that nice green raincoat. The rainy season is about to start."*

Suddenly Nina wondered how Marta had known about the coat. Nina had bought it on the day she was shot; she'd seen the sales slip. Yet Marta had been in Switzerland with Julien then. Or had she?

Something shifted in Nina's mind. She almost heard a click, as if a door had opened.

And then she had her memory back.

Her peril, the pain in her arm, even her fears for Mike were forgotten for a moment in a rush of sheer joy and thankfulness. For two weeks she'd been stumbling in the dark in a strange house. Now the lights were on and she was home. She remembered her life, and for a moment she was flooded with memories: being carried in her father's arms to see the Christmas tree in Rockefeller Center, Charley surreptitiously teaching her how to drive in their mother's car, holding her mother in her arms at her father's funeral.

There was none of the drama that had accompanied her visions, none of the white flashes and vivid pictures. The change had been as smooth as stepping from one room to another. And the pain in her head was subsiding. Nina guessed that the blow from Irons's gun, which had landed right where she'd been shot, had somehow triggered the return of her memory. *Good does come out of evil,* she thought. *But I don't think I'll thank him.*

Nina was finally able to forgive Mike for his lingering doubts about her honesty. For now that she had recovered her memory, she felt a great rush of relief at the knowledge that she hadn't been part of the smuggling ring. There were no dark secrets in her past. For two weeks she'd been living with the fear that she might have done something terrible. And if *she* hadn't been able to banish that fear altogether, how could she have expected Mike to do so? He'd been doing his job, and doing his best to protect her at the same time.

Now Nina knew the truth about the emerald she had mailed to her brother. She had found it in Julien Duchesne's office.

She'd gone there one afternoon two weeks ago to borrow a jeweler's loupe....

Nina had taken her loupe home the night before to look at some garnets for a pin that she was designing for her mother's birthday. She'd forgotten to bring it back to the office with her, and now she needed it. She knew that Julien was out of the office—he'd gone to Switzerland on some family business. She'd borrow his loupe.

She didn't see it on his desk, so she sat down in his chair and opened the top drawer of his desk, the one where most people keep pens and paper clips. She didn't feel that she was doing anything wrong. The drawer wasn't locked; Julien must not keep anything very private in it.

The loupe must be in here, Nina had thought. She'd seen him take it out of the drawer dozens of times. Her fingers closed on something round and heavy at the back of the drawer, and without thinking she pulled it out. It was a large, roughly cut emerald. Nina knew at once that she'd never seen this particular stone in her life. It was a big stone. Even with a less-than-perfect cut, it was worth a couple of hundred thousand dollars.

Her mind raced. She knew that she should simply put the emerald back where she had found it and pretend she'd never seen it. It was Julien's business. But she kept thinking of things she'd noticed about Julien lately—little things, but they added up to an ominous pattern. The whole company knew that he'd lost a lot of his investments, but he'd been spending money wildly. And his behavior had changed. She'd never particularly liked Julien, but in recent months he'd become almost unbearable, alternately manic and moody. He was especially excitable on their buying trips to Colombia, during which he sometimes disappeared for hours at a time on "personal business." He had been more than usually nervous on the last trip, in June. Nina had wondered if Julien was using cocaine; she'd even thought about talking it over with Armand.

But maybe Julien's problem wasn't drugs. The emerald burned coldly in her palm. It didn't match anything in the Z and D workroom or inventory. Nina knew that it wasn't logged on any purchase or work order. It had almost certainly come from Colombia; the color and the crude cut suggested as much to Nina's expert eye. But she had personally examined all of the stones bought for Z and D in Colombia. And both she and Julien had declared no personal purchases at customs. Everything pointed in one direction: Julien had smuggled the stone. If he'd smuggled one, he'd probably smuggled more. He'd been behaving oddly even before their most recent trip; maybe the smuggling had been going on for some time.

Nina didn't know what to do. She wanted to go to Armand—but what if he were involved? She shrank away from that thought because she loved the Zakroffs, but she had to be sure. She was afraid to confront Julien directly. His hostility and unpredictability were getting worse. Just yesterday he'd practically taken her head off when she'd walked into his office while he was on the telephone. He'd grilled her suspiciously about what she'd overheard and seemed not to believe her when she swore to him that she hadn't heard anything.

The best thing would be to turn the problem over to the authorities, but what authorities? Nina couldn't go to the police—she didn't have enough proof of wrongdoing. Julien could bluff his way around the presence of a single stone.

She decided to hang on to the stone until she had figured out what to do. Julien wasn't due back in town for a few days; that gave her a grace period. She slipped the emerald into her jacket pocket and left Julien's office.

Then a chilling thought struck her: What if Julien weren't working alone? Armand—or someone else, she amended hastily—could come looking for the gem. She'd better not try to keep it in her office or apartment. But if she did nothing, if she put the emerald back where she'd found it, Julien would dispose of it and there'd be no evidence at all. She made a snap decision and sent the stone to her brother in Chicago. She enclosed a photocopy of the valuations from the last buying trip in case Julien tried to fiddle with the paperwork to make the stone look legitimate. And she sealed the whole thing inside a double wrapping, with a note to Charley asking him to hang on to the inner package until he heard from her—

"We're here" came Irons's voice, and Nina was jerked back to the present. The car stopped.

"You get her," Julien said, "and I'll take this." He hefted the attaché case.

Irons opened the door to the back seat. One hand was in his coat pocket. He saw her looking at it and said, "It's the gun. I'll kill you unless you do exactly what I say." He handed her a key. "Unlock the cuffs and unhook yourself from the car."

Nina's arm had gone numb. As soon as she moved it, she felt the crippling pain of restored circulation. She rubbed her wrist and tried to straighten and flex the arm. "Now cuff your wrists together in front of you," Irons ordered. Fumblingly, Nina obeyed. "Throw me the key. That's the way. Get out."

She struggled to her feet and Irons draped the scarf over her wrists. "Now come with us."

Nina saw that they were at the ocean—they must be somewhere on the Jersey coast. The sea was gray. Spatters of rain fell from an overcast sky, and a cold wind was blowing. They were at a dockyard. Dozens of boats were bobbing at the docks, colorless and forlorn on the dreary autumn day.

"She's not here," Julien was saying distractedly as he looked around the parking lot.

"She's probably on the boat. Come on." Irons prodded Nina, and she walked carefully down a ramp and onto the dock. It was a floating dock; it bobbed and swayed sickeningly under her feet. The water looked as cold as death.

Nina's recovered memories dovetailed with what she had learned from Mike and what she had overheard between Irons and Julien. Irons and Julien were in on the smuggling operation together. Julien acted as the courier; maybe he also helped dispose of the stones, either on the black market or by providing faked provenances.

She seethed with fury, remembering those trips back from Colombia with Julien. She'd stood there in the airport, innocently presenting her invoices and valuations and purchases to the customs agents, while Julien smiled blandly and acted the part of the big-shot businessman, chatting with the agents about the state of the gem business and the difficulties of a border guard's job. And all the while he'd been carrying a fortune in contraband—gems that represented drug money.

But something had upset Julien's profitable applecart. Based on what she had heard that day, Nina guessed that when the international investigation got too close, Irons had ordered Julien to stop smuggling the stones. Julien, unwilling to give up the easy money, had defied Irons and brought in another lot of illegal emeralds. He'd been careless with them, though, and Nina had found one.

Then the last piece of the puzzle fell into place for Nina....

It was late at night, the night of the day on which she'd found the emerald in Julien's office. Nina received a hysterical phone call from Marta Duchesne, Julien's sister. Nina didn't know Marta very well, and Marta had never called her at home before. But now she sounded beside herself with worry or fear.

"I need you to help me," she cried.

"What do you want me to do? What's wrong?"

"It . . . it's so difficult to explain. But I have to talk to someone. I need your advice. Can we go somewhere and get a drink?"

Nina wondered whether Marta was suspicious of Julien. Maybe Marta, too, had found some piece of incriminating evidence. Marta urged her to come out to a restaurant for a talk, and Nina agreed, feeling that Marta might calm down more quickly in a public place. Marta picked Nina up. "I know a new place on the waterfront," she said. She refused to answer Nina's questions, saying, "I'm too upset to talk about it while I'm driving—wait until we get to the restaurant."

But Marta took an out-of-the-way route through the deserted streets of the North Philly warehouse district, and Nina started to get nervous. Marta's manner was so strange, so tense and febrile. She kept looking at Nina out of the corner of her eye, not like someone seeking a confidante but calculatingly, like someone assessing a risk.

The car began slowing for a red light. Marta said, "I was in Julien's office today. Were you?"

All at once Nina was scared. She didn't care how big a fool she might be making of herself if her fears were unfounded: She wanted to get away from this woman, and she wanted to get away now. Without pausing to think she threw open her door and jumped out. But the car was still moving, and Nina stumbled and fell to her knees on the pavement. The car's brakes screeched, and Nina looked back in fright. The last thing she saw was Marta's face, distorted with anger as she aimed a gun.

Now Nina knew. It was Marta who had shot her. Marta must have been in on the smuggling scheme all along; Nina remembered how close the Duchesnes had always seemed, and how Marta had always appeared to be the dominant member of the duo. Marta had probably found the emerald missing and gotten suspicious of Nina; maybe someone at Z and D had innocently mentioned seeing Nina in Julien's office. Maybe Marta herself had seen Nina leave the office and soon after discovered the jewel missing. However she had found out, Marta had decided to kill Nina. She must have thought that her first shot was fatal. There'd been no time to check—in North Philly, her foreign sports car was as conspicuous as a UFO, and Marta wouldn't have wanted to take a chance on being spotted at the scene of the shooting. So she'd left Nina for dead. Nina wished that she could have seen Marta's and Julien's faces when they learned that she was still alive.

The little procession had reached the end of the dock. Nina's mind went blank with helpless terror. She thought that Irons was going to shoot her in the back and shove her off the dock. Instead he pushed her roughly toward a big sailboat. "Get aboard," he said. Julien jumped lightly onto the boat's deck, and Nina realized that this must be his boat.

She scrambled aboard awkwardly, hampered by her bound wrists and by the motion of the boat, which was straining at its moorings, tossed by the sea's angry chop.

Irons followed her. He picked up the attaché case from one of the side benches and, with a scowl at Julien, carefully stowed it in a cuddy under the bench.

Julien laughed. "Look, I know you don't like boats, Irons, but it's perfectly safe. Things don't just fall overboard. We're tied up at the dock, for God's sake." He opened the hatchway and hurried down into the cabin. Irons motioned for Nina to follow.

"Marta? Marta?" called Julien. He turned to Irons, alarmed. "She's not here."

Irons shoved Nina onto a seat and shrugged. "So? We still have a job to do."

"I don't like casting off without her," Julien said worriedly.

"We'll pick her up later. We need to get moving. *Now.*" The menace in his voice was unmistakable, and he had taken the gun out of his pocket. Its barrel was still trained on Nina, but Julien went pale.

Now it's your turn to be afraid, Nina thought vindictively. The alliance seemed to be breaking down.

The boat gave a little lurch, and the room bobbed up and down. Nina felt a shock of recognition: The tableau in front of her matched the first of the visions she'd had, the one she'd experienced while eating lunch with Mike on the first day of her amnesia. She'd seen Julien and Irons talking in a small, moving room, and here they were. Unfortunately, the vision hadn't shown Nina how to prevent what was going to happen next.

"Back on deck," Irons ordered her. "I want you where I can keep an eye on you."

The three of them trooped back up the stairs and out the open hatchway into the cockpit. With a sullen look at Irons, Julien began preparing to get under way, checking the engine's fuel gauge and casting off the mooring lines. Irons sat down on one of the side benches, motioning with his gun for Nina to sit opposite him.

"I hope you like boats," he said to her with a hard smile. His eyes were two beads of obsidian, as heartless as those of a reptile. "We're going to go for a little boat ride. But I'm afraid you won't be coming back with us. Once we get out far enough, you're going into the drink."

He watched her, waiting for her to show fear, and Nina defiantly kept all expression off her face. She'd be damned if she would give him the satisfaction of seeing her cry again, or beg.

"Oh, I'll take the cuffs off, first," Irons continued. "I don't think your body will ever be found. I hear there are a lot of sharks in these waters this year. But even if they find enough to identify you, there won't be anything to suggest foul play. You'll just be a tragic drowning victim who hit her head on something—" he hefted the gun "—and fell overboard. Too bad."

Julien started the engine and took the wheel. The boat churned slowly away from the dock and then headed out to sea. The wind freshened, whistling through the rigging and blowing Nina's hair across her face. The boat bounced as it cut across the choppy waves. Irons turned up the collar of his coat and grimaced. "And some people do this for fun. Jesus!"

Nina gazed back as the coast receded into the distance. Her eyes stung from the tearing wind and her whipping hair. She knew that Irons and Julien were going to kill her and give her body to the sea once they were far from shore, but she was unafraid. She had passed beyond fear into a numb, hopeless grief. Facing death, she thought only of the life that she and Mike would never share. He would never know what had happened to her. And she would never know what had happened to him. She had never told him that she loved him. She regretted that now. From the depths of her being Nina sent up a silent, heartfelt request: *Let him be alive. Please, let him be all right.* She asked for nothing for herself. All her thoughts now were for Mike. Her sorrow for the life they might have had together was lost in the intensity of her prayers for the one who was dearer to her than her own breath and blood.

Julien left the wheel and stripped the canvas cover from the boom. He started untying the lines that lashed the big mainsail down.

"What're you doing, you idiot?" yelled Irons. "Leave that thing alone. Just use the motor, damn it!"

Julien grinned at him, a manic glitter in his eye. "You want this done fast, don't you?" he called mockingly. "Well, I can double our speed with the sail up." With a series of sharp tugs he raised the mainsail. He tied off the line and jumped back into the cockpit, and the sail bellied out with a loud snap.

Again Nina was startled by a sense of recognition that was far stronger than déjà vu. For an instant Julien's profile was silhouetted against the white, flapping sail, exactly as she'd foreseen it in her vision. *Number five,* she said to herself. Now they've all come true.

But they hadn't! What about the last vision: the one of Mike and Irons fighting? Nina swallowed hard, trying to make some sense out of her clamoring thoughts. The fight she'd seen in her vision could have happened already. Irons could have grabbed Mike when Mike left the cabin this morning to telephone Hecht. They could have fought then, and Irons could have killed Mike or turned him over to confederates. Nina's imagination ran wild. Maybe Mike was now in the hands of drug dealers who were extracting revenge for his years as a vice cop—

She didn't believe it. For one thing, all of the other visions had come true *just as she'd seen them.* They weren't about things that happened somewhere else; they foreshadowed things that she was going to see. So the fight between Irons and Mike couldn't have taken place without her knowledge. Besides, Irons had been unrumpled, positively dapper, when he showed up at the cabin, and Nina just wasn't willing to believe that he could have tangled with Mike Novalis and walked away without a scratch. *Or walked away at all,* she added.

She looked up, startled. While she'd been trying to figure out whether her psychic visions were sufficient grounds for hope in a desperate situation, Julien and Irons had started arguing again, and now Julien sounded half-hysterical.

"What do you mean, we're not going back?" he cried.

"I told you, it's over. Thanks to your screwup, there's too much heat. My bosses will be looking at you, and they'll be looking at me."

"We could ride it out," Julien pleaded.

"I'm not taking the chance. You're getting us out of here. We're going to dump the excess baggage and then work our way south to the islands. We've got a fortune in stones—we can disappear down there and live like kings."

"But what about Marta?" Julien's face was haggard.

"You're awful damn worried about that sister of yours," said Irons. "You know, I was starting to wonder about the relationship between you two. Maybe you're a little closer than a brother and sister should be?"

A howl of animal rage erupted from Julien's throat, and he tensed as if to spring at Irons. But Irons swiveled the gun and Julien stopped in his tracks, his face working convulsively.

"Hell, I don't care if you are making it with your sister," Irons said contemptuously. "She's not a bad-looking broad, if you like the bitchy type. But get this, you fool. She'd double-cross you in a second."

"She wouldn't." Julien ground the words out, and then screamed, "Not Marta! She wouldn't!"

Irons laughed. "While you were in Switzerland, you poor chump, she came to me and offered to cut you out if I split fifty-fifty with her. She even offered to do me on the spot, any way I wanted it, just to seal the deal."

The hatchway door slid up and Mike Novalis stepped through it into the cockpit. Nina's first wild blaze of hope died as quickly as it had been born. Mike's hands were clasped behind his head. Behind him stood Marta Duchesne, holding a gun.

"Don't believe him, Julien," she said.

Julien stared at her. "Marta! Thank God you're here. It was Irons, he made me leave without you."

She ignored him and spoke to Irons. "Did you really think you could double-cross me and get away with it, you piece of—"

"I didn't say anything about double-crossing you, Marta," Irons replied smoothly. "We were going to send for you."

"I'm sure you were." She laughed. "And split three ways instead of two? Or maybe you planned to dump Julien, too, once he got you to safety, and keep it all for yourself?"

Irons was as still as a statue, but she must have seen the answer in his face, because she said, "I thought so. Well, isn't this an interesting situation? There truly is no honor among us."

Julien's eyes were riveted on Marta. "Is it true? Were you really going to...to sleep with him?"

"Forget about that and get his gun!"

"But—"

"Do it!" she shrieked.

Marta and Irons stared at each other with naked hatred in their eyes, covering each other with their guns. Julien looked from Marta to Irons, gnawing his lip in indecision. Locked in their standoff, the three conspirators seemed to have forgotten Mike and Nina, but Nina knew that if she moved an inch, or if Mike did, one or both of those guns would instantly turn on them. She looked at Mike. Drizzle and spray were plastering his thick black hair to his head and neck, and the contours of his cheekbones and jaw stood out sharply. In the pallid light his indigo eyes looked almost black. He shot her the roguish grin that she loved so much, and her heart turned over. She knew that he wasn't going to go quietly.

The boat breasted a big wave and dropped into the trough. Marta swayed on the narrow top step of the hatchway. Just then Mike drove one elbow back into her stomach as hard as he could and launched himself across the cockpit at Irons. He hit the FBI man in a flying tackle as Irons fired. The shot went wild. Then Mike and Irons were rolling on the deck of the cockpit, grappling for control of the gun in Irons's hand.

Marta lurched into the cockpit and raised her gun toward the melee on the deck, but she couldn't get a clear shot at either Mike or Irons. Julien had left the wheel and thrown himself into the struggle, trying to pull Mike off Irons.

"Get out of the way!" Marta screamed. She looked like a wild thing, desperate with rage. In a second, Nina knew, she'd start firing and not care who got hit.

Scrabbling under the seat with her shackled hands, Nina seized the attaché case and opened it. She grabbed the strongbox and stood.

"Stop!" she cried. She jumped up onto the seat and knelt awkwardly on the gunwale, holding the box out over the deck rail. She was just inches away from the dark water swirling and hissing past the boat's hull.

"Stop it!" she screamed again. "Or I drop the box!"

Julien rose. "Give it to me," he begged. "I'll let you go—"

Mike wrenched the gun from Irons, knelt on the man's chest and clouted him in the head, knocking him out. At the same instant, Marta took aim on Mike from behind.

Nina hurled the strongbox at Marta with all her strength. As Marta fired, the box struck her heavily in the shoulder, and she staggered and fell back across the gunwale, hanging half out of the boat.

The *Diamantina* lurched and wallowed as a heavy wave caught her broadside. Marta flailed for the deck rail but couldn't reach it in time. She was thrown overboard. Julien made a grab for the strongbox, which was lying on the slippery gunwale. The box slid smoothly under the deck rail and into the sea. With a single shrill cry, Julien dived over the rail. Nina was never sure afterward whether he was going for his sister or the stones.

Mike was lying on the floor of the cockpit in a pool of blood and water. But he was alive; his eyes were open and he was clutching his left shoulder. Nina knelt at his side. He grinned weakly and said, "My heroine."

"Oh, Mike, I've been so scared. I thought I'd never see you again." She looked fearfully at his shoulder. "How— how bad is it?"

"I'll live. In fact, you saved my life. Marta was gonna blow my head off, but you spoiled her aim and I got away with a nice clean little shoulder wound. Cheer up," he said, hoping to ease the anxiety he saw on her face, "I'm going to be around for a while."

She managed a tremulous smile.

"That's better," he told her. "Now we've got to do some things." He looked at Irons, who was still unconscious. "First we'd better deal with him."

At Mike's direction, Nina went through Irons's pockets, looking for the key to her handcuffs. She was shaking with revulsion as she pawed through his wet clothes, afraid that at any second his eyes would snap open and he would seize her hands. But he didn't move, and after heaving him onto his side she managed to extract the key from his hip pocket. She handed it to Mike, who unlocked the cuffs, wincing and trying not to gasp with pain as he moved. Nina was desperately worried about him. Despite his bravado—kept up largely for her sake, she was sure—he had lost a lot of blood.

"Now we'll use the cuffs on Irons." Mike told her what to do. Puffing a little, she wrestled Irons's limp body over to the nearest deck cleat and fastened one cuff to the cleat, the other to his wrist. As Irons had taught her, she made sure that the cuffs were good and tight.

The rain was now increasing and the sky was completely overcast, a uniform dark gray. Mike couldn't be sure which direction was east and which west. As they didn't know their position relative to the coast, it was dangerous to remain under way. Their best chance for rescue was to stop moving. He told Nina to cut the engine. Only then would he let her help him down into the cabin, where it was dry, if not warm.

Mike collapsed onto one of the leather benches. His strength was fading fast. "The radio," he said. "This boat must have ship-to-shore. We'll call for help."

Nina looked around feverishly; after a moment she located the radio on the bulkhead near the chart table.

"Know how to use it?" Mike asked. She shook her head.

He talked her through it. She opened a channel and spoke into the microphone: "Mayday, mayday. This is the sailboat *Diamantina,* out of Shore Haven Marina, Long Beach Island. We have an emergency. Repeat, emergency. Two people overboard and a gunshot wound in need of medical treatment. We are approximately three miles offshore and drifting under sail. Please send aid."

Nina repeated the message three times and activated the radio's distress beacon. Then she went looking for a first-aid kit.

She stripped Mike to the waist and wiped away the blood from around the singed black hole where the bullet had entered his flesh. She nearly wept at the sight. He was so strong—but even strength and honor, Nina reminded herself, were vulnerable. She ached to take away his pain, to protect him and keep him safe so that nothing could ever hurt him again. But that, she knew, was impossible. The best she could do was to love him.

She placed an antiseptic dressing on the wound and bandaged it, then brought two blankets from one of the staterooms and covered him well.

"Sit down with me," he said. "Put my head in your lap."

She raised his head, as gently as she could, and did as he had asked. He sank back into her with a sigh as if he'd won a long battle.

And then he began to talk.

"There's something I've got to tell you, Nina." She held her breath, hoping that he was going to tell her that he loved her.

"Something about me. I want you to know the truth about me."

"I already know about you," she told him lovingly, placing her palm on his cheek.

"No. Not this. You gotta know...." His voice faded and his eyes drifted shut. Then, visibly gathering his strength, he continued. "I told you about Jack. My partner who died?"

She nodded.

"What I didn't tell you was that I killed him."

He watched her through the haze of pain, waiting for her face to change, waiting for her to take that warm, soft hand away. But she said softly, "I know you better than that. Tell me."

"I didn't shoot him. But I made it happen. The raid we went on that night—it was a setup. And it was my fault." Despite the pain and shock of his wound, Mike felt clearheaded, as clearheaded as he'd been in years. He was confronting a much deeper and older pain, and he thought that this time he had a chance to emerge victorious. Strength flowed into him from Nina's hands, from her voice and smile, from her spirit. Would she take that strength away when she had heard it all?

"There was a woman. Her name was Karen. I met her when I was setting up the bust. She was the sister of one of the dealers. She hung out with them all." Mike paused to catch his breath. Nina gazed down at him, full of compassion. She knew what was coming next, but she let him speak. He was giving her the greatest gift of all, entrusting her with the darkest part of his soul.

"I thought I was in love with her," he said, voice cracking—with fatigue or emotion, Nina didn't know which. "It wasn't really love, I know that now, but I was crazy about her. Karen was smart. I should have stayed away from her, but I spent way too much time around her. It didn't take her long to make me for a cop."

Again Mike labored for breath. His voice had grown faint. He could barely keep his eyes open. But he forced himself to go on. If he didn't finish this now, maybe he never would.

"She told me that she hated the high life, wanted to get away from it. But one of the top bosses had something on her brother. She said that if her brother tried to stop dealing, his boss would see that he went to prison. I told her I'd help her. The big bust was going down.... I warned her to stay away from the warehouse that night. And I told her to keep her brother away, too. I shouldn't have done that, Nina, I shouldn't have done that."

Mike started to cry, harsh gasping sobs that racked his injured body and knifed into Nina's heart. She hushed him and soothed him, kissing the tears away from his eyes. "Don't say any more," she told him.

"No, I want you to hear it all." He wiped his face with his good hand and went on. "You know what happened. The bust went bad and Jack got blown away. Karen had tipped off the drug bosses. I never even in my wildest dreams thought that she would ever do that." There was a universe of savage self-reproach in his voice. "I held Jack in my arms while he bled to death, Nina. He knew what had happened. He knew right away. Do you know what he said to me, Nina? He said, 'Don't let this destroy you, Mike.' The guy was dying, and he was worried about me."

His eyes closed wearily. "Now you know, Nina. That's why I couldn't trust you, couldn't believe in you. I was afraid you were another Karen. It wasn't fair." His voice faded to a whisper. "I'm so sorry."

"Mike, there's something I have to tell you." He looked up at her groggily.

"I got my memory back."

"Did you? That's good." He was fading fast.

"And everything is okay, Mike. I'm not in any trouble. But you were right to be worried. I might have been involved. Don't be sorry...." Nina's voice trailed into silence. Mike was unconscious.

Nina waited, and as she waited she once again saw the flashes of white light that had signaled each of her visions. This vision, like the others, didn't last long. It was just a glimpse of something—something that might come to be. And when it was over Nina knew, without quite knowing *how* she knew, that it was the last vision she would ever have. Her gift had served her well—it had saved her life and Mike's. Now it was gone. The future was as much a mystery to her as it was to every other human being. But in its place she had been given back her past.

Mike's head rolled limply in her lap. Nina saw that blood was already beginning to seep through the dressing on his shoulder. His breath was deep and even, and his heartbeat, when she pressed her hand to his chest, was strong and steady. But he felt so cold. She tucked the blankets more closely around him and bent over his still form, cradling his head in her arms.

The boat was wallowing. Its steady side-to-side motion was almost comforting, as though the sea were a giant rocking chair, lulling them with its eternal rhythm. Rain continued to fall, not in a howling storm but in a straight gray soaking. Even in the cabin the air was dank and chill.

Nina wondered briefly about Irons. He was sure to be drenched by now. But earlier, when Nina had said something about trying to get him into the cabin, Mike had flared up, a steely glint in his eyes.

"Let him drown," he said savagely. "Let him freeze. Only he won't, the bastard. He can't reach the wheel or anything else, so he can't do any harm. Just leave him where he is. If he'd hurt you, Nina, really hurt you—" he paused, and suddenly his drawn face looked ten years older "—I might have killed him." He pulled her to him then, groaning as the sudden movement pained his shoulder. So Nina had led him to the bunk and thankfully left Irons manacled to his cleat. For all she knew, he was still unconscious.

Above the smack of the waves and the rattle of the rain she thought she heard another sound. A moment later, there it was again, clearer now. It was the *thuk-thuk-thuk* of a helicopter, getting closer.

Mike stirred restlessly in her arms. Nina murmured, "It's all right, darling. We're safe. You're going to be okay," as she stroked his damp hair. She traced his dark brows and the planes of his face with trembling fingertips. How pale he looked. Nina remembered how he had looked when he knelt above her on their tumbled bed in the fishing cabin; she had touched him then, too, stroking his face and gazing into his eyes as if she'd never seen him before; and then she had tangled her hands in his hair and pulled him into her with a cry, and he had loved her.... Only hours ago. "Hang on, honey, please," she said.

The black lashes swept up and Mike's eyes blazed blue in his white face. "Nina," he slurred. "Listen. 'Simportant.''

"I'm here, Mike. I'm right here."

"Love you," he gasped. "I love you."

He passed out.

"I know," she whispered. Then the helicopter roared overhead. Its earsplitting racket was the second most beautiful thing Nina had ever heard.

Epilogue

Mike woke up in a white room filled with flowers. The first thing he saw was Nina. As soon as his eyes opened she surged up from her chair.

He widened his eyes and made his face go blank. "Who are you?" he said, putting a hand to his head. He groaned and blinked at her. "Where am I? *Who* am I?"

She stopped dead in her tracks, an expression of incredulous dismay on her face. "Oh, no," she wailed. "Not this. I don't believe it!"

"April Fool," he said with his widest grin.

She stamped her foot. "Don't you ever, *ever* do that to me again," she warned. "And anyway, it's October—just in case you've forgotten the month, too," she added sarcastically.

"I'm sorry, sweetheart, I couldn't resist," he said. "But I promise—no more amnesia jokes ever again. Now come here."

"Well...all right." But she was smiling, and her eyes were bright with happiness.

Mike wanted to take her in his arms, but the left one wasn't working just then, so he had to settle for gathering her to him with his right arm only. She came to him tentatively.

"I won't break," he growled into her hair, and with a joyous laugh she lay next to him and held him tight.

"I'm glad you haven't forgotten *this,*" she murmured.

He answered, "Never." And meant it, too, more than he'd ever meant anything in his life.

He smelled again the smell of her, that hint of soap and sandalwood, and felt her smiling into his neck. Her breasts were deliciously full against him, one long leg rested across his thighs...and Mike noted bemusedly that his body was reacting to hers just as though he hadn't recently taken a beating and a bullet.

In the *hospital?* he asked himself, and knew that where Nina was concerned, his answer had to be: *Anytime, anyplace.* Still, he could at least *try* to act like a respectable patient.

"You'd better get up for a minute, sweetheart," he said regretfully, "or you'll have to find a Do Not Disturb sign for the door."

Nina sat up and threw back her hair, eyes sparkling wickedly. "*I* wouldn't mind, but the doctor did say you shouldn't, um, overdo it for a while. You need to build up your strength."

"It's already built up," he muttered, but beyond an impish glance down the bed Nina pretended not to know what he was talking about. She pulled her chair to the side of his bed, sat down and took his hand.

"I think you're up to a little hand-holding."

"Get back on this bed, and I'll show you what I'm up to," Mike invited.

She shook her head. "Some other time," she said, and there was a promise in her eyes. Mike demanded an update on everything that had happened during the eighteen hours he'd been asleep. His first question was about Sig.

He relaxed when Nina told him that Sig was at her apartment, happily drooling on the bed and gnawing on the last remains of the much-abused sofa cushions.

Then they talked about Irons. He was under arrest. In all the confusion, the key to the handcuffs had been washed into the boat's bilge, and the Coast Guard had had to get a special tool and unscrew the cleat to get Irons clear. It should have been funny, but it wasn't. Nina shuddered, remembering the venomous glance he had thrown her as they led him away. She was glad there was to be no bail.

A federal prosecutor had arrived from Washington, accompanied by a retinue of DEA, FBI and Treasury officials, all eager to talk to Mike and Nina. A probe of Irons's link to Colombian drug money was under way. In the meantime, Irons had been charged with kidnapping, attempted first-degree murder and conspiracy to murder. The trial would be a long drawn-out circus, but in the end Irons would face a long prison sentence.

"The Duchesnes?" Mike asked.

"Nothing. The official verdict is lost at sea."

Shark bait, Mike thought, and was not sorry for it. He laughed a little harshly. "The emeralds," he said. "When the story gets out, every scuba diver on the East Coast will be trying his luck."

"The Coast Guard divers are already out there," she told him. "But the currents are strong, the mud on the bottom is deep and that box wasn't very big. Somehow I don't think those stones'll ever be found." She thought of Julien's upturned face vanishing astern. "At least I hope not."

The sad irony of it all was that everything that had happened to her, from the shooting on, had been unnecessary. Nina hadn't known enough about the smuggling operation to get anyone in trouble. The single stone she'd found in Julien's desk wasn't enough to incriminate him; he could easily have explained it away. But he panicked, thinking that Nina knew more than she did. He flew to

Switzerland as planned and established an alibi there while
Marta shot Nina. And once they had gone that far, the
conspirators were committed. They couldn't be positive
that Nina really did have amnesia; she could nail them for
attempted murder, if not for the smuggling. Their only
hope was to find out what she knew and get rid of her before she could turn them in. They had almost suc-
ceeded—until a stubborn rogue cop had gotten in their
way.

Mike jerked a thumb at the largest and most elaborate
floral arrangement. "Where'd this stuff come from?"

"Mostly from Armand," Nina explained. "This whole
thing has been a nightmare for him, too. But at least everyone knows he didn't have anything to do with the
smuggling and the drug money. He just ran the design side
of the business. In fact, he's relieved to be rid of Julien."

Nina gave Mike the highlights of a long talk she'd had
with Armand Zakroff that morning. "I'm too old to run
this business by myself," Armand had said, "and too
young to give it up. I need a partner I can trust, someone
whose ideas are like my own. I want you to be that partner, Nina."

The offer was appealing. Except that Nina knew that she
did not want to measure her work by dollar values and
profit margins alone. She had seen with brutal clarity the
dark side of the world of precious stones, the fatal power
of gems to corrupt and destroy. So she had accepted Armand's offer—but only if he agreed to turn the import
dealership into a training center for gemology and jewelry
making.

"And he loves the idea," Nina said enthusiastically.
"He wants to get students from all over the country, and
experts to come in and give seminars. We'll still do some
buying and selling, but the emphasis will be on design. I'll
get to teach some classes on semiprecious stones—"

"Like spodumene," Mike teased.

"Exactly like spodumene," she said firmly. But her heart was singing, because Mike had remembered their silly little joke. So this is what it's like, she realized with sudden wonder. This feeling that everything that happens between us is ours alone, that nothing like it has ever happened before.

She squeezed his hand and concluded, "We've worked out a deal where I'll earn my share of the business over time. I think it's going to be great."

He raised her hand to his lips and kissed it. "To your success."

"And Armand's," she added dutifully.

"If you think I'm going to kiss Armand's hand—"

"Just kiss mine again."

He did so. "So the company will still be Z and D," he said thoughtfully. "Zakroff and Dennison."

Nina looked at him, remembering her first glimpse of him in this same hospital. He still needed a haircut and a shave. She studied the deeply etched lines in his forehead: evidence of a lot of frowns over the years. Oh, there was no doubt about it. Mike Novalis was arrogant, hot tempered and very used to being on his own. But he was also funny, and kind, and brave, and passionate. And she knew that once he had given his word and his heart, he would be faithful to the end of time. She loved him.

And love made her want to offer him the best she had. Mike had taken a leap of faith when he told her he loved her. Now it was her turn to be greatly daring for him. "Actually," she said, "I'm pretty sick of the initials Z and D after everything that's happened. I was thinking of changing them." She drew a deep breath and was surprised at how fearless she felt, how right. "How about Z and N? For Zakroff and Novalis."

He went utterly still, and her heart almost stopped. She'd taken the leap—but was he going to meet her, after all? Or was she wrong about everything?

"Do you mean—" He cleared his throat and tried again. "Do you mean you'll marry me?" His voice was almost a whisper, but it was full of uncertain hope, and in his eyes she saw a hunger and a need that matched her own.

"If you'll propose," she said.

He pulled her close. "Will you," he said between kisses, "marry me?"

"Yes," she answered breathlessly.

"Did you foresee this? Did you know I wanted to marry you?"

"No. Not like the visions. That's over, now that I have my memory back. I don't know how I know that, but I'm sure of it."

He stroked her hair. "Are you sorry that the gift is gone?"

She looked at him, and her face shone with love and joy. "How could I be? Look at all I've gained." Someday, she knew, she'd tell him about that final vision she'd had while she waited with him on the boat, the vision that had filled her with hope and made her believe that dreams can come true. For in that vision she'd seen herself and Mike in a hospital room. Their heads were together, and Mike's arms formed a circle around her shoulders, her haven of safety and strength, and in her arms she held a baby. That was their future; she knew it. She blinked tears of happiness out of her eyes and smiled at the man she loved.

Mike took her face in his hands and kissed her again, knowing as he did so that a lifetime of sleeping and waking with this woman, of sharing her life and her heart, would not be enough. It wasn't a gentle kiss. His mouth moved urgently against hers, claiming her, and she answered his deepening passion with her own—until he drew back to ask with mock wariness, "You're not going to want an emerald engagement ring, are you?"

She gazed up into azure eyes and said dreamily, "No, I think I'd like a sapphire. If I can find one that's exactly the right color."

"Whatever you say, sweetheart," he said, holding her tight again. "You're the expert. But be sure you find one you really like. Because you're going to be wearing it for the rest of your life."

* * * * *

Next month, check out

featuring
Paula Detmer Riggs

Paula Detmer Riggs returns to the Intimate Moments lineup in October 1995 with *Her Secret, His Child*, IM #667, a powerful story with an EXTRA edge.

For sixteen years Carly Alderson had lived with a secret, embodied by her daughter. Yet she'd never dreamed the past would catch up with her—or that father and child would one day meet. Mitch Scanlon had changed her life one all-too-memorable night...and now the truth threatened to rip her heart—and family—to shreds.

In January 1996, INTIMATE MOMENTS EXTRA features Kathryn Jensen's *Time and Again*. Don't miss any of these breakthrough novels by the genre's best, only in—

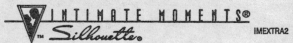

IMEXTRA2

Introducing
a new Intimate Moments
trilogy by

Beverly Barton

Ashe McLaughlin, Sam Dundee and J. T. Blackwood...three rugged, sexy and dangerous ex-government agents—each with a special woman to protect.

In October 1995—*Defending His Own*
                    (Intimate Moments #670)

Ex-Green Beret Ashe McLaughlin had never forgotten Deborah Vaughn and the night of passion they'd shared—or the way her father had railroaded him out of town. But he had never known about the son he'd left behind. Now Deborah needs Ashe to keep her safe—and the safest place for her is in his arms.

Coming in January 1996—*Guarding Jeannie*
                    (Intimate Moments #688)

Embittered former DEA Agent Sam Dundee has a chance at romance. Hired to protect Jeannie Alverson, the woman who saved his life years ago, Sam is faced with his greatest challenge ever...guarding his heart and soul from her loving, healing hands.

And look for J. T. Blackwood's story in spring 1996.

Trained to protect, ready to lay their lives on the line, but unprepared for the power of love.

OFFICIAL RULES

PRIZE SURPRISE SWEEPSTAKES 3448

NO PURCHASE OR OBLIGATION NECESSARY

Three Harlequin Reader Service 1995 shipments will contain respectively, coupons for entry into three different prize drawings, one for a Panasonic 31" wide-screen TV, another for a 5-piece Wedgwood china service for eight and the third for a Sharp ViewCam camcorder. To enter any drawing using an Entry Coupon, simply complete and mail according to directions.

There is no obligation to continue using the Reader Service to enter and be eligible for any prize drawing. You may also enter any drawing by hand printing the words "Prize Surprise," your name and address on a 3"x5" card and the name of the prize you wish that entry to be considered for (i.e., Panasonic wide-screen TV, Wedgwood china or Sharp ViewCam). Send your 3"x5" entries via first-class mail (limit: one per envelope) to: Prize Surprise Sweepstakes 3448, c/o the prize you wish that entry to be considered for, P.O. Box 1315, Buffalo, NY 14269-1315, USA or P.O. Box 610, Fort Erie, Ontario L2A 5X3, Canada.

To be eligible for the Panasonic wide-screen TV, entries must be received by 6/30/95; for the Wedgwood china, 8/30/95; and for the Sharp ViewCam, 10/30/95.

Winners will be determined in random drawings conducted under the supervision of D.L. Blair, Inc., an independent judging organization whose decisions are final, from among all eligible entries received for that drawing. Approximate prize values are as follows: Panasonic wide-screen TV ($1,800); Wedgwood china ($840) and Sharp ViewCam ($2,000). Sweepstakes open to residents of the U.S. (except Puerto Rico) and Canada, 18 years of age or older. Employees and immediate family members of Harlequin Enterprises, Ltd., D.L. Blair, Inc., their affiliates, subsidiaries and all other agencies, entities and persons connected with the use, marketing or conduct of this sweepstakes are not eligible. Odds of winning a prize are dependent upon the number of eligible entries received for that drawing. Prize drawing and winner notification for each drawing will occur no later than 15 days after deadline for entry eligibility for that drawing. Limit: one prize to an individual, family or organization. All applicable laws and regulations apply. Sweepstakes offer void wherever prohibited by law. Any litigation within the province of Quebec respecting the conduct and awarding of the prizes in this sweepstakes must be submitted to the Regies des loteries et Courses du Quebec. In order to win a prize, residents of Canada will be required to correctly answer a time-limited arithmetical skill-testing question. Value of prizes are in U.S. currency.

Winners will be obligated to sign and return an Affidavit of Eligibility within 30 days of notification. In the event of noncompliance within this time period, prize may not be awarded. If any prize or prize notification is returned as undeliverable, that prize will not be awarded. By acceptance of a prize, winner consents to use of his/her name, photograph or other likeness for purposes of advertising, trade and promotion on behalf of Harlequin Enterprises, Ltd., without further compensation, unless prohibited by law.

For the names of prizewinners (available after 12/31/95), send a self-addressed, stamped envelope to: Prize Surprise Sweepstakes 3448 Winners, P.O. Box 4200, Blair, NE 68009.

RPZ KAL